The Fugitive Trail

The Fugitive Trail

Zane Grey's New Western Series™

ZANE GREY™

Sagebrush
Large Print Westerns

Library of Congress Cataloging in Publication Data

Grey, Zane, 1872-1939.
    The fugitive trail / Zane Grey
    p.   cm.—(Zane Grey's new western series)
    ISBN 1-57490-248-2 (hardcover: alk.paper)
1.Large type books. I. Title

PS3513.R6545 F84 2000
813'.52—dc21   99-05497

Cataloguing in Publication Data is available from
the British Library and the National Library of Australia.

Sagebrush Large Print Westerns are published in the
United States and Canada by Thomas T. Beeler, Publisher,
Box 659, Hampton Falls, New Hampshire 03844-0659.
ISBN 1-57490-248-2

Published in the United Kingdom, Eire, and the Republic of
South Africa by Isis Publishing Ltd, 7 Centremead, Osney
Mead, Oxford OX2 0ES England. ISBN 0-7531-6246-6

Published in Australia and New Zealand by Bolinda Publishing
Pty Ltd, 17 Mohr Street, Tullamarine, Victoria, 3043, Australia.
ISBN 1-74030-013-0

Manufactured by Sheridan Books in Chelsea, Michigan.

CHAPTER 1

THE TOWN WAS FULL OF TRAIL DRIVERS AND LABORERS just paid off and looking at red liquor. In the back room of Lafe Hennesy's six men sat at a big round table and played poker for table stakes. Two of them were cowboys making a night of it, and blowing their roll early, one was a stranger in those parts. The gambler, Quade Belton, dark, swarthy, and with sharp eyes, had the biggest pile of silver and gold before him. His sidekick, Steve Henderson, was doing well too. The sixth man was trying hard, and sweating freely, but he was getting trimmed. He was in his twenties, soft of face and hands, obviously not a horseman and, judging from the way he played, not much of a gambler. His name was Barse Lockheart.

Suddenly a few onlookers were shoved aside and a young man stepped up to the table. Except for his hardness and the steel in his eye he was a dead ringer for Barse Lockheart. His voice, when it came, had bite in it.

"Barse, get up! Quit this game pronto!"

The six men looked up, questioning, wary. Barse flushed red. "What the hell's eatin' you?" he burst out.

"You're in bad company. Shake it now," came the reply.

"But I'm a loser. I won't quit. You've got a gall to brace me in the middle of a game."

Henderson banged the table and turned to Barse. "Tell him to go where it's hot."

"Bruce, you can go to hell!" shouted Barse. But the wavering of his eyes belied the defiance in his voice.

1

The stranger looked up at the intruder with a sneer on his lips. "Say, are you your brother's keeper?"

"You're damn right—when he keeps company with Steve Henderson and an outfit any trail driver would know is shady as hell."

All six men flipped their cards on the table. Several chairs scraped back. The two cowboys looked uneasy.

"Lockheart, I resent that," growled Henderson. "I'll just have to call you out."

There was no bravado in Bruce's cold, matter-of-fact reply. "Don't make the mistake of trying it."

The stranger slowly rose from his chair, his right hand crooked low near his gun. Belton pocketed his winnings. The two cowboys left their seats and joined the group of onlookers backing away from the table.

"Mr. Lockheart," snapped the stranger, "did you include me in the outfit you called shady?"

"I did. But I was flattering you."

"Ahuh! Jest how?"

Bruce replied with a smile. "Shady might do for you in this easygoing town. But down on the trail where men are hard you'd be just plain crooked."

The stranger's gun was out in a flash, but with the same incredible speed Bruce had drawn his and squeezed the trigger. The bang of his gun seemed to lift the roof and the stranger fell across the table, which upset, letting him slump to the floor. A second later Henderson's gun was out, but he never had a chance to aim as Bruce shot him. The third roar was Henderson's gun going off in the air as he toppled over backward.

Bruce backed away, his gun smoking, and was swallowed by the crowd that pressed forward around Henderson. Quade Belton and Barse Lockheart slipped out the door and went for their horses. The older man

2

mounted and turned to the other.

"Are you coming, or does your brother call your shots?"

The sting went home. "My brother can go to hell!" Barse replied angrily. He mounted quickly and rode after Belton into the fading light.

In the early spring twilight Trinity sat on a log above the swift stream waiting for a lover who was always unreliable and late. The murmuring stream mirrored the fading rose and gold of sunset; a mother duck with her brood paddled under the overhanging foliage; late birds twittered sleepily in the tall trees; there was a fresh, damp sensation in the cool air. Behind her were distant sounds from the Spencer ranch, where she lived, and from beyond that the low roar from the town of Denison, more than usually raw and elemental this spring night by reason of the railroad construction camp on the outskirts and the arrival of trail drivers and cattle herds from the south.

Looking southward always fascinated Trinity. It was from the south that she had come and from there the future vaguely called. A wide gap in the dark line of trees opened to the vast wild Texas rangeland. By day and by night, when she waited at this trysting place, she seemed to see down to the Trinity River where she had been found abandoned as a child and rescued by these good Spencers. They called her Trinity and nothing had ever been learned about where she had come from nor who she was. She remembered long rides in wagons; endless plains of waving grass; black herds of buffalo; camps and fires along dark rivers; fierce bearded men; gunshots, and the blood-curdling war cries of Indians.

A dreaming, brooding loneliness spread south from

3

the stream. And never had the beauty of that Texas land struck her so poignantly. Purple dusk moved silently from the wooded stream bottom, over the undulating range, toward the golden afterglow of sunset. Almost, Trinity preferred the peaceful and wild unknown southland to the tumult and trouble of the Spencer ranch and the wide-open town of Denison.

The distant noise of that town brought her mind back to Barse. He had changed, there was no denying it. The lovable, gay, thoughtless, improvident boy had taken to evil companions and a dissolute life. He resented her talking about it, too, and more than once had turned on her with stubborn violence when she brought up the subject. And yet there were flashes of his old self, like the time he had insisted on buying her that expensive dress. She had been thrilled, but when she asked him how he had got the money he had become angry and defiant. It worried her. "I feel like Barse's mother," she thought. "He's a little, irresponsible boy."

Then her thoughts turned to Bruce, as they had more and more lately. He was so different from Barse, tough, hard, and serious, with a reputation as a buffalo hunter, trail driver, and yes, a gunman. Trinity wondered at the talk she had heard of Bruce's prowess as a gunman. She had not seen much of Bruce until lately as he had always been away hunting or trail driving. But in the last few months he had come to the ranch often, more to see her, she knew, than to see her parents. And, in spite of her affection for Barse, there was something solid about Bruce that she found very appealing. The last time he came, she remembered with a pang of guilt, she had almost let him kiss her. And even now she found the idea disturbing and exciting. No, he couldn't be a killer. But her duty was with Barse. She had to try to get him

4

to change his ways and settle down. He needed her, and if he promised to straighten out she would marry him.

She knew that Barse was not going to come tonight, so she left the riverbank and picked out the familiar trail through the darkness. As she crossed the meadows, the grazing horses lifted their heads to snort. Horses had played a large part in her life. Few of the boys could outride her. Then she remembered that Barse was one Texan who did not own or love horses, and she suffered a pang.

Trinity entered the grove that surrounded the ranch house. The peeping of the frogs in the pond made a sweet, sad music she had loved as long as she could remember. There was a light in the sitting room of the rambling house. She went in, wanting to seek the seclusion of her room, but resolved to tell the Spencers of her decision.

"Trinity, you're in early," said Mrs. Spencer, a gray-haired, sturdy woman.

"Barse did not come," replied Trinity. "Where's Dad?"

"He's out somewhere. Hal rustled off to town. One of the riders fetched news of a holdup. Bandits, I reckon. Denison was pretty bad before the railroad work came with its gold an' riffraff laborers, an' gamblin' hells an' dance-hall hussies. But now it's the worst Texas town I ever lived near."

"I've decided I—I'd marry Barse," stammered the girl.

"Oh, no, Trinity!" expostulated Mrs. Spencer.

"But I'm almost distracted!" exclaimed the girl. "Hal is the best of them all, if I only cared for him. I—I like Bruce too well and I've let him be sweet on me. Barse has the only claim on me. He needs me."

"Don't be upset, Trinity," rejoined Mrs. Spencer. "I feel sorry for you. Too many beaus! It's no wonder. Reckon there aren't many girls as pretty as you. Or as good. An' you can lay your hand to any ranch wife's work. Not to say a cowboy's knack with hawses, an' a rope an' gun! I say take the boy you want most."

"Mother, I think it's Barse," returned Trinity.

"You're not shore, though."

"Oh, no, I'm not. I've sort of babied Barse for years."

"You've tried to mother him, boss him, reform him, because he's bad. Beware of that, Trinity. It doesn't work out often."

Mr. Spencer's heavy tread sounded on the porch and through the kitchen. He entered the sitting room, a typical Texan of lofty stature, lean face, white hair, and piercing eyes.

"Howdy, lass. You shore look forlorn," he said in his hearty voice.

"Dad, I've been telling my troubles—and what I'm going to do," said Trinity, and she blurted out her situation and her conviction about what seemed best.

"Wal, lass, you've settled it. Now abide by it an' don't worry no more."

"Do you—you approve, Dad?"

"I cain't say thet I do, Trin. But it's yore life an' you've got to decide it. Time was not long back when Barse was a fair-to-middlin' boy. But he changed, same as Denison changed with growin', more money an' cattle, an' now this durn railroad."

"But Bruce said the railroad would make Hal rich."

"I cain't gainsay thet. When the work's done an' this mushroom camp is gone, I reckon Denison will settle down. But now it's tough. Why, tonight at six when the railroad paymaster was about to pay the laborers a gang of masked riders rode down an' held him up. Got away slick with thousands! Not a shot fired!"

"Thet easy!" retorted Mrs. Spencer, with scorn. "Where was Bruce Lockheart an' some of these other fightin' Texans about then?"

"Mother, I'm sure Bruce wasn't in on it," interposed Trinity.

"No, I saw Bruce after, luckily for him," replied Spencer. "He wasn't one of them bandits, though some of us rangemen reckon this two-bit robbin' an' rustlin' around heah lately ain't been done by old hands."

"Dad!" cried Trinity, aghast.

"Wal, lass, don't let it fuss you."

"But how can I help that?"

"You cain't at thet, mebbe. I cain't. It doesn't all look so good. I've seen reckless cowboys break out many a time. There's always some reason. Money scarce or else too much money in sight. Hobart Smith, who saw this holdup, swore there was only one heavy matured man in the outfit. The rest lean, young riders!"

Trinity was thinking, with a queer sinking of her heart, that of late Barse had been unusually well supplied with money and careless of it. Without another word she went to her room and, without lighting the lamp, threw herself on her bed. She pondered this thought. One day she had met Barse in town when he had been drinking and he had tried to buy her everything in the store. When she grew curious, he said he was unlucky in love but lucky at cards. She always endeavored to forget his evasions, but this had stuck. And now it came back with redoubled force. Bruce, in his bitterness about her love for Barse, once said she did not know the half. Seldom did he speak ill of anyone. Much less of Barse. At other troubled times she had been too strong and loyal for doubt. This time she failed to rise above it. There was something deeply wrong. She reflected on many instances to which she had blinded herself. Almost all of them threw discredit on Barse Lockheart.

Still, though Trinity admitted she might be a fool, she would stand by Barse and trust him to be above anything worse than drinking and gambling. She would silence her fears and doubts. She would try to avoid seeing or hearing any more to make her unhappy.

Suddenly there was the sound of horses. A team was driving in. Peeping out the window Trinity saw a buckboard with a spirited brace of blacks pounding to a halt at the gate. Caleb Green, a neighboring rancher, held the reins and his companion was Hal Spencer. Trinity's father joined them. Green spoke. Trinity was quick to sense something amiss. Then she saw that Hal was bareheaded and pale. Her father led the way indoors.

Trinity hurriedly went to the sitting room. Mrs. Spencer looked startled, and was staring at Hal, who evidently had just finished speaking. Spencer's gray eyes were on fire.

"Howdy, Trinity," said Green, with a smile. "You shore grow prettier every day. Where'd you get those red spots in your cheeks?"

"Good day, Mr. Green. Thanks for the compliment. I reckon I'm excited."

"Quick to get a hunch, eh? . . . Wal, Spencer, I'll be rustlin' along. Want to tell the news." And Green went out the open door. Spencer went as far as the door and closed it.

"Now spill it, Hal," he said curtly.

"Trinity, you better leave us," spoke up Mrs. Spencer

nervously.

"Nonsense. She'll have to heah it," returned the rancher sharply.

"Mother, I'd better tell Trinity. I saw the whole thing."

"Oh, Hal! . . . What?"

Hal faced her, quite white, and his eyes were dark with feeling.

"Trin, it needn't upset you. . . . Bruce Lockheart just shot two men. Killed a stranger who butted into the argument. And shot Steve Henderson—mortally, so they say."

"How—dreadful!" gasped Trinity. "Bruce! . . . What for? Where?"

"It just happened, Trin. Bruce was drawn on first, to be sure. But he must have been hunting trouble. He was terrible—wonderful! Denison will never doubt again all those trail drivers' stories of his fights. His speed with a gun! Whew!"

"Wal, tell us, son," interposed Spencer.

"Barse! Was he—there?" asked Trinity breathlessly.

"Ha! *Was* he? Barse was to blame for the fight. Damn bullhaided fourflusher—"

"Oh!" cried Trinity, in distress. "But then he couldn't have been in on the holdup," she said, relieved.

"Hal, talk sense," ordered his father. "What come off?"

Hal sat down and wiped the sweat beads from his pallid face. "I'm sorry, Dad. I reckon I'm flustered. Sit down and don't look so scared. . . . It was this way. Just after Jeff Hawkins got shot—"

"Hawkins?" ejaculated Spencer, amazed. "When was thet?"

"Dad, I plumb forgot you left town before," replied

9

Hal. "It must have been soon after the holdup. I didn't see that fight. Hawkins was shot by a strange gunslinger who later made the fatal mistake of bucking up against Bruce. But, by golly, I saw that!"

"Son, would you mind comin' out with the facts?" interposed Spencer impatiently.

"Give me time!" Then Hal told them of the incident at Lafe Hennesy's. He was still excited, and the story came out in a rush.

"Wal, I'll be damned!" exclaimed Spencer.

"Oh—how dreadful!" cried Trinity.

"Well, there was an uproar," continued Hal. "Belton and Barse skipped out. I didn't see Bruce any more. Men crowded around Henderson. He was alive, but shot clean through. He'll die most likely. They took him to the doctor at the construction camp."

"What did the crowd say?" asked Spencer.

"Gosh! I couldn't remember. But there was excitement, believe me. After the atmosphere cleared, the dead gunman was identified as the one Hawkins had tried to arrest. Then Bruce came in for a lot of praise."

"But, Barse—what became of him?" begged Trinity.

"Nobody seemed to know—or care," responded Hal gruffly. "Later I heard he rode out of town with Belton, probably went to Belton's camp."

"Bruce had it right," said Spencer. "Belton's outfit is shady."

"Well, Dad, they're two less than they were," observed Hal significantly. "Mother, let's have supper quick. I want to go downtown again."

"Hal, I'll go with you. . . . Trinity, what's on your mind?"

"I—I hardly know," faltered the girl.

Suddenly Trinity had conceived the idea of playing

the spy herself. Find out what Barse Lockheart's relation was to Belton's outfit! It shocked and then fascinated her. She thought over her capabilities. She was strong, supple, and she could ride and follow tracks with any cowboy. She could slip through the brush like an Indian. No sense of fear impeded her.

"I'll do it!" she thought. "After supper I'll ride down the trail and find Belton's camp."

Trinity went in and changed to her riding overalls and boots. She often rode to town in the early evening. And when she met Barse she sometimes stayed out late. She could do it. She could discover something, if not that night, then on another night. Her blood raced and she tingled with the secret intention of allaying her fears or learning if there were grounds for them.

An hour later, when she rode down to the river on her mustang, Buckskin, she found her mind was crowded with thoughts and resolves. There had not been any horses on the trail since those she had seen earlier in the day. Putting Buckskin to a lope, she headed down the river in the direction she had seen Belton go several days ago. The trail kept to the timber, and that grew heavier until, with the darkness, she could not see far ahead. Thereupon she dismounted and, stepping a little way from her mustang, listened intently for hoofbeats. Trinity's ears had long been keyed to catch the sounds of the open.

In five miles she halted ten times. She had now entered the wild river bottom, where she dismounted at intervals to listen and peer low to discern tracks.

She was fully seven miles from home now. Considering that, Trinity was about to turn back when she smelled smoke. After a little she heard the ring of an ax. It was farther down. She proceeded slowly for perhaps a quarter of a mile and presently was rewarded by spying the flicker of a campfire. Slipping out of her saddle, she led Buckskin off the trail and tied him. Then she faced up the trail and marked the spot by the dead branches of a tree against the sky.

Once back on the trail, Trinity leaned on a log and took cautious stock of the situation. It seemed natural to be thrust upon her own resources. By inheritance and training she was well adapted to this kind of lonely work. But up to now her many jaunts had been concerned with hunting and fishing, trailing lost horses and cattle, and playing at being pursued by Comanches. She was now tracking men and, she felt convinced, men who were evil and dangerous.

Trinity stilled her agitation and figured that she must not make the slightest sound or move which would betray her to sharp-eared outlaws. For she had concluded that Belton's gang were outlaws.

It was a cool spring night and very quiet. She became aware of the peep of frogs, the soft murmur of a swift stream, the cry of night hawks, and stealthy rustles in the brush. Once more locating the campfire, she began to steal silently toward it. She became absorbed in this stalk. She had a gun, but she was going to make sure she would not need it.

For a while the timber was fairly open, consisting of big trees through which she could glide from one to another. She avoided cracking twigs or rustling brush. The campfire grew brighter. She lost it sometimes and then found it again.

After a long, careful advance, circling a little, she found the fire obscured for some moments. Suddenly, on rounding a thicket, she was amazed and frightened to see it clearly not more than a hundred steps distant; and

12

the bright blaze disclosed three men in plain sight. One was the bold dark-faced Belton. One she had never seen before. The third was Barse.

Trinity felt a cold shock and fought to keep her courage. The men were talking.

Belton had a deep voice and he was not cautious. She distinguished: "gunslinger messed our plans . . . we got a bank job." The others spoke low in earnest tones. Barse shook his head, evidently not agreeing with Belton.

She was too far away and she determined to crawl closer, to a point behind some logs. The grass and weeds looked deep enough to shield her. But her heart thumped and she shook when she started across that open space.

Making for a small clump of bushes, she got it between her and the campfire. Gaining that, she grew brave again and then elated. Belton's voice sounded nearer. She sank flat and strained her ears— "luck changed—we better pull bank . . . an' rustle tomorrow . . . leary of this. . . ." Trinity strained to hear more. Rob the bank? Oh, no, not Barse.

Trinity heard a slight noise close at hand. Her heart leaped, then seemed to stop. There came a soft footfall right upon her. It paralyzed her—curdled her blood. Then two gloved hands, hard as iron, seized her, one in a viselike grip on the back of her neck and the other clamped tight over her mouth.

CHAPTER 2

IN A MOMENT, WHILE TRINITY WAS BEING TURNED FACE up to the starlight, a desperate instinct to save herself overcame her fright. Slipping her hand in her coat

13

pocket, she tried to turn the gun against her assailant.

"Say, boy, what were you up to?" came in a fierce whisper.

Trinity recognized it. She lost her rigidity, and as she sank back her sombrero came off exposing her face and curly hair. At sight of them her captor released her with a sharp expulsion of breath.

"*Trinity*!"

"Hello, Bruce," she replied in a whisper. "You nearly—broke my neck."

He bent down to peer at her in amazement. Then, remembering the proximity of the outlaws, he enjoined silence and pulling her to her feet, led her away, keeping the clump of bushes between them and the men. Once back in the timber he halted and faced her.

"Girl, what were you doing there?" he asked in a low voice.

"Same as you—I'll bet," she replied.

"You were spying on Barse?"

"Yes."

"Well, you little fool! But you've got nerve, unless you've no idea what hard hombres these are."

"I know. I wanted to find out if Barse was with them. So did you!"

"Wrong. I *know* he's in with them."

"Oh, Bruce, I feared it!"

"He needed a scare. If today wasn't enough, I'll give him another."

"Today!" she whispered tragically. "You spilled blood on his account."

"Who told you?"

"Hal saw it all."

"Uh-huh. I might have figured that d—— rooster would be around. I had to do it, Trinity, or Barse would

14

have been in trouble.—Come."

Bruce led her silently through the timber to the trail and then asked her where she had left her horse. Then he led on. When they reached the dead tree he said, "My horse smelled yours when he passed heah."

"Come home with me," she entreated.

"No. I'm going to sneak up on that outfit. I've a hunch they're plotting some deal. If I can find out what it is I can spoil it."

"Yes, Belton means to pull something," replied Trinity, and told Bruce what little she had overheard.

"The bank tomorrow—not if I can help it. . . . But never, mind, Trin. You go home now."

"Bruce, you're going to run risk again? Fight—and—and maybe be shot!" faltered Trinity, suddenly prey to unaccountable emotion. His nearness affected her. Catching hold of his sleeves, she gazed up at him. How dark and stern he was.

"Sure I might get shot," he replied in harsh bitterness. "Anyone would think you weren't a Texan. And a lot you'd care—"

"Hush! Don't say it. Bruce Lockheart . . ." Her voice trailed away while her hands slipped up to his shoulders. They were longing to go round his neck and she would be powerless to stop them unless he repulsed her. His strong fearlessness attracted her much more than Barse's weakness ever had.

Bruce uttered a short hard laugh. "That's like a woman. Now the damage is done—and your conscience hurts—you let on—"

"Let on, nothing!" she interrupted passionately, deeply hurt. "I never said I *didn't* care, Bruce."

"What about Barse?" he asked quietly.

"I don't know. I'm so mixed up." Suddenly she stood

15

on her toes and kissed him. She left him standing there as motionless as the tree, and running back to her mustang she untied him and mounted to urge him into the trail.

"Trin!" called Bruce poignantly.

But she dared not go back then. What had she been about to do? She was shaking all over, hot and cold by turns, appalled by a realization that she must really love Bruce Lockheart. No matter what her regard was for Barse or how she felt responsibility to save him, the fact was clear now that she loved Bruce. Events of the last two days had clarified her mind. The difference between these brothers had come home to her. Barse was not even a shadow of Bruce. Another backslide from Barse would earn a sickening contempt. And another fine gesture on the part of Bruce would upset her equilibrium disastrously.

It required several miles of keeping her mustang at a walk or slow trot for Trinity to fight down her feelings and gain composure enough to put her faculties onto this by no means safe return trip. Fortunately, she met no riders. When she got to more open trail she put the mustang to a lope, halting now and then to listen and peer ahead.

Several miles below the ranch Trinity turned off the trail and, climbing out of the hollow, crossed a section of range to a road that eventually brought her home. It was late. She unsaddled Buckskin and went quietly indoors. The excitement had exhausted her and she went to sleep promptly.

Next day she went about her tasks deeply pondering the backlash of her sentiments. Try as she might, Trinity could not dismiss an insistent call of her heart. Loyalty, pity, and responsibility urged Barse's claim on her, but these were not love.

Spencer and Hal had gone to town. Trinity dreaded their return for fear of hearing more disturbing news. To delay this she went down to the river, hid in her shady bower, and thought and thought. Something more was going to happen before she could change her definite stand, which intuitively she dreaded she would. It had to happen.

Early in the afternoon a clip-clop of trotting horses coming on the trail from downstream brought Trinity up, keenly curious and watchful. She peeped from her leafy covert. Presently four riders hove in sight. The leader was Belton. But he looked different. The others appeared strangers to Trinity. Before they passed out of sight her sharp eyes made the observation that the men were garbed alike in black sombreros, dark vests and shirts, and blue overalls. They rode horses Trinity had never seen. She would remember a horse, his build, his color, and his gait more surely than she would his rider.

"That's peculiar," muttered Trinity, as she watched them disappear. "Those were fine horses. Spirited and racy. Outlaws' horses. . . . What can Belton be up to? It can't be any good—and I've a hunch . . ."

She pondered the matter. If Spencer had been home, she would have hurried to tell him. She had happened on something dark afoot and should do something about it. But what? She was inhibited by Barse's connection with these men and by her fear for Bruce.

"Oh, if Bruce would only come along! Maybe he will. I'll wait."

Hardly an hour had elapsed when Trinity heard rhythmic, swift hoofbeats of shod horses coming on the trail from town. They were approaching fast. Then she saw them. Four horsemen in single file. Fleetly as the

17

horses sped by, she recognized the dark bays and the garb of their riders. Masked! The riders were masked with red scarfs. Despite this, she knew the last rider—Belton. He kept looking back. Then they were gone and only the ringing hoofbeats proved to Trinity that she had actually seen the flight of outlaws who had surely committed a crime.

No sooner had the sound of hoofs died away downstream when she heard others coming from upstream. Almost at once she espied two horses abreast, with their riders fighting. Then one of them caught the bridle of the other horse and hauled back on it. Both horses pounded to a stop in the trail scarcely fifty feet from Trinity. She stifled a scream and then fell prey to terror. The aggressive rider was Bruce Lockheart, white with passion, his eyes burning. The other man, in spite of a red mask, was easy for Trinity to recognize as Barse.

"Leggo! What d'you—mean—runnin' me down?" panted Barse hoarsely.

"You know damn well. Pile off!" replied Bruce, cold and grim, as he leaped from his saddle.

"No! . . . What 'n 'ell for? I'm slopin' with Belton. Cain't you see that?"

Bruce snatched the red scarf off Barse's face and threw it down. Barse was pale and sweating. Then Bruce jerked him violently out of the saddle.

"Barse, you've no guts for a job like this. Belton made a sucker out of you. . . . Then rode off an' left you. What's in that sack? The holdup money?"

"No. Just my share."

"Barse, did you drop that black sombrero during the raid on the bank?"

"It was shot—off my haid. See heah!" And Barse

18

stuck a shaking finger through a bullet hole. "But I picked it up again."

"Ahuh. Narrow shave. Suppose it had hit you? Left you lying in front of the bank for all the town to see! Fine for Mother and Trinity!"

"Aw, shut up. I tell you I'm slopin' with Belton. If he misses me he'll come back."

"That's what you think. An' if he does, I'll kill him damn pronto. . . . Barse, it's all over town that one of the Lockheart boys was in the holdup."

"Yeah? All the more reason for me to slope. I cain't see why on earth you stopped me."

"No, you couldn't," returned Bruce, in contempt. "If I'd been able to find you this morning I'd have stopped you before." And when Barse tried to mount his horse, Bruce knocked him down. "Maybe you can savvy that. . . . Simmons, who shot your sombrero off your head, swore he recognized one of the Lockhearts, but could not tell which one."

"Aw, you needn't worry about bein' accused. They'll never think you was in the bank holdup."

"I'll make them believe it," said Bruce, grimly, as he snatched Barse's sombrero and traded his for it. "Get out of that vest and shirt."

"You cain't—mean—" gasped Barse.

"Yes, I do. . . . Heah, take mine. . . . Pronto now or I'll slug you again." Bruce tore the garments off the dazed Barse and with lightning-swift action made the exchange. Then he leaped astride Barse's horse. "Listen sharp. Take my horse. Go home by the back way. Don't let Mother see you change those overalls. Hide them. Then go in town, as if you didn't know what's happened. Savvy?"

"Yes—but—Bruce . . ." Barse choked out in agony.

19

"It's for Trinity's—sake and Mother's," rejoined Bruce unsteadily. "Trin loves you. . . . Marry her—and go straight. Try to be a man instead of a yellow dog! Rustle now. . . . Don't ever let Trinity know."

Bruce spurred the horse down the bank into the swift stream. It was shallow and easy to wade. Bruce did not look back until he was climbing out on the other side. His dark face flashed. Then he was gone into the brush.

Trinity came out of her stupefaction and tried to cry out to call Bruce back. She was unable to utter a sound. When she turned she saw Barse ride out of sight. Trinity sank to the grass, prostrated by conflicting tides of bewilderment and distress.

Amazement, grief, and passion claimed Trinity in turn, and the last abided with her even after she had gained an outward calm. The facts burned into her mind. Barse was a thief and a coward. Bruce had sacrificed himself for love of her and a mistaken sense of loyalty, blindly believing he could save Barse and her happiness.

Barse and the situation there at home would not yet stay before her consciousness longer than a moment. Bruce swayed her now. She asked herself a hundred questions and answered nearly all of them. Bruce had taken the stolen money because that had been the only thing to do. He would become an outlaw; he would fight if cornered in order to save his life; then he might fall to the use of that bank money. But never before!

Into Trinity's dark boding thought flashed an inspiration. Before it was too late she would trail Bruce, find him, share his fugitive life, prevail upon him to take her to faraway Arizona, and there begin anew. "Marry Barse now?" she soliloquized, with passion. "Never! Not if he was the last man on earth!" Whatever she had felt for Bruce leaped into worship. This realization and her resolve changed every aspect of past and present. It exalted her. It beat down her distress, her conflict. It gave her something to do that was worthy of Bruce. There was almost an ecstasy in the adventure, the hardship, the peril that must be met in trailing Bruce Lockheart into the vast wilds of Texas.

Trinity put off reveling in that dream to address herself to the immediate present. A few stern moments of concentration sufficed to make her plan and to decide how best to go about it. She would wait to see what developments unfolded the next day or so, and then she would leave.

Sunset was coloring the rolling landscape when she returned to the ranch. Supper was soon ready, but the men did not come home. After the meal Trinity sat out on the porch, consumed with anxiety and speculation. About dark the Spencers drove in. They looked taciturn and had no word for Trinity. Later, when they had a belated supper, she went in.

"Dad—Hal, why so glum?" she asked.

"Bad news, lass," replied Spencer.

"Trin, the bank was held up today by five bandits," added Hal.

"That's no especial bad news," said Trinity.

"But this hits you, dear."

"How so?" she asked, affecting surprise.

"One of the masked bandits had his hat shot off. He was recognized. It—it was Br—one of the Lockheart boys," stammered Hal.

"Hal, you were going to say Bruce," returned Trinity sharply.

"Yes. . . . I'm damn sorry I was."

"I don't believe it."

"Nobody did at first. But we had to."

"Because Barse was around right after the holdup in his old clothes. Those robbers had on new outfits. Blue overalls and black hats."

"And Bruce?" queried Trinity tersely.

"He was the last of six riders running his horse hell-bent down the river trail. Some boys saw him. Also Mrs. Perry. She heard horses tearing by her house. When she looked she absolutely recognized Bruce. He hasn't been seen since."

Spencer shook his head sadly. "If it hadn't been for that! . . . It looks bad."

"Hal, did you see Barse?"

"Yes. About an hour after the robbery. He had heard and he was upset."

"What did he say?" asked Trinity, intensely curious.

"Well, naturally he blew off. Said he was sorry for his mother. But he wasn't surprised. Those years with the buffalo hunters had ruined Bruce."

"So—Barse said that!" ejaculated Trinity, hardly able to conceal her rage.

Mrs. Spencer heaved a deep sigh and interposed: "It was easy to see Bruce had changed. That hard, wild life on the ranges! He could never settle down. But a bandit? It's a pity. He was a real Texas lad. Worth ten of that lazy Barse! Oh, this Texas since the war!"

"Mother, you're right," agreed Spencer regretfully. "But it's a queer deal I cain't savvy."

"Trin, what do you think about it?" asked Hal, eyes keen and kindly upon her.

"I—I hardly know—yet. I'm shocked," returned Trinity.

"Don't take it too hard, lass," said the rancher. "Bruce was almost a stranger to us. Heah so little time. But for

22

the disgrace an' grief it wouldn't have been so bad for his mother."

"Barse was her favorite," rejoined Mrs. Spencer. "Case of mother love for the weaker son."

"Wal, in thet case it's better it was Bruce who turned out bad," said Spencer.

"But, Dad, Bruce was a grand fellow," expostulated Hal resentfully. "Barse is no damn good!"

"Oh, son, I wouldn't say that," put in his mother.

"I'm sorry, Trin," added Hal, fire in his eyes as he gazed hard at Trinity. "But it's true. Aw, it all makes me sick."

"Hal, I like you the better for what you say," replied Trinity soberly. And she hurriedly went to her room, fearing she might betray more than she thought wise.

Trinity began at once to pack her clothes in a bag, and her few treasures, and to get out her savings, which she had not counted for a long while. She was elated to find that she had several hundred dollars. It seemed a fortune. She had been working and saving for her marriage.

She heard Hal say: "Trin took it kind of cool. I wonder . . ."

"The girl was flabbergasted," replied his mother.

"No wonder. So was I."

Spencer added in his deep voice: "Son, I'll bet she never marries Barse now. Then your chance will come."

"Never for me, Dad."

Trinity saw in this another reason why she had to run away. Hal knew her and he suspected that all about this bank robbery was not as it seemed. When Trinity had gone, he would guess the truth. But Trinity did not care about that.

She turned out the light and went to bed. Sleep did

not soon come. Before she succumbed to it she had conquered her emotions. She would leave Denison on the morrow, stopping the stagecoach at the crossroads near the Spencer ranch. She wanted intensely to see Barse, but if he did not present himself in the morning she would wait no longer.

Trinity slept so late that Mrs. Spencer had to call her. "Get up, you lazy girl! Barse is heah an' wants to see you."

"He can wait," answered Trinity. By the time she had dressed she was ready for Barse Lockheart.

Mrs. Spencer said, "Mawnin', Trin. Your friend is all spruced up like he was goin' to a party. I'd think more of him if he'd been down in the mouth."

"So would I, Mom. . . . I'll see him before I have breakfast." She went out. Barse was sitting on the porch. He had on his best suit and was clean shaven. Trinity was hardly prepared for his almost debonair manner. She remembered him as he had spoken his last broken words of shame or regret to Bruce. But Trinity had steeled herself for anything. The easiest way for her was to deceive him.

"Howdy, Barse. You're up early—for you," she greeted him brightly.

"You've heahed—about Bruce?" he asked hesitatingly, but he was hopeful. He had not expected to find her like this.

"Yes. Hal told me last night. I'm horribly disappointed in Bruce."

"You can bet I was too," replied Barse hurriedly, and the uneasy uncertainty left him.

"How'd your mother take it?"

"Ma hasn't been told yet."

"Oh! Are you going to keep it from her?"

"Long as I can. . . . Trin, this thing has jerked me up hard. Bruce had me fooled, same as he had you and everybody. His preaching and trying to reform me was all a blind. His shooting Henderson and that card sharp was all in line with his plan. It'd have worked, too, if he hadn't been recognized."

"Bruce seems to have had it all planned," replied Trinity, gazing serenely at Barse.

"Trin, you—you won't let this make any difference between us?"

"Why no, Barse, I certainly won't."

"That's great, Trin, and mighty sweet of you. I reckon then we needn't wait any longer?"

"Wait? For what?"

"Why—to be married," he returned, swallowing hard. Despite his nerve, that was hard to get out.

"I suppose not, Barse," she said in the same even voice. "Come over tonight, and we'll see."

"Aw, Trin, that's just great!"

"I've plenty to do and I haven't had any breakfast yet."

"I'll go right home and be back tonight."

"Good-by then, until—" Trinity left more unsaid and went in.

"Trinity, did you settle it with Barse?" inquired Mrs. Spencer, a little caustically.

"Yes, I settled it," rejoined Trinity briefly.

"Well, I cain't help saying that it's a pity you settled on Barse Lockheart," went on the older woman bitterly. "You—who had the pick of the young men! . . . Take Hal, for instance. It's beyond me how and why you chose Barse instead of my son. Hal is worth a dozen Barses."

"He is, indeed. But it's not a question of worth."

25

"Then you love Barse so well you don't care how worthless he is?"

"Love him! . . . I despise Barse Lockheart."

"Girl! Are you out of your haid?"

"You'll think I am, Mother."

"I certainly don't savvy you. For Hal's sake—and all of us—I'll be glad when you're gone." Mrs. Spencer, usually kindly, spoke with a heat unusual for her.

"That—won't be long!" Trinity broke down, and weeping bitterly went to her room. But she recovered quickly. Mrs. Spencer's statement made the situation easier for her. Presently she went out to her breakfast.

"I'm sorry, Trin. Don't mind what I said. You've been a good girl and we all love you. Too well, I reckon." Mrs. Spencer spoke contritely.

"And I love you all. Don't forget that," answered Trinity.

"I'm going to town today," returned Mrs. Spencer. "Want to go along?"

"No, indeed, I don't."

"Well, I don't blame you. There'll be a lot of gossip. And everybody will be curious about you."

What with her tasks and state of mind, Trinity found the hours short. The stage usually left Denison about one o'clock and was due at the forks shortly afterward. She felt relief that she was alone. It was difficult for her to write the few words to her foster mother explaining her action. And she left that task until it was almost time to go. After eating a hurried lunch she went to her room and put on her best dress and bonnet. She realized she was forsaking the only home she had ever known, but such was her absorption in her adventure that she did not then feel any grief. She was in a hurry to go. Someone might come. Taking up her bag, Trinity went out. She was astounded to be confronted by Barse Lockheart.

"Hello, Trin! . . . What's this? All dressed up—and a bag!" he ejaculated.

"Barse, I'm going away for a little while," she replied, and walked off the porch.

"What the hell!" he burst out, in consternation. "Going away?—Like hob you are!" And he blocked her path.

"I said I was taking a trip," continued Trinity spiritedly. She felt the rise and spread of a hot wave in her breast. It would be dangerous to cross her at this time. Still she hoped to avoid a quarrel.

"And *I* said you are like hob!" he retorted, anger succeeding amazement. "It's got a queer look—your going away without telling us."

"I don't care what it looks. I decided I wanted to go."

"Trin, I'll bet you decided more than that." He had paled and the freckles stood out on his sallow face. His eyes were narrowing with an ugly look. "But I won't let you go."

"*You* won't? Barse Lockheart, you can't stop me," she cried, losing her temper.

He tried to snatch the bag out of her hand, but Trinity held it and jerked away.

"You didn't mean it!" he burst out.

"No!"

"You were going away on me?"

"Yes."

"You never meant to marry me?"

"I meant to once—but never now!"

"What? . . . *Now*! You double-crossing cat!"

"Sure I was double-crossing you."

He slapped Trinity, and she returned the blow with

27

stinging good measure.

"How in hell can I figure you?" he shouted, shamed and infuriated.

"Barse, let's talk straight. . . . I was out on the river trail yesterday."

"Yeah! And what of that?" he raged.

"I was hidden. I saw you and Bruce."

"You couldn't have been close to us. And I reckon you imagined a lot."

"Such as what?" retorted Trinity, in scorn.

"Lord only knows. The fact was, Bruce tried to ring me in on his bank-robber deal."

"Just how did Bruce try that?"

"Why, trading horses with me—taking my sombrero and vest—"

"What for?" cut in Trinity bitingly.

"'I—I reckon to disguise himself—to get away—"

"You liar!" Trinity's voice rang out in passionate contempt. "Bruce took your horse, your clothes, your stolen money to save you—*you thief!* You let him shoulder your crime. You coward! You haven't a spark of manhood in you. . . . Bruce had a delusion that I cared for you. He wanted to save you. He was noble—great. And I love him. I love *him*! . . . I'm going to trail him—find him—share his life . . . . Go back to town and tell. Tell the truth. Ha! I bet you won't. If I could prove it I'd tell them myself. Now get out of my way, you white-faced sneak. I'm going and I'm happy to see the last of you."

Trinity saw Barse sink to a seat on the porch, his head bowed, his whole frame shaking. Then she wheeled and ran out to the lane; slowing to a swift walk, she made for the road. In that fiery outburst she had rid herself of congested feelings. She was the better for surrendering

28

to fury. She was glad Barse had come.

It was a mile out to the road. By the time she had reached it she was herself again. She saw the stage coming. To get in it would be an ordeal, if any passengers knew her. Facing around, she took a last look at the ranch, at the home she was forsaking, at the cattle and horses along the river. "Good-by! Oh, good-by!" she murmured, as her eyes dimmed and her heart pounded.

Trinity had decided to go to Doan's Post and listen for word of Bruce. To do this she had to spend the night at Ryson and catch the Red River stage in the morning.

The ride to Ryson was uneventful. Settling herself comfortably, Trinity watched the landscape roll by, feeling with each mile a slow detachment from the Spencers and all they had meant to her. Ahead was a new life, one of duty, honor, love; and she prayed with the utmost faith that she would find Bruce before he became hardened and drifted toward evil.

The range the stage traversed was rolling plain, crisscrossed by streams and fertile bottom land, with the levels beginning to give a green tinge to the waning gray. Cattle dotted the range; here and there a ranch house showed amid trees; farmers were plowing fields; the undulating country stretched away illimitably, in the dim hazy distance hinting of the reach and wild that was Texas.

Trinity at last fell asleep. She was awakened by the jar of the stage coming to a halt. They had arrived at Ryson, a wayside hamlet where the branch stage line ended. There was a tavern, with the inevitable saloon and lolling, bold-eyed cowboys. Trinity was glad to finish supper and hurry to her room and bar her door.

Strange surroundings and voices, and loud revelry from the tavern saloon, kept Trinity awake a long time. But she got to sleep at last and awoke refreshed and eager. She had always longed to travel, to see new places and faces, and to experience all of Texas.

The main-line stage arrived just as Trinity finished breakfast. It was a huge vehicle drawn by four horses. She hastened to pack her bag and make ready for the long day's ride, at once thrilled and concerned by the prospect. The innkeeper got her transportation and carried out her bag, very kind and attentive.

"Are there many passengers?" asked Trinity.

"Always packed, miss," he replied. "But you'll get the best seat. Don't mind the cowboys. They're nice fellows."

Trinity was the first one to get in. She felt shy to be the cynosure of many eyes. Several passengers followed. Evidently all had disembarked there for breakfast. Then she became tinglingly aware that four cowboys were throwing dice to see who could win a seat next to her. They were quite serious about it and their talk abashed her. Still she thought she had better take stock of them. They were typical Texas cowboys, young in years but old in range experience, tall, slim, round-limbed, three of them towheaded and blue-eyed, with darkly tanned faces. They wore heavy sombreros, high boots, and overalls. Trinity did not miss the fact that they all packed guns.

Presently the four piled into the coach from the side opposite Trinity. The one who carefully deposited his long length next to her removed his sombrero to disclose a keen, handsome face, with intent eyes and a smile which softened the stem features.

"Mawnin', miss," he said pleasantly. "I reckon I'd

30

better introduce myself now than later. It's a long day ahaid an' we're shore packed in heah. . . . I'm Lige Tanner from down Nueces way."

He was so sincere and winning that Trinity felt impelled to reply in like spirit.

"Trinity! Wal, I've heahed thet name before. Somebody mentioned it to me. Shore is onusual an' pretty. . . These boys heah are my pards. We're part of the Nueces cattle outfit rollin' home from a tough drive to Dodge with three thousand haid of longhorns."

"Three thousand head! Somehow I knew you were all trail drivers."

"Aw, thet's not so good," replied one of the two who had pushed themselves into a seat opposite Trinity. "Cowboys haven't the bad name common to trail drivers."

"I never heard of a distinction," said Trinity.

"Miss Spencer, it's just thet us drivers have graduated into hard ridin', drinkin', an' fightin'," added Tanner.

"Couldn't you be hard riders without the other?" asked Trinity, her eyes twinkling.

"Laws no, miss. When we reach the end of the three months' drive up thet turrible Chisum Trail we gotta get drunk an' blow off steam. Else we'd never forget the work an' heat an' flood—the Injuns an' the rustlers."

"It's a pity. But some riders have to take cattle north. That's what is saving Texas."

"Heah thet, pards? There's a girl for a trail driver's wife!"

"No such luck," responded Tanner ruefully. "Miss Spencer, may I ask where you're bound for?"

"Doan's Post is my first stop," replied Trinity, awakening to possibilities for information and help.

"Now, boys, ain't thet fine? Two whole days with

31

Miss Spencer on this stage! Our luck's shore in. . . . But if you'll excuse me, what you mean—yore first stop?"

"I may have to ride all over Texas."

"Indeed. Lucky you. . . . Sorta onusual for a young girl like you. . . . Tryin' to find someone?"

"Yes," sighed Trinity.

"Parents or relative?"

"No. I have neither."

"You're an orphan?" he queried incredulously, his blue eyes kindling.

"Yes. I was raised by kind people named Spencer. . . . When I was a child I was lost or deserted on the Trinity River. Spencer found me. Called me Trinity."

"Say, now I remember!" he exclaimed, with great zest. "I've heahed of you. I know yore story."

"You do! Texas is a small world, after all. Who told you?"

Tanner appeared to forget the others, he was so deeply stirred. "Best pard I ever had! Greatest hombre I ever knew! He saved my life down on the Colorado. Say, was he swift with a gun! . . . I spent half a year huntin' buffalo an' fightin' redskins with him. Then he took a trail drive with me. It ended only six months ago. An' just before he left me he told me about Trinity."

"Buffalo hunting—you said?" faltered Trinity, feeling the hot blood beat and swell along her veins.

"Yes. Thet was the job he liked best. . . . You must have knowed him."

Trinity hesitated before replying. She had to know if news of the holdup had traveled on ahead of her; if Bruce's name had been connected with it yet. She decided to take the chance.

"Was your friend's name—B-Bruce Lockheart?"

"Wal, I should smile! An' you're thet Trinity? I shore

32

am glad to meet you. . . . Boys, we didn't meet up with a stranger. This girl is a friend of the best pard I ever had. You've heahed me talk of him. Bruce Lockheart?"

"Lige, I reckon we have. Many a time," replied one of Tanner's comrades.

"Specially when things was goin' bad an' you needed some humdinger of a hombre," added another.

Trinity was powerless to resist the impulse that swayed her. "Bruce is my—my—friend. . . . We—we quarreled. He rode away. I am going to find him."

"Bruce's girl!' Wal, if this ain't the best ever!" shouted Tanner, and he gripped her hands. His eyes shone upon her. "I cain't figger how Bruce could ever have rid away from you. But he was a queer, proud fellow. Sort of touchy about his reputation."

"Yes, he was."

"Wal, Bruce could never hold out against you," avowed Tanner cheerfully. "When did he leave?"

"Three days ago. Last Saturday."

"You'll ketch up with Bruce at Doan's."

"He was in a hurry. Suppose I miss him?"

"Thet'd be bad. When he takes to the trails you cain't follow him."

"Why not? I can ride, track a horse, make camp, take care of myself."

"Wal, I don't doubt thet. You shore look capable. But south and west of Doan's it's buffalo country for hundreds of miles. Too dangerous for a girl alone."

"I make a good boy rider, Mr. Tanner."

"Aw, you're too pretty. You could never fool me."

"I'll bet I could."

"Let's hope you'll not have to disguise yoreself. Why, thet'd be a downright shame. Wait till we get to Doan's. Mebbe you won't need to borrow more trouble. . . . Tell me about Bruce. Then I'll tell you what I been through with him."

The ensuing hours and day sped by for Trinity on the wings of story after story of wonderful adventure, related by a stanch admirer of Bruce Lockheart, and which in the simplest words made him a hero. How little had Trinity really known about the work and exploits of Bruce Lockheart. He was famous on the frontier. It was terrible to realize that soon he would become infamous. She must find him, at any risk, and take him far away from Texas.

They spent the night at a ranch house fifty miles south of Ryson. Next day they traveled beyond the ranch country into the real Texas wilds. Trinity saw her first herd of buffalo, a black dust-raising patch moving north on the horizon. The sight flushed her cheeks and brought a lump to her throat. The keen Tanner called her a buffalo hunter in the making. The endless purple plains fascinated Trinity. She gazed until her eyes ached.

Late in the day the cowboy pointed to a meandering line of green' timber and groves of trees in the distance.

"Thet's the ole Red River runnin' there, Miss Trinity, an' do I hate her? . . . Shore glad we don't have to cross her again this trip. Doan's Post lays beyond the timber to the left. We'll get in about dark."

Darkness did settle down before Trinity could view Doan's Post. But she saw campfires and clumps of horses and heard the bawling of cattle.

"There's a trail herd in, miss," said Tanner. "Haided north, of course. Doan's will shore be interestin' to you. Show whether you're a tenderfoot or not. Ha! Ha!"

Soon yellow lights flared out of the gloom, disclosing

a huge square edifice which was the trading post. The driver hauled up his two teams with a grand flourish.

"Doan's Post! All out!" he called lustily.

A circle of Indians and cowboys sprang up as if by magic.

"Jim, look after Miss Trinity while I run in an' see if Bruce is heah," said Tanner, leaping out of the stage.

"Come, miss. . . . It's a high step an' I reckon you're stiff from thet long ride," spoke up the cowboy Jim, helping Trinity down. "There. Right this way."

He led Trinity through a gauntlet of sloe-eyed Indians and bold smiling cowboys into the building. A huge colorful room, bright with yellow lights and an open fireplace, greeted her pleasantly. There were shelves and counters laden with merchandise, and from the rafters hung a multiplicity of utensils and tools. But Trinity's eager glance sought among the men assembled there one dark face she yearned, yet dreaded to see.

Lige Tanner came quickly toward her, ahead of several men.

"Bruce left heah yesterday," he said hurriedly and low. "An' am I glad! You savvy, Trinity?"

His eyes were sharp, sympathetic, warning.

"Oh—yes. I savvy!" she whispered.

Then the others came abreast of Tanner. "I'm Tom Doan," said the foremost, a stalwart bearded man, unmistakably curious. "So you're Trinity Spencer?"

"Yes, Mr. Doan, I am."

"Right glad to meet you, miss. I know yore folks. My wife will look after you. Supper's about ready. But first let me introduce Captain Maggard, Texas Ranger. He rode in today on thet hurry call from Denison."

Trinity steeled herself around a sinking heart. Tanner had warned her. The ill news had reached Doan's Post.

35

"Good evenin', Miss Spencer," spoke up the tawny giant beside Doan. He had the uncompromising face of a Texas Ranger. She felt the flame of his eyes, but his manner was cool, courteous, gallant. "I'd shore have been pleased to meet you any time. But this is most opportune for me. I want to heah all about these holdups at Denison. I sent two of my Rangers on the trail of this Bruce Lockheart. What do you know about him?"

CHAPTER 3

TRINITY FACED THE TEXAS RANGER WITH AN INNER trembling that the thought of Bruce enabled her to hide. This Ranger Captain was Bruce's enemy and therefore hers.

"Captain Maggard, I heard all about the bank holdup at Denison and probably I know as much about Bruce Lockheart as anyone," she replied to his question.

"Then indeed I shore am lucky," he answered. "I've only a meager report an' what gossip I've heard since I rode in here. It wasn't much."

"Well, I remember it this way," Trinity started, carefully choosing her words. "There were five robbers. They rode dark horses, wore blue overalls and black sombreros with red scarfs over their faces for masks. Four of them came out of the bank and handed a bag to the bandit who had stayed with the horses. As they mounted, someone in the bank, the cashier Mr. Sims, I think, began to shoot. One bullet knocked the hat off one bandit's head. It loosed his mask exposing his face. The man doing the shooting claims he recognized one of the Lockheart boys. This one recovered his hat, leaped astride, and rode away after the others."

36

"Short an' sweet then," said the Ranger. "Was this robber hit by any bullets?"

"Not that I heard," answered Trinity.

"One of the Lockheart brothers," mused Captain Maggard. "Is there any suspicion that both brothers were in the holdup?"

"No," replied Trinity steadily, thinking swiftly and trying to follow the outlines she had planned. "Barse Lockheart was around town afterwards it was reported."

"The logical conclusion then was that the other Lockheart is implicated."

"Yes, that's the gossip, but I believe the cashier was mistaken. I know Bruce Lockheart. The fact is, he is a dear friend. I don't believe he was in that bank holdup any more than I could believe it of Hal Spencer—or you yourself, Captain Maggard."

"Young lady, you shore are positive in your opinions," the Ranger captain went on. "The report seems to be pretty general that it was Bruce Lockheart. He was here as late as yesterday afternoon. He was in an awful hurry to get away an' rumored takin the trail to the south."

"Captain Maggard, someday you'll find it all a mistake," said Trinity earnestly. "What do you actually know about Bruce Lockheart?"

"I've heard a lot. He's very well known down south as a buffalo hunter an' Indian fighter, one of Loveless' righthand men, a hard-ridin', hard-shootin' Texas cowboy. Nothin' was ever said until I got here at Doan's Post that was against him. An' then I couldn't find anybody who'd give me much information."

"Bruce is proud—hotheaded. When he learns what he's been accused of he'll be liable to kill someone."

"You don't believe he knows we're after him?"

"No. If you could only call your Rangers off until you find out who the guilty parties really are!"

"I can't do that very well all in a minute. My boys have gone an' probably I won't hear from them until they catch up to Lockheart. I wish I could have talked to you before I sent them."

"There's something else, Captain. I haven't told anyone yet because I wasn't sure," went on Trinity. "I had a sort of hiding place I used to go to as a child, along the river near my home. I still go there to watch and think. A trail runs down off the bank towards the brakes not too far away. During the last several weeks I've often seen horsemen going to and fro along this route. One of them, the leader, I've seen in Denison. His name is Belton."

Captain Maggard started to say something, then evidently thought better of it. He motioned Trinity to go on.

"Some time ago the railroad construction company was held up and the payroll stolen. I think Belton and his men pulled this job. The day of the bank holdup I was there by the river watching. I didn't know what had happened, but what turned out to be about an hour after the robbery four riders passed heading away from Denison. They wore black overalls, black sombreros, and they had red scarfs. They were pretty far away, but I think I recognized Belton."

"Ahuh! Five rumored at the bank, an' you only saw four riders?" the Ranger asked.

Trinity realized she was on dangerous ground. "That's all," she said. "But the fifth could have been close behind them. I left at once. I could have missed him. I'll gamble none of them have been seen since."

"Wal, anyway, Miss Trinity, that was an important

observation you made," responded the Ranger. "It shore may be Belton has a gang of outlaws an' that the accusation against Bruce Lockheart is a case of false identification. I don't know the name Belton, but Texas is full of outlaws an' they change their names everywhere they go. Did this Belton outfit get well acquainted in Denison?"

"Yes, they did. They spent their time gambling and had a bad influence on some of the cowboys and young men who lived there. Barse Lockheart was one of them. He got too thick with these men and drank and gambled too much. Both Bruce and I tried to get Barse to stop this wild living."

"If Bruce hadn't of ridden away, it would be much easier not to suspect him in this robbery. If he's innocent *why* did he ride off?"

"Bruce never stays home long. This time he had more than his usual reason for going away. Both the Lockheart boys have been attentive to me and I—I hardly knew which one I liked best. Anyway, I refused Bruce and he left."

"When did you last see Bruce?"

Trinity thought swiftly. If she said she had last seen Bruce before the holdup, it would be difficult to retract if later she found reason to tell of the meeting between Bruce and Barse. She decided to gamble.

"Early the same morning. That was when we quarreled. I believe he rode away at once."

"Could that be proved—his leaving *before* the holdup?"

This Ranger was penetrating. "I—don't know," she breathed.

"Might I ask if your presence here in Doan's Post has anything to do with Bruce Lockheart?"

"It certainly has. I want to find him and persuade him to come home and prove his innocence."

"That's commendable of you, Miss Trinity, and shore speaks well for Bruce. An' thanks for bein' so good an' tellin' me all this. I'll see you after you have had a rest and somethin' to eat."

Trinity was shown to her room, where she removed the stains of, travel and changed her dress, all the time running over in her mind all she had told Maggard and wondering if she had said the right things. She was assailed by doubts. Perhaps she should have related the full details of the meeting between Bruce and Barse. She had been wild, crazy to run off after Bruce without first establishing the damning guilt of Barse. But it would have been, and would still be, only her word against Barse's. Until she found Bruce! He could make Barse tell the truth. And he might in his mistaken loyalty give the lie to her story. She would have to wait. At least she had given the Ranger Captain a good deal about which to ponder.

Presently she went out to meet Mrs. Doan and the cowboy Tanner and one of his friends. When Mrs. Doan excused herself and left, Tanner turned eagerly to Trinity and whispered, "That was a tough place for you. Maggard is an old buzzard. I'm anxious to know how you got on with him."

"I was scared to death at first," replied Trinity. "But now I'm glad I met him. I deceived you and Captain Maggard though when I said Bruce and I had quarreled and I refused him. Now you know better."

"We understand, Trinity, an' it may help some. As for me an' my pards here, we don't think Bruce ever held up any bank. Now listen. The opinion here is that Bruce rode north. That is, some of the Indians said so, but

Doan claims that he rode south. Personally, I think Bruce will go west. If I know him, he'll make for the brakes of the *Llano Estacado*. It's my idee that he'll hole up at the head of one of those rivers, an' if you're bent on findin' him, bear this in mind. It'll be a pretty hard job to find Bruce, but you ought to get track of him if anyone can. I advise you to go on south with us at first an' we'll help you to make inquiries everywhere an' of anyone that might have seen him. He had lots of friends an' it ain't likely any of them will put the Rangers on his trail. Some places will be hard for you to get to. You cain't go alone."

"I'll have to go alone," replied Trinity. "I can't afford to pay a cowboy or anyone to accompany me. Besides, I don't want anybody."

"Then it's shore a desperate undertakin'," responded Tanner, shaking his head. "I'm worried about you, but I don't want to force myself on you."

"You've been very kind," rejoined Trinity gratefully.

After supper Trinity, accompanied by the cowboys, went into the big hall of the post and there Captain Maggard, who evidently had been waiting for her, accosted her with deep earnestness. "Miss Trinity, I want to talk to you very seriously."

He led her to a bench over in one corner somewhat out of the bright light and, handing her to a seat, faced her with a regard quite in contrast to his former attention.

"I've been talkin' to Tom Doan about you and I'm tremendously interested. Please forgive me for being personal but this might mean a great deal to you. Is it true that you're not really Trinity Spencer?" he asked.

"Captain Maggard, my name is not Spencer. I don't know what it is. Spencer found me when I was a child at

41

a deserted camp on the Trinity River and he named me Trinity. He and his family brought me up and have been very good to me."

"Wal! Then it's true? I'm shore interested. Now listen, you're the livin' image of the girl an old pard of mine, Steve Melrose, married twenty-three years ago. When I first saw you I was struck with the resemblance. Her name was Mary Hutchinson. She and Steve lived several years at Shreveport and there they had a little girl. Steve came west to buy cattle an' find a ranch. After he had located, he sent for her. I remember at the time he told me he should have waited until there was a big wagon train comin' on. But he was eager to have Mary an' the child home. He instructed her to get men an' wagons and come on. It was proved that she left with one wagon an' driver. She was never heard of again. That was over twenty years ago. When at last he gave her up for lost Steve married again. They have a wonderful ranch at the head of the Brazos River. Steve is rich in cattle now an' the few times I've seen him in the last ten years he always spoke of his lost wife an' little girl. Miss Trinity, by all means you should hunt up Steve Melrose! Tell him I sent you."

"Oh, Captain Maggard!" exclaimed Trinity breathlessly. "Do you think it possible that he might be my father?"

"Indeed I do. Stranger things have happened in these wild times. My reason, of course, is that you look so much like Mary. She had an exceptional beauty, which indeed you have. Then the fact of your bein' found on the Trinity River. There's a ford on the Trinity, or I should say there was, on a road that went through to Fort Worth from the east. The important thing is, have you anything at all that would identify you?"

42

"I have the little dress they found me in and a locket that I wore on my neck by a string. Unfortunately the locket was empty."

"Is there any mark on this locket?"

"Yes. It has an enameled figure of flowers and it is very worn."

"That's somethin'. Whoever put that around your neck would probably recognize it. Have you any idea how old you were at the time you were found?"

"Spencer said I could have hardly been three. I have vague memories of campfires, of horses and wagons, of strange yelling voices. I have often wondered if that childish memory could be of Indians?"

"It could very well be. Now, Trinity, I think this might result in a wonderful thing for you. By all means go to see Steve Melrose. Take the stage here and ride till you come to the post on the Brazos River. You can mention my name and you will be well taken care of. Wait there until there is a cattle train or a wagon train makin' for the head of the Brazos. Find Steve Melrose an' if he's not your dad you'll be very glad you met him anyhow, for he's an old Texan an' a grand man. Mrs. Melrose an' her children would be happy to meet you. Promise me you will go?"

"I shall indeed, Captain Maggard. Oh, I am thrilled. If it really happened that I could find my father! I have often dreamed that it might come true. . . . Thank you with all my heart."

"Wal, that's just fine. I will be ridin' up Brazos way someday and I will hear how it turned out. Let's hope that you find a home."

Trinity almost burst out, "And let's hope I find Bruce. This could be the way." But she kept silent.

When Trinity was called in the morning, to rise at

43

once and dress and hurry out, she found Tanner and his companions at the breakfast table with other men she had not met. Tanner gave her a friendly greeting, paying her a fine compliment, and told her that the southbound stage would be ready to leave pretty soon. The Rangers had left already on their journey north. While Trinity was partaking of a hurried breakfast Mrs. Doan came in with a basket which she gave to Trinity. "Good morning," she said, smiling. "I've put up some things for you to eat on the way. Don't let these starved cowboys get into this basket. And when you come back to the Post, we want you to stay longer."

Very soon Trinity was bundled into the stagecoach by Doan, who made her a present of a lightweight Indian blanket which he said would add to her comfort. "I reckon a norther, the *del norte* of the Mexicans, is going to blow down in a day or so, and you may have some trouble keeping warm." He leaned towards her and whispered, "Every wagon train and cattle drive that comes through here will have some scout who is a friend of mine. I'll tip him off to make inquiries every place they stop about Bruce Lockheart. Sooner or later he'll find out you're hunting for him. I hope it all turns out well. Good-by and good luck."

Tanner and the cowboys were the only companions to ride with Trinity in the stage. There was a cattleman on top. The stage driver was a rangy, sallow-faced Texan with a long drooping yellow mustache and a rollicking laugh. The Doans bade them good-by and soon they were off. Timber soon hid the Post from view, and looking southward Trinity saw the seemingly endless, plain of waving grass. The sky was overcast and the air was chill. Tanner said he would not be surprised if they had bad weather that day. It was a good hard road and the four horses drew the stagecoach at a steady trot. Tanner and his associates exhausted themselves in their efforts to entertain Trinity. There were no cattle on the range. Tanner said there would be sure to be some buffalo traveling north of the Brazos. Jack rabbits, deer, and various birds came into sight at intervals. The day grew darker and the wind increased. Trinity had recourse to her blanket and she was glad to have it. "It shore is a *del norte*," said Tanner. "An' that's too bad because it's pretty country. When the norther blows you can't see anythin' for the low clouds an' rain. Sometimes, though, northers blow out of a clear sky."

Toward noon the cowboys got out their lunch and Trinity shared some of the delicacies of hers with them. After they had satisfied their hunger the cowboys went to sleep and Trinity, sliding down under the blanket, succumbed to her own drowsiness. After that she dozed on and off but she was awake when the norther caught up with them with clouds of dust and a pattering of hail on the stage and the roar of wind. Not till late in the afternoon when they stopped at a wayside station did Trinity grow fully awake. The evening was gray and cold and the warm fire that greeted the travelers was very welcome. For all Trinity could see, there were a couple of white men and several Indians at this place. The accommodations were poor and the fare was coarse but it was hot and satisfied the pangs of hunger. There were blankets and a buffalo robe on the bed given Trinity and she slept warm. Once or twice during the night when she awakened the wail and mourn of the wind made her shiver and wonder sorrowfully if Bruce were well sheltered that stormy night.

The next day's ride was made through intermittent gusts of rain and sleet and snow. The landscape was obscured, the steadily trotting horses splashed through the water on the road. But the road was still hard and the horses made good time. There was nothing to do but try to keep warm and sleep and hope for the passing of the hours. The cowboys extended themselves to give her comfort. That night, they stopped at a post, not so pretentious as Doan's, but still a good-sized trading post with its usual complement of Indians and hangers-on. This place, the cowboys told Trinity, was on the Jesse Chisholm cattle trail and the road from that point followed a trail to Fort Worth, where they would arrive, provided there were no washouts, the following evening. Another day from there would take them to Robertson on the Brazos River. "This norther will blow out in another day or two an' then the sun will shine. You'll have good weather for a spell then an' your ride up the Brazos should be somethin'!" Thus Tanner assured Trinity and she reveled in the thought.

Robertson's Post was not particularly different from Miller's except that it was picturesquely located on the banks of the Brazos. They had arrived there late at night and Trinity had to wait until the next morning to see what the place looked like. She was delighted to have the sun shine warm and golden once more and to see the shining river gliding on between the green banks. At breakfast Trinity had her first treat of buffalo meat and she confessed to the cowboys that she liked it. At this place the Mexican cook was really good and Tanner assured Trinity that if she had to stay there any time she would have good things to eat. Her room, too, was plain but clean and neat, and her open window looked out upon the river. The trader Robertson was absent at the time and his womenfolk made Trinity welcome and comfortable. There were several Texans there and some Mexicans, but not any Indians. Some little time after breakfast Tanner sought Trinity to tell her: "All good luck, I reckon. There's two supply wagons belonging to Melrose leaving here tomorrow or next day. You can get a tent here an' blankets. Melrose's men are pretty shore to be good fellows. They'll take care of you. When you get tired of riding on a wagon seat you can fork a hawse. An' let me tell you the farther up the Brazos you travel the more you'll come to love it."

"It certainly is a pretty enough river here," Trinity said. "How far do you think it is up to Melrose's place?"

"Oh, a long way," replied Tanner vaguely. "Two hundred miles an' more. His ranch, you know, is clear at the haidwaters of this river. I'd like to see it myself. At that, I'd go with you if you'd let me."

"Thank you very much, but I don't think I should let you do that. I have a gun and I can take care of myself."

"Wal, you don't say," returned Tanner with a grin. "I'd just like to see you stack up against some tough hombre. . . . Now, Miss Trinity, the rest of the good news is this. I've questioned everybody I met since we got to Doan's. Not one trader or scout or Indian or anyone I talked to has seen anyone that could possibly be Bruce. As a matter of fact, me an' my pals are the only young riders come through here lately. At Doan's you know there were conflictin' reports about Bruce. Some said he hit south. I don't believe he went north either, as Maggard seemed to believe. I finally got it out of Doan's clerk that Bruce had given him ten dollars for a good-sized pack of grub an' made him promise not to tell about it. That makes me reckon that Bruce would head straight west across the plain for the high country, just as I told you. Buffalo huntin' is about over an' there

47

won't be many camps of buffalo hunters. He'll make for the brakes of the Staked Plains, and he'll hide out in some lonely place. Bruce likes to hunt an' he likes to fish. For the present it's just as well you're goin' to Melrose's because you stand little chance of hearin' about Bruce till he takes to the trail again, an' you'll be goin' closer all the time in the direction I'm shore he went. He'll get out of grub an' he'll get tired of bein' lonely an' he'll *have* to move; an' after that somewhere, sometime, you are goin' to heah of him. We all hate to say good-by to you, Miss Trinity, but we have a hunch that you're goin' to come out happy."

As luck would have it, Melrose's supply wagon got into Robertson's that night and announced they would make an early start in the morning for the Brazos Head ranch. There were three cowboys, two young long-legged Texans and a Mexican vaquero, as dark as an Indian. The teamster Slade had his wife with him, a rather comely and agreeable young woman, and she was more than glad to have Trinity go with them. The other teamster, Sam, was a more than middle-aged Texan who had been with Melrose for many years. He was one of the loquacious, cheery type of individuals that was friendly with everybody. At once he took a great interest in Trinity, and she saw that she was going to get along well.

She was called early next morning, and when the wagons rolled off up the river the sun was just tipping the crimson grassy horizon. Trinity sat on the front seat of the second wagon with Sam and she stood up on the driver's seat to wave good-by to Tanner and his friends. They were divided between satisfaction at her good luck and disappointment they had to lose her. "Don't forget, Trinity, I've a hunch. It'll all turn out well."

One morning Sam raised his long whip and pointing said to Trinity, "Look there, lass. Now we are gettin' somewhars."

"What? And where?" asked Trinity.

"You ain't lookin' sharp enough. Don't you see thet dim gray outline way ahaid an' high up, like as if it was clouds? Wal, it ain't clouds."

"Oh, I do see something," replied Trinity eagerly. "That is land, and it is high."

"Wal, I should smile. Thet's the bold face of the Staked Plain. It's higher along there than anywhere in West Texas. Right down under thet bluff lays the Melroses' ranch. I'll bet you never want to leave it."

Greatly intrigued, Trinity peered at that hazy gray outline until her eyes grew tired. But, as the hours passed, she made sure that it grew more distinct. That evening round the campfire there was more than usual cheerful talk about tomorrow being the last day.

Slade got them up very early the next morning and they were under way by sunrise. Miles on miles of waving grass stretched back and eastward like a crimson sea sloping away. In the clear light of the early morning Trinity had her first sight of the wonderful *Llano Estacado*. It seemed very close in the rare atmosphere, but Sam said it was fully twenty miles away. "Howsomever," he added, "we don't hev thet much drive an' the road is tolerable good an' not so much uphill as it was."

There were not many moments in the morning or the early hours of the afternoon that Trinity's gaze did not revert to the beautiful prairie and the several lines of green trees that spread away like fingers to head up into dark canyons underneath the bold gray bluff. Away to the south along the slope began a great patch of black, which Sam explained was timber and which the Texans called brakes. "Them brakes run all along the edge of the bluff for hundreds of miles, an' in them the outlaws an' Indians find a refuge. No cowboys or Rangers ever get any man who holes up there." Those significant words struck Trinity with a shock. To see that wild country was to understand Bruce's love for it and why it was a safe cover for any fugitive. By some strange fate she had come directly to the wildest part of Texas.

In the afternoon the sun hung like a ball of red fire over the rim of the escarpment and cast an increasing color upon the rugged ground below and the rolling slope of plain that heaved up to the base of the gray wall. They came at last to where the stream forked again and they followed the northern branch, which Sam said was the main one. The yellow road ran on and turned out of sight about a mile distant. Trinity could not wait to see what was around that corner. And when at last they rounded it, she uttered a low exclamation of delight. To north and south the last steppes of the plain, split by several lines of green, heaved to the great slope. In the foreground, the road led to a long line of adobe, flat-roofed buildings and long fences and corrals of peeled logs that shone yellow in the sunlight. Above them a grove of trees stretched out from the river and showed the white gleaming walls nestling among them. The ranch with its varied color and broken rolling levels appeared overshadowed by the magnificent upflung gray escarpment, for the most part barren and rough and unscalable, but which showed one deep green-lined canyon where evidently the Brazos River had its source.

As they neared the brown buildings Trinity became absorbed in these and was hardly able to contain her excitement. She did not really expect to find Captain

Maggard's strange prediction true but there was one chance in a thousand, and that filled Trinity's heart to overflowing. At the last, as the cowboys drove the horses into one of the open corrals and Sam finally hauled up his teams before the end of the long line of brown structures, Trinity managed to control her emotion. She was all eyes at that moment. Several bareheaded, shirt-sleeved cowboys awaited the caravan; several Indians lolled on the porch; there were Indian mustangs standing with halters down and saddled ponies hitched to a rail.

Sam threw down his whip and reins and clambering over the wheel, he bawled out: "Heah we air!"

A tall stalwart man came out on the porch. He was bareheaded and his thick silver hair caught the breeze. To Trinity's intense scrutiny he embodied all the attributes that seemed so splendid in a Texan. He had a fine, clean-shaven face, lined and drawn, hard and craggy from contact with the elements, but softened on the moment with a smile. "Ho, Sam, I see you're back ahaid of time."

"Shore am, boss. Got everythin' an' came through aflyin'. An' I fetched some company for you Melroses."

"So I see," replied the rancher, slowly stepping off the porch, his piercing eyes transfixing Trinity. "And she's more than welcome. Young lady, get down and come in."

Trinity felt her face burn and her eyes droop as he helped her to descend from the wagon and led her into the store. It was a spacious colorful place, but Trinity did not see anything distinctly. Once inside, she removed her sombrero and her scarf and, smoothing her hair back from her face, she looked up at him. He was staring down at her with the gaze of a man who might have seen a ghost.

"Lass, you must—excuse me," he said unsteadily. "Who are you?"

"Perhaps you can tell me," returned Trinity, her voice breaking. "I have traveled far to find that out. . . . Mr. Melrose, do you know me?"

"Know you! Indeed I do not."

"Do I resemble anyone you once—used to know?"

"Yes, you do," he answered huskily.

"Captain Maggard of the Rangers sent me to see you. He said I was the living image of your first wife."

"Maggard! He sent you? This is strange! Girl, you *are* like—Mary. Tell me—who are you?"

"I have lived under the name of Trinity Spencer," went on Trinity breathlessly. "But the Spencer part was given me by the man who found me, a child scarcely three years old, lost on the Trinity River. He rescued me—called me Trinity—took me to his home and brought me up."

"Good Lord!" burst out Melrose, his face turning white. He seized her shoulders and bent over her with a piercing beautiful light in his eyes. "Is that all you know of your childhood?"

"All. I remember campfires, wagons, horses, and yelling voices which sometimes I thought must have been Indians. The only thing that I have that could possibly identify me—is this." Trinity's hands shook as she untied the knot in the silk scarf she took from her jacket; she handed the little locket to him. Melrose straightened up as he received it. It seemed to Trinity in that moment that her heart stopped beating and her blood stopped pulsing in the intensity that, for her, was a growing certainty. Melrose took the little locket and as he turned it over in his palm a sharp catch in his breath

52

preceded his gaze returning to her. The piercing light had given way to something beautiful and soft. His face worked. He said, "I gave this locket to Mary the day we were wed in New Orleans. I recognize it absolutely. I bought it from a jeweler who was a dealer in antiques. This was a rare piece and was worn by someone in the French court in the time of Louis Fifteenth. . . . How unbelievable—how wonderful! Trinity Spencer, you are my long-lost daughter. You are my Mary come to life again!"

Hours later Trinity stood at the open window in a room of the ranch house where she had found a home. All her doubts had been dispelled, and the last one, whether she would be welcomed in this family and received joyfully or not, had been answered to the fullness of her heart bursting with gratitude. It was incredible! But it was true! She looked up at the white stars blinking above the rim of this grand gray wall, and the place, the time, the peculiar circumstances, all voiced this truth and her good fortune. Silently she prayed in her thankfulness. Her dreams, which after all had been her prayers, had had their fulfillment, and if the spirit that had guided her had given her a father and a home, surely she could invoke that Infinite Power in behalf of Bruce, the fugitive who had shouldered shame and ruin for her sake and who on this dark night hid somewhere alone in the wilds, his dark face up to the skies. Trinity prayed for him, and out of that and the beauty of what had come before she gained something far deeper than hope and faith. She lost some of her fear for Bruce. She would wait there in her new home until she heard news of him or until, in the strange fulfillment of their fates, he would find her there.

CHAPTER 4

BRUCE LOCKHEART SAT BESIDE HIS LONELY CAMPFIRE on one of the headwaters of the Canadian River. He knew the country, having hunted buffalo there. He had gotten well up on the slope toward the rough foothills and he calculated he was not over two days' ride from Spiderweb Canyon, a hiding place for outlaws that had never been penetrated by Rangers. But he did not want to hole up there unless driven.

"Reckon I've given Maggard's Rangers the slip at last," thought Bruce. "But they made a Comanche of me."

The time was somewhere along in midsummer, he did not know what date. It was a cool night and the heat of the red embers felt pleasant to his outstretched hands. The place was as wild and lonely as he could wish. Deer grazed with his horse, coyotes prowled around near at hand; soft-footed cats bent green eyes at him from the brush; night hawks shrilled their weird cry from on high and the hum of a multitude of insects along the stream presaged the melancholy approach of autumn.

"What to do!" muttered Bruce. "Ride down into the brakes of the Brazos or make for the Pecos in New Mexico? Or safer still—the ranges of Arizona?"

He pondered the question. His fire burned down and he replenished it. He had a pack of supplies that, with the meat so easily obtained, would last till winter.

"That's the rub—winter." He hated the cold. He did not care to camp in the snow and ice. For the present he could stay right there, fish and hunt, while away the hours dreaming of the girl he had loved and lost, and forget if he could the human bloodhounds on his trail.

"I'll hole in here till the leaves turn and then head for those warm Arizona canyons I've been told about," he decided with relief.

This moot question out of the way, Bruce reflected on his long and irregular flight from Denison. The weeks had been crowded with incidents, some of which were bitter to remember. He had been forced to fight, but only with old enemies of the trails, cowmen, desperadoes, and gamblers who would have provoked a saint. His notoriety made him a mark for drunken men who had an itch to promote themselves in camps and gambling halls. He had been cornered by Rangers, but had escaped without drawing a gun on these officers of the law. His hands were still clean. He had not spent a dollar of the Denison bank money that was a burden around his waist, and to his conscience.

For the present he was safe. If he got to the Tonto Basin of Arizona he would probably be safe for the rest of his life. The wild canyon country had been settled by Texans, many of whom had been driven from the Lone Star state. But getting there on horseback was no easy job. He did not know the way. Cattle camps and towns could not be avoided.

The Rangers had advertised his flight and the outlaws knew he carried a small fortune with him. It helped his situation that neither Captain Maggard nor any of his Rangers had ever seen him. On the other hand, a range-wide wager between Maggard and Luke Loveless, the most successful buffalo hunter in Texas and now a big cattleman, had incensed the Ranger, hurt his vanity, and had made Bruce a marked man. Bruce had ridden for Loveless almost three years during the wildest range strife Texas had known. Loveless' riders had been a hard crowd, and Bruce had been his best marksman and rider. There was no love lost between Loveless and Maggard. The hunter, standing at the bar of Tom Doan's saloon and heated by liquor, had laughed the Ranger to scorn. Bruce had been told by men who had seen and heard that meeting: "Maggard, you're on one of your wild-goose chases. You fellers always have to be trailin' some pore devil. If Bruce Lockheart becomes a killer an' outlaw, you'll make him one. But Bruce is as honest as I am an' as fine as my own son. You'll never take him alive. An' when you corner him, which I shore doubt, some of you Rangers are goin' to cash in yore checks."

"Loveless, will you back your championship of this favorite of all your hard-nut riders in more than big talk?" asked Maggard, in anger and derision.

"You bet I will," replied Loveless.

"I'll bet you I'll arrest Lockheart or kill him inside of a year."

"Taken, Ranger, for all you got. An' easy money! What's more, I'll bet a like sum thet it'll come to light Bruce never was in on the Denison holdup."

A heavy wager was made then and there, with Tom Doan holding the stakes. Loveless' faith warmed Bruce's heart. He swore he would win the wager for his old boss. But his innocence he could never establish. He had to keep that stolen money. His sacrifice had been made to save his brother and thus ensure Trinity's happiness. For Bruce the saddest part was to realize how easily he could be forced into evil, as he had been into outlawry.

Bruce spent a month in that secluded dale. The rest for himself and his animal was sorely needed, and the sense of security and peace was infinitely good for his soul.

56

But when his food supplies, except salt and meat, were almost gone and frost had long since nipped the leaves, he knew it was time to move on. And he hated to leave and hated to renew that old hard vigilance. So he bade good-by to this golden Indian summer camp and struck out north.

He kept to the escarpment that paralleled the plains. Every few miles a ravine or canyon cut deeply into the bench and in each one he found water. Not once in a long day's ride did he cross a trail made by man or Indian.

Three more days' travel brought Bruce out on the rim of that endless bluff to a high point where he could see the most northerly of the Texas roads leading out of the Panhandle. And soon he sighted dust clouds and then a wagon train of fourteen huge canvas-covered prairie schooners. That was entirely too small a train to risk in the Indian country at that time.

Bruce had to search for miles to find a place where he could get down off the cliff. When he succeeded and drew near the train he came upon a young rider driving a herd of horses. Bruce hailed him and received a friendly reply and wave of hand.

"Howdy, Texas Jack," said Bruce. "Can I ride along with you?"

"Shore can, stranger," came the reply. "How'd you know my name?"

"Oh, I can always tell Texas Jacks. I know most a hundred. . . . Where you bound?"

"Las Vegas an' Santa Fe."

"Seen any redskins?"

"Yestiddy we had a brush with a small bunch of Kiowas."

"Lose any stock?"

"Few hawses, thet's all. Shore lucky."

"Who's your trail boss?"

"Hank Silverman."

"Where you from?"

"Waco. We left the main road below Doan's Post. The Red was in flood an' we couldn't cross."

Bruce calculated that he was fortunate so far. He had never run into Silverman, but knew him to be a real Texan and an old trail boss and scout. When the wagon train halted at a brook to camp, Bruce lost no time riding up to the circle of wagons.

"Where's your boss?" he asked of the first man he met.

The piercing scrutiny of gray eyes like those of a plains hawk met Bruce's and then lost their intensity. Hank Silverman needed only one good look at a Texan.

"Howdy, stranger," he said, in reply to Bruce's greeting. "I seen you pile off the bluff. Kiowas after you?"

"No, I'm glad to say."

"What's yore handle?"

"I'm riding nameless these days. But I sure want you to know I was `Luke Loveless' right-hand for three years."

"Wal, thet's a strong recommend even if Luke wasn't any friend. Tell me, is it true what I heahed—thet he made a fool bet about one of his boys?"

"I heard that too, Silverman, and I'm afraid it's true," replied Bruce, the very marrow of his bones warming to the twinkle in this Texan's eyes.

"Wal, don't worry none about it. I reckon Luke never lost a bet in his life. I shore couldn't win one from him."

"Thank you, Silverman. Can I ride along with your caravan awhile? I'm pretty lonely and hungry."

"You're welcome," returned the scout heartily. "Fact

58

is, if those Kiowas ketch up with us I'll be damn glad you happened along. You said yore name was Saunders, didn't you? Wal, git down an' come in."

Like Loveless, this Texan was the salt of the earth. He knew whom he was harboring. Bruce left his saddle, pack, and blanket under one of the wagons and sallied out to offer his services. The caravan was not large in number of wagons, but there were an unusual number of men, heavily armed, and a formidable outfit for rustlers or redskins to attack. It was, in fact, a pioneer crowd moving west in charge of the scout Silverman. There proved to be a dozen families, men, women, and youngsters. The children were quick to make friendly overtures, and several blooming girls made eyes at Bruce.

He had supper with Silverman and the teamsters, doing more than justice to the wholesome food. Listening intently to the talk, Bruce thought how good it was to be among his kind once more. Before dark set in he felt at home with these Texans and had made sure that he was safe for the present. When this caravan came to camps, towns, or met with other wagon trains, or was joined by strange horsemen, then it was time for Bruce to look sharp.

After supper he sat in the circle by the general campfire.

"Wal, them reddies will shore trail us if they git some more of their kind," said one old plainsman.

"Hank don't 'pear to reckon thet way," replied a grizzled Texan.

"But we're not out of Kiowa country yet," said a third.

"Reckon we will be soon."

Bruce quietly interposed: "Kiowas seldom range west of the Canadian."

"Wal, we crossed thet days ago."

"Course we cain't rest easy till we're out of this dinged Injun country," said another.

The company broke up early, some to go on guard duty and the rest to bed. Bruce sought his blanket under a wagon and, with his head pillowed on his saddle, soon fell asleep. But once more in flight, his slumbers were not deep and the slightest sounds awakened him. Each time he had to adjust his thought to the welcome fact that he was not alone.

The slow leisurely tranquil days passed. Only at intervals did Bruce recall the bitter fact of his real identity and the false character under which he had cloaked his brother's guilt.

By the time the caravan had joined the main road, the Santa Fe Trail, the members had accepted Bruce as one of them. Silverman had been most friendly. Once he said enigmatically: "Son, I reckon it was a good idee yore workin' out of Texas." But Bruce knew his presence could prove an embarrassment to Silverman, and he resolved to leave him at the next stop.

Silverman's outfit pitched camp on the outskirts of Couchos before noon one day. It was a gala occasion for the members of the wagon train. There were trading posts and stores, saloons and gambling halls in full blast. Bruce tried to keep out of sight of the many visitors. He thought he recognized one of a group of riders who came to trade horses. He could not be sure, but he had sharp eyes, a retentive memory, and he grew intense and keen. The others had eagerly gone to the posts and stores, leaving Bruce the freedom he desired.

Just before supper Silverman sent for Bruce.

Hurrying over to the circle of wagons, Bruce did not need to see the scout's grave face to sense something was amiss.

"Son, I wasn't shore of yore bein' Bruce Lockheart, but I know now."

"Yeah?" queried Bruce, trying to keep his voice steady.

"Reckon you remember Tom Gaillard?'

Bruce cracked a hard fist into his palm.

"Shore you do. Loveless' worst enemy, if I recollect."

"Loveless swore Gaillard was a rustler."

"Yes; only he couldn't prove it. Wal, Galliard was heah with his outfit, tradin' hosses. He seen you an' he's been talkin' loud. Some of my men heahed him. I'm damn sorry. You'll have to ride."

"Of course. What did he—say?"

"Connected you with thet Denison bank robbery last spring. Swore he was goin' to send word to Captain Maggard. An' if the Rangers get you, he'll claim the reward."

Bruce gave way to cold fury. He had been living in a fool's paradise. It was just as well to be rudely shocked back to his real self. He met Silverman's gaze squarely.

"Son, was you in thet bank deal?"

"No, Silverman. But I got blamed for it. And I can't prove my innocence. Keep that secret, and thanks for everything."

"Listen," went on Silverman, speaking low. "I'm droppin' most of these men on the way. I'm headin' for the Tonto Basin in Arizona. Only Higgins an' Davis are comin' with me. I've two brothers in the Tonto. Work yore way through an' hunt me up there."

"Aw, thanks. That's good of you. But I can't impose on you."

"Texas Rangers haven't got to the Tonto yet," the trail boss replied significantly. "Git now an' good luck!"

Bruce went out to secure his new horse, a big rawboned bay that Silverman had traded him for Barse's horse. He was much taken with the bay. "Legs! That's your new name. I'll bet it'll take some running to catch you." He saddled Legs and tied on his other things, including the empty pack. Then he sat down to wait for dusk.

All approaches to town were dark and the one street was certainly not light with its yellow flares thickened by dust clouds. He dismounted at the first store and, taking his pack inside, bought necessary supplies, then returned to his horse. This made a bulkier pack than Bruce was accustomed to carrying, but Legs was a big horse and he would not feel the weight.

After that Bruce leaned on the hitching rail for a few moments, yielding to the stern urge to pay his respects to Loveless' enemy, Tom Galliard. It was an excuse and opportunity not to be overlooked. After that, other outlaws and men unfriendly to him might be a little closer lipped. Once he had decided, Bruce strode up the street.

It appeared to be busy, noisy, dusty everywhere. Evidently a main-line wagon train had camped outside of town. A few cowboys mingled with the motley crowd of teamsters, pioneers, travelers, and Indians.

Bruce entered the largest saloon, a huge barnlike hall, well lighted, full of drinkers and gamblers. The first man he saw was the dark-bearded Galliard. He sat at a gaming table with five other men. Bruce reached a favorable position before Galliard, who sat facing him, glanced up. He was shuffling a deck of cards. His hands stiffened, the cards dropped. All of Galliard's visage not hidden by beard turned a livid hue.

"*Quiet!*" thundered Bruce. The noise of glasses,

coins, voices ceased until the contrast was remarkable. All faced guardedly toward the intruder.

"Galliard, I'm lookin' for you!" cried Bruce in ringing tones.

"Yeah! An' who the hell are you?" blustered Galliard.

"I'm the man you've been talking about today."

"Lockheart, eh? What you want?"

"Just to waste two more words on you."

"Wal, let's hear them."

"Rustler!"

"I return the compliment. . . . Bank robber!" shouted Galliard.

"Draw!" hissed Bruce.

The five players with Galliard dove to the floor. Galliard, his eyes balls of fire, heaved up with a crash of chairs, his arm lurching for his gun. As he got it out Bruce's shot broke all his tense action. The gun clanked to the floor and Galliard sank face down over the table. Bruce waited a moment, smoking gun extended, his eyes like compass needles, then backed out of the saloon. The silence inside burst into a babel of voices. The pedestrians outside gave the door a wide berth. Bruce hurried away, mounted, and rode out into the dark melancholy night.

CHAPTER 5

FROM THAT COUCHOS EPISODE MISFORTUNE HOUNDED Bruce Lockheart's fugitive trail for a whole year. Wherever he rode or stopped to hide or worked on a cattle ranch or got a job in some out-of-the-way town, his identity was sooner or later discovered. Now and again the limelight was thrown upon him by some notoriety-seeking would-be gunman, and he had to ride on.

So far he had escaped contact with Rangers and so did not have to fight them. But he was drawn into other encounters, all of which made greedy men see in him a counterpart of the bank robber for whom a large reward had been offered. He could not hide his striking appearance. At last in chagrin and revolt he headed back toward the wild brakes of the *Llano Estacado*.

Low in spirits and supplies, and tired from many days in the saddle, Bruce approached a fair-sized settlement about midmorning one day. On the outskirts cowboys were bedding down a herd of cattle. The bawl of cows, the yells of riders, were music to Bruce's ears. He encountered a bow-legged youth leading an unsaddled horse.

"Howdy," said Bruce, reining in. "Mind telling me what town this is?"

"Howdy, stranger," was the hearty reply, accompanied by a grin. "This here burg is Mendle."

"Mendle? And where's that?"

"Wal, it's pretty far from anywhere. . . . Reckon you're from out Lincoln way. How's the cattle war?"

"Getting too hot for comfort," rejoined Bruce easily. "Driving Texas longhorns, eh? That bunch looks dusty and tired. . . . Circle M. Don't recall that brand."

"Never seen it myself, stranger," replied the rider. "Texas outfit just rolled in from the range. Barncastle is the boss. Canadian River cattleman. Know him?"

"Barncastle? Nope. I'd have remembered that name. Is he driving on north?"

"Nope. Sold out to my boss, who's a buyer for Chisum."

"So long, cowboy. I'm on my way," returned Bruce, and rode on.

"Good day, stranger," returned the other genially.

Bruce rode boldly into town because he was forced to take such risk. Soon he entered a wide street, dusty and active with bustling life. The place appeared to be identical with any other western cattle town. He dismounted before the first store, tied Legs to the hitching rail, and stalked casually through the door. "Howdy," he said to the storekeeper. "I want a pack of supplies pronto."

"Hello, young man. Reckon you're the second of thet Barncastle outfit who was in a hurry," drawled the other.

"Nope. I'm not with Barncastle," rejoined Bruce curtly, and proceeded to name the supplies he wanted.

"Wal, thet's a reference, if you was askin' for one," said the merchant enigmatically.

"Yeah?"

"You're a Texan, son, an' so am I. Thet's enough."

"Sure it is, reasonably. But isn't this Barncastle a Texan?"

"He is not," rejoined the storekeeper, as with his back turned he began swiftly to fill the order.

"I rode by his outfit as I came along. Just drove in, I heard, and sold out pronto. . . . Who runs that Circle M brand?"

"Cattleman named Melrose."

"Melrose?" echoed Bruce. "That's a well-known Texas name."

"Yes. He 'pears to be a Texas rancher who ranges between the headwaters of the Brazos an' the Big Wichita," rejoined the storekeeper. "He settled in thet part of Texas not long ago. Runs a big outfit."

"I know that country," said Bruce thoughtfully. "Kiowas and Comanches range north of there, and raid down into the Panhandle. Wonderful rich cattle country, but still unsettled." Then he inquired, "Barncastle sell here before?"

"Yes. Twice last spring."

"What did Chisum pay for this herd?" Though Bruce asked this question he could have made a fairly good estimate.

"Five dollars a haid."

"No!" exclaimed Bruce sharply.

"Fact. Barncastle told me so, not a half hour ago. Eleven hundred haid odd, at five pesos a haid!"

"And no questions asked?" queried Bruce sarcastically.

"Hell no!"

"Chisum will drive those cattle on to Dodge and get twenty dollars. . . . Same old fishy cattle deal."

"Wal, it might look fishy," agreed the other, "but Jesse Chisum can do it. He'll buy from anybody."

"Pretty slick old fox."

"Yes. . . . Wait. Let me tie up that pack, please. . . . It's pretty bulky. . . . Now a blanket. Fold it flat around a small frying pan and coffeepot. . . . six boxes of shells, half .45 Colt and half .44 Winchester.

"Son, I see shells in yore belt are thinned out some."

Bruce nodded somber agreement, then burst open a box of shells and filled the vacant places in his belt. The few left over he put in his pocket. "Tobacco and matches, boss. That'll be about all. Sure I'm forgetting something."

"Mebbe you'll remember. Let me carry this pack out for you." He followed Bruce from the store to the rail. "Son, thet hawse suits you somehow. . . . What'd you

66

say yore name was?"

"What'd you say about this Barncastle being a rustler?" countered Bruce.

"See heah, Texas Jack, I didn't say no more'n you," protested the storekeeper, leaning over the rail while Bruce tied on his pack with nimble fingers.

"Hell you didn't! But don't worry. I'm not the talking kind."

"I'll bet you belong to thet outfit of Texas Rangers who rode through heah ten days ago."

"Listen, old-timer," replied Bruce grimly. "If anyone asks about a rider on a long-legged bay horse, you didn't see him!"

"Son, I never saw him atall."

Bruce swung into the saddle, and suddenly, as a thought struck him, he bent a hard gaze upon the Texan.

"Where might I get a look at this Barncastle?"

"Wal, he hangs out up the street at the Elks Hotel, mostly in the barroom. . . . Hey, son, what's in your mind?"

"I'll hit him for a job. . . . So long, old-timer."

Bruce rode up the wide dusty street fighting the fierce idea that had struck him so wildly. To focus attention on his arrival in Mendle and his possible sudden departure would not be a wise procedure. But he was in the grip of a powerful and irresistible impetus. If this Barncastle did not measure up to western status, Bruce would see through him in a very few moments. How would he reply to terse queries? If he was crooked, as Bruce was already convinced, he would betray himself. The idea intrigued Bruce. It grew upon him. He did not know why.

Dusty riders and creaking vehicles passed him on the street. It was the noon hour, with but few pedestrians in sight. Bruce saw the huge horns of an elk adorning a sign on the town's most pretentious building. He put Legs to a trot. There were loungers around the wide-open front of the hotel, several riders, townsmen in their shirt sleeves, a tall heavy man in black garb. His back was turned. Reining Legs at the curb, Bruce slipped off, dropped the bridle, and stepped round the horse to the wooden pavement.

"But, Barncastle, I can't make a deal—before I see—" One of the shirt-sleeved men was speaking anxiously to the black-garbed individual. He broke off haltingly.

"Aw, hell! Sure you can," came the reply, in a sonorous voice a little thick with liquor.

Like a ringing bell that voice pealed through Bruce. He felt his skin tighten. A leap of his heart, a flash of hot blood succeeded the shock. Then an iron will clamped down upon his emotions. Bruce recognized that voice. His instinct had been like a lodestone.

The lean rider next to Barncastle jumped as if stung.

"That cowboy!" he rasped out, pointing at Bruce with a shaking hand. His swarthy visage paled. "*Look!*"

Barncastle's tall form wheeled unsteadily to disclose the bold features of Quade Belton. He looked older, more lined and sodden of face. His hard blue eyes popped; his mouth gaped wide. Then astonishment changed to consternation and fear.

"BRUCE—LOCKHEART!"

With an alarmed imprecation the lean rider went for his gun. He was quick, too, and got it out, but Bruce's shot broke his aim and tenseness. He slumped forward, his gun belching low, his bullet scattering the gravel in the street. He fell with his weapon clattering on the

68

boardwalk. Belton, with distorted visage, attempted to draw right in front of Bruce's menacing gun, which on the instant again belched fire and smoke. Belton's sombrero sailed off his head and he plunged flat on his back.

Then came a pause, after which shuffling feet and jingling spurs attested to bystanders getting out of the way. Shouts followed the rush. Horses snorted and pounded the ground.

Bruce leaped into the street. Legs had reared to plunge back. But he thudded down and stood. Bruce swung astride and gathered up the reins. With gun extended he faced the hotel front. Except for the two prostrate men, the space was deserted. Belton was writhing in what appeared the throes of death. Then at a touch of spur Legs was off like the wind. Bruce turned at the first corner and looked back. Men were running, collecting in a group before the hotel, yelling and gesticulating, approaching the prone forms on the pavement. He could still see Belton, black-garbed and full-bodied, flopping about like a slaughtered chicken. Then the scene vanished beyond the corner wall. Bruce flew on at a hard gallop and in a few moments had left Mendle out of sight.

Then the fierce, viselike storm in his breast broke to mingled emotions. All the bad luck of his fugitive days had been paid for in this single stroke. But he was on the run again. Belton's riders would raise a posse to chase him. He gazed back up the yellow road. It was empty, except for dispersing clouds of dust.

Bruce was old in experience at that game. He doubted that he could be run down in a straight race, even if he risked that. Legs was Indian bred, strong and fast, and tireless. But Bruce meant to leave the road at the first point where he could swerve without leaving tracks. He was a past master at hiding his trail.

Once more attending to the ground behind him, Bruce made the discovery that the road and its borders were freshly trampled by many hoofs. The Circle M herd had been driven along this route. Presently it crossed a stream bed for a hundred yards or more, then led into the cedars. He might be trailed, but he would never be caught. Southeast was his direction. Somewhere beyond lay the vast trackless *Llano Estacado,* its wild brakes under the rim with endless river bottoms. Like an Indian he studied the lay of the land ahead; like a cowboy he saved his horse and bent all his faculties toward a certainty of escape. When he topped the range he looked back to see the yellow road winding snakelike across the sage-gray and cedar-green plain. Out there ten miles this road split, the nearer fork sheering widely to the south. Range on range of gray and black billowed in that direction, gradually wearing down to a dim purple void, which was the prairie.

Far back along the winding road low streams of yellow dust appeared on the move. At that distance dust clouds from cattle or wagon train would not have streaked out at length, and movement could have been barely perceptible. Horsemen at brisk pace were riding on the road.

Watching this moving yellow against the green, Bruce pondered. The thing for him to do was to anticipate the worst—that the dust arose from the hoofs of a posse of riders. They would split at the forks of the road, which conjecture would make certain his suspicion. And grimly, sardonically he watched the onsweep of dust streamers, like the tail of a comet, until short of a half hour he saw it separate into two lesser streamers, one of which turned south.

"Couple of days' riding for nothing," he mused. "They'll get tired and ride back. Then what?"

Captain Maggard and his Rangers sooner or later would ride through Mendle. They would hear all about Bruce's visit there. Surely one or two of the men standing in front of the Elks Hotel would have heard Barncastle's trenchant call.

CHAPTER 6

SEVERAL DAYS LATER BRUCE MADE A LATE CAMP AND when he awakened the next morning the sun was high and warm. Legs cropped the grass along the brookside. Bruce made short work of his own needs. But at this camp he filled both canvas waterbottle and canteen. Refreshed by the stay there and spurred anew by the old plan, he packed eagerly and rode up out of the gully to the ridgetop.

Bruce reined Legs abruptly in his tracks. And he exclaimed aloud. Clear and sharp to his vision arose the magnificent heave of a high, gray-sloped, black-seamed plateau. It was far away, but distinct in that rarefied air. The plateau he had traversed now dipped for many leagues, and ended in level prairie that sloped endlessly to the bold escarpment—the rugged northern front of the famed Staked Plains of the Spanish explorers.

Bruce, on his earlier flight from the buffalo country toward the Pecos Valley, had watched for days on end the southern bulge of this *Llano Estacado*. But it had been dim and mystic, far away, a ghostly barren upflung wall which only the Comanches dared climb. Here it had beauty and sublimity. It beckoned and called to

71

Bruce. Somewhere beyond that wild rampart, in one of the canyons breaking out of the rim, there would be a lonely refuge for him, where he could hunt and fish, and wait, and lull himself into dreams of a possible future.

He watched that changing gray upthrust all day, as if it lifted imperceptibly higher, while he descended the long slope of the plateau. Sunset found him making dry camp. While the light lasted he hunted for a deer, but all he could shoot was a jack rabbit. Hungry for meat, he cooked and ate most of this rabbit, saving what was left for the next day.

Next morning he was up and away before the east tinged red. All day he carried his rifle across his saddle, keen eyes alert for a deer or bear. But game of all kind was remarkable for its absence. And all the arroyos and creek beds were dry. This fact gave him great concern. He would not dare ascend the Staked Plains without having watered Legs and filled his vessels. His fears were unfounded, however, for at the base of the great slope he came to a fine brook, where grass was abundant and game plentiful. That night he had venison, and he sat up late roasting strips to pack with him. He pondered over the thought of carrying a haunch of deer meat in addition to what he had cooked. But as it would weigh close to thirty pounds, and the strips of meat would last longer than the water he could carry, he decided against the needless burden.

Bruce lingered long at that watercourse next morning. Legs ate and drank all he could hold. When the time came to start the ascent Bruce felt grave anxiety. He had heard Texans talk about the *Llano Estacado*. In summertime it was a death trap. This season was early fall; there had been late rains on the heights; he felt convinced that he could cross the point of the great escarpment, in a southeasterly direction, to come out on the rim somewhere north of the headwaters of the Brazos. Anyway the die was cast, and he started the climb on foot, indomitable and strong.

The ascent of this escarpment was far longer than he had calculated from below. At last he surmounted it, winded and hot, at once aware of a cooler, keener atmosphere. Near at hand the ground rolled away westward fairly even, not quite devoid of brush and stunted cedars. Southward, in the direction he must take, white deceiving stretches bellowed away to a dim horizon. Looking to the north, he found the plateau by which he had come a thousand feet or more beneath him. Plainward there was a void, streaked by wandering dark lines in the foreground, that led on and on to gray nothingness.

The day was dull and cloudy; no sunlight appeared to come through anywhere; a cool mist blew on the wind. It was a propitious day for travel and Bruce made up his mind to profit by that. Tightening his saddle cinch, he mounted Legs and headed out into the unknown.

Bruce's plan was not to travel inland more than a day from the rim. But when once he got out into the wasteland he realized that this would be exceedingly hard to do. To find water and what little grass there might be he must get back farther. Scattered blades of meager grass waved in the wind; cactus and a dwarfed sage vied with an occasional bush for the sustenance to exist on that flinty soil; stunted dead trees spread spectral arms. Not a living creature did his roving gaze catch.

The day passed. Legs put sixty miles behind him. At sunset the gray cloud bank broke, letting the sun gleam red and sinister out upon the rolling plain of barrenness, changing it strangely. Bruce found water in a rocky depression. Legs snorted his displeasure at the alkali taste, but like a wise horse he drank it. A weedy sedge and an unhealthy growth of grass did not augur well for feed for the horse.

"Could be worse," declared Bruce, and his voice, breaking the silence for the first time that day, struck him singularly. How deadly quiet this plain! But that and the loneliness comforted him. No need to sleep with one eye open this night! Hungry, and cheered by this camp, when bad as it was he had anticipated worse, Bruce built a good fire, though he had to fare forth for wood, and prepared and ate a substantial meal. He must save his water, but keep up his strength by eating. A few days at most should see him across to the rim again.

The night was cold, with a peculiar penetrating sting. He sat over his bed of red coals, grateful for their heat. The place had an oppressive something that Bruce felt and could not cast off. It was a weight. Nevertheless, for a fugitive this solitude was perfect. Still in the absence of worry there came other feelings, baffling and vague. If he had given in to them, succumbed to introspection, he would have suffered the old hard bitterness. But he scraped earth over his campfire, laid his saddle blankets upon the spot, made his bed, and went to sleep.

Late in the night he awoke, his sleep out, and the cold intense. Before dawn he was up, stumbling over the desert in search of firewood. Far afield from his camp he found a dead tree, and that solved his problem of the hour. Dawn broke. The sky was clear. A ruddy effulgence spread over the eastern length of the plain. He was in for a sunny day, and did not like the prospect.

Legs had grazed all the green and gray verdure to its roots. He stood waiting to get out of that place. He whinnied; and contrary to most horses, he let Bruce coax him to drink. Before sunrise Bruce was on his way.

Legs made fast time over the scaly ground, which scarcely left marks of his hoofs. The keen horse wanted to get through with this job. He kept veering almost imperceptibly toward the east. And that worried Bruce because he knew about the uncanny instincts of some horses. So presently he let Legs have his head.

A monotonous similarity of every mile of the plateau at length dulled Bruce's attentiveness. But the absence of birds, rabbits, lizards, every kind of life forced itself upon him. In the dust of bare patches of ground he espied coyote tracks, and that was as remarkable as the dearth of other living creatures.

The sun had not been an hour high when Bruce began to realize its heat. Legs' flanks were still dry, but they felt hot. The wind was going to blow. Wisps of dust whipped up here and there and curled over the gray shingle. Trees became scarce and at length failed. A scanty sagebrush and cactus grew thinner.

Without being aware of any change in the topography of the plateau, Bruce came suddenly upon a wide bare depression, miles across; and in striking contrast, in the center there appeared a patch of green. Legs scented water and did not need to be reined off his straight course. Soon Bruce rode up to a waterhole with margins of white alkali circling it. The horse refused it at first. Bruce got off to taste the water. It was salty, though better than none. Legs drank a little, snorted and shook his head, tried it again, left off, and finally took a long full drink.

All around this waterhole Bruce saw mustang and moccasin tracks. The signs were old. They led from the southeast to the west. He decided to backtrack them as far as possible. Not until he had halted here did he appreciate how hot was the sun. He removed his coat and tied it over his pack; then resumed the journey. Legs was now sweating freely. He followed the mustang tracks. In places Bruce made out a trail. No doubt it came up over the rim, leading to some secret place the Indians knew of in the interior.

Long before noon Bruce fell prey to deeper anxiety. The rays of the sun beating down and the refraction of heat radiating from the bare hard ground grew increasingly burdensome on man and beast. The heat veils rose like smoke. Gusts of hot wind, like blasts, blew thin fine alkali dust in his face. At length he had to cover his face with a scarf. All the while the tireless horse kept to his swift gait across the desert.

As the day advanced, heat and wind increased, both of which would have been endurable but for the flying dust and sand. Often Bruce had to have recourse to his canteen. At intervals he uncovered his eyes to look ahead and at the ground. If there were still a trail, he could not see it through the thin layer of sand. Legs had covered at least fifty miles that day, when all at once his rhythmic action and the steady clip-clop of hoofs perceptibly changed.

They had reached the sand. Ghostly swirling sheets and veils could not hide the wonderful billowy sea of dunes that hid the horizon. Legs slowed to a walk. The hours lengthened interminably.

There was no sunset, but a darkening of the light and a cessation of wind told Bruce that day was done. The flying sand settled; only along the knife-edge crest of sand dunes did a moving silver curve prove that the wind had not altogether stopped. He kept on, hoping for a swale in which to camp. He searched in vain. Darkness came on stealthily. He halted on a flat bench in the lee of a dune. No water, no grass, no firewood!

"Legs, you're great, but I don't know," he said, unburdening the horse. Another day like this one would put them in dire straits. Bruce ate some strips of venison and dried fruit. His canteen was half empty. A long pull at it proved to him what thirst really was. The sun had taken a lot out of him, simply dried him up. He recalled hearing how men lost on the desert could lose fifty pounds and more a day.

In none of his past flights had Bruce ever been so done up as he felt now. Wearily and moodily he lay down to sleep. Oblivion came at once. Like a log he lay, never awakening until dawn. Legs was not in sight, but his tracks showed. Bruce soon found him nibbling at some brittlebush.

Returning to where he had left his saddle and pack, Bruce was stunned to find that the latter had been rifled by marauding coyotes. Empty parcels and bags were strewn over the sand. All his supplies except a bag of salt and a few handfuls of dried apples had been stolen. Bruce sat down, overcome. Need of water for Legs and, secondly, for himself—that was imperative. Two days or at the most three like yesterday would finish the most superlative of range horses, let alone a man.

Legs was not daunted. He wanted to be on the march. Bruce straddled him, with the certainty that his life depended upon the horse. They progressed onward six or eight miles, into a bewildering labyrinth of sand dunes. But with the sun the wind rose, and in another hour Bruce faced an inferno. He lost track of time as well as direction. He had all he could do to preserve his eyesight. The sheeted blasts burned as if they had been ejected from a furnace. He almost strangled for lack of air. All day Legs plodded on, as if he knew what objective to make. Like a nightmare that ghastly day passed with the waning wind and settling sand. Bruce fell off his horse and lay in the sand. At length he got up to wash the sand out of his eyes and drink what was left in his canteen. Then he made a deep dent in his sombrero, and filling it with water from the canvas bottle he put that to the nose of the horse. Three times he did this.

"Not much—old pard. But—keep you—from choking," he said.

Legs appeared tired, though far from beaten. He did not want to tarry there. Again Bruce trusted the horse. If he did not want to rest, Bruce knew he could not force him. He got into the saddle again and rode on. Night fell. The sky was a vast blue-black dome with countless white stars that cast silver streaks across the wastes of sand. It was unearthly beautiful. He fell asleep in the saddle, to awaken and fall asleep again. The time came when he fell out of the saddle. Legs stood with head bowed. Bruce slept until the burning sun on his face awakened him.

It was another day, fierce, red, with rising wind. Bruce drank a pint of water, and gave the quart and more that was left to the horse. The ghastly features of the preceding day were magnified. The sun, burning into Bruce's skull, made him lightheaded. Half the time he was out of his senses. The other half he felt the sand-laden wind, the hot blasts, the burning of his eyeballs, the curding of froth in his mouth.

If night had not come again, with its cessation of these terrible rigors, Bruce would have gone crazy and fallen from the saddle to die on the sand. But the horse kept on. And Bruce was as one pursued over the wasteland by furies. This was what it meant to be an outlaw, a fugitive. To suffer all that the physical and mental man could stand! Such a life was not worth living. He would rather die a hundred violent deaths than go through this again. It would have been better had he never been born. Only let him get out of these sand dunes that the Spaniards had called the place of desolation and death!

Such passionate thoughts and pangs at length gave place to physical sensations of pain and thirst and hunger. To hunch in his saddle, hanging onto the pommel, grew to be about his only intelligent reaction. Distance and time had ceased to exist.

But that awful night ended in dawn. And soon Legs, heading toward the reddening in the east, came out on the rim of the plateau. He snorted and sent the froth flying from his clogged nostrils.

Bruce stared, slowly realizing. He rubbed his weary eyes and looked and looked. Far below, a green and gold canyon opened out of the vast slope of the gray barren plateau. Scarlet and yellow and purple vied with the green. The wide canyon opened out upon the verdant prairie. A winding lane of trees and the gleam of a bright stream stretched out upon the prairie, to fade away into the gray of distance. Far over to the south Bruce made out a herd of buffalo. To the north a vast stretch of prairie was dotted with thousands of cattle.

CHAPTER 7

FAR BELOW AND DEEP IN A SIDE CANYON OF THE *Llano Estacado* Bruce and Legs rested and slept all day. In the late afternoon Bruce washed in the crystal-cold water of the spring, and just before the sun went down he shot a rabbit for his supper. Later, by the roaring fire which he had no fear of being seen, he pondered his next step.

The cattle he had seen that morning must belong to Melrose. He needed supplies, and he would like some news. The chances were slim that anyone there would know him. At any rate, he would have to risk it. And maybe he could take a job there under a different name—at least for a time. It would be nice to talk to people and live in a bunkhouse again. His mind made up, he turned in and went right to sleep.

Dawn had just broken when Bruce emerged from the glen to take the right bank of the brook and ride out upon the open prairie. A belt of timber, marking the watercourse, hid the ranch house and buildings and corrals from his sight. He felt secure in the confidence that no eye had seen him come out of the glen. It behooved him to make fast time down to where the road crossed the brook. There were no cattle in sight on the south side of the brook. He crossed two smaller brooks coming down from his right, and he observed that other branches ran in from the north. From that junction the main Brazos began, and grew to be a sturdy fast stream, roaring down between the lines of trees. When he reached the bridge from which he planned to approach the ranch as though from the prairie, his range-keen eyes caught sight of riders far down the road. He decided to wait for them. It would be well to ride into Melrose's ranch in company.

Bruce dismounted and ate biscuits and bits of meat he had stored in his pocket. Then he sat down to go over the part he had to play.

"Might last only an hour—and then, maybe days,"

muttered Bruce.

He had elected to play a type like that Texas cowboy, Jesse Evans, right-hand rider for Chisholm, and one-time comrade of Billy the Kid. Bruce, in his ragged cowboy garb, looked the part. There was a zest and a devil-may-care defiance in the pretense. Maybe he could fool even the old fox Maggard! But not, of course, if anyone saw his meeting with Belton.

In due time the riders approached. There were four of them, leading two pack animals. On closer view Bruce saw that one was a Mexican, a supple-limbed vaquero, swarthy, sloe-eyed, and long-haired. Two of the riders were rangy Texans, flaxen-haired, lean, and brown of face, with still clear eyes like amber. He knew none of them.

"Howdy, stranger," spoke up one. "Was you just holdin' down this here bridge, or waitin' for us?"

"Howdy. I reckon I was doin' the first till I seen you."

"Where you haidin'?"

"Wal, I'm this far to thet Brazos ranch, but I'd sort of like to ride up with company. I'm Lee Jones, from down Uvalde way."

"Yeah? One of them Big Bend Joneses?" replied the cowboy, with a grin. "Shore glad to meet you. My name's Serks, Tex for short. Heah's my brother Jim. Meet this heah unprepossessin' hombre, Peg Simpson, who shore beats his looks. . . . An' Juan Vasquez."

With Bruce on foot and the others mounted they shook hands all around, in a meeting that seemed nonchalant, but far from casual. Bruce sensed that they wanted support as well as he. Perhaps Brazos Head range had a hard reputation. Mounting, Bruce found himself riding beside Simpson, a bowlegged little cowboy, in gaudy garb, and remarkable for a ruddy round comical visage.

"Say, Lee, it ain't escapin' me none that you don't pack thet gun fer comfort," was this worthy's initial remark.

Tex Serks glanced over his shoulder. "Hell, no. I made that observation myself."

"Wal, I heahed this Brazos range had the Pecos backed off the map," drawled Bruce. "Sizin' yore outfit up I reckon you all look like a good hard-ridin' bunch to tie to."

"What're we up agin heah?" queried Jim Serks bluntly.

"Wal, I don't know any more'n I heahed," replied Bruce. "Not bad among the buff hunters. But there's some hombres along them brakes thet'd make any range tough."

"So you come up along the brakes, eh? How far?"

"All the way. I haided out of Fort Worth last spring."

"Then I reckon you haven't heerd Melrose's call for Texas breed riders?"

"Nope. Thet's new to me."

"All right. Word came south thet Melrose is havin' his shirt rustled off his back. Thet grass an' water's rich heah between the haids of the Brazos an' the two Wichitas. Room for a million steers! He'll welcome all the cattlemen thet want to tackle this hard-nut range. But he warns them of the rustler outfits lately rid in."

"Short an' sweet," commented Bruce. "Did you heah of any cattlemen that hankered to throw in with Melrose?"

"Shore. Bescos is on his way from Red River, drivin' a good herd. An' if we report to my uncle Jed thet Melrose is talkin' sense, why, he'll come."

"I see. Reckon thet's why you brothers tackled this

82

proposition?"

"Eggzackly. An' another reason why we want to get friendly with some real hombres. We four fellars aim to stick together."

"Fine idee. But gosh! You shore wanta lay off me. I'm a real hombre all right, an' no good atall."

They all hawhawed at that, which proved they hardly agreed with Bruce. His appearance always favored him, and he hoped it would when he had to line up in front of Melrose and his foreman, Slaughter.

It developed later that one of the larger clumps of timber, like an island in a ripply sea, had obstructed sight of the ranch house and environs.

"Thar! Doggone my soul!" burst out Tex Serks.

It was indeed a heart-lifting sight for a young man, cattle and range bent, who had dreams of success and a home. The scene tugged at Bruce's sore heartstrings.

"What air them long low buildin's?" inquired Peg curiously.

"Bunkhouses, you pore dumbhaid!"

"Hell, they look like forts to this hombre," returned Simpson.

Indeed, it was a shrewd deduction. Those two very long buildings were situated far apart, fronting obliquely the wide space before the ranch house. As the riders drew near, Bruce observed that the bunkhouses had been built of solid logs. A long row of doors and small square windows, like portholes, faced a wide and continuous porch. Red rock chimneys stood up from the rear. A hitching rail ran along each front. Big corrals, built of peeled logs and with adjoining covered open sheds, further added to the ranch scene. Beyond the far group, in the edge of the timber, showed corrals and barns.

83

"Lee, I'll do the talkin', if you don't mind," said Tex, as they rode up.

"I'd be darn glad, Tex, but I'll bet this Melrose an' his foreman will make us all talk."

"Won't betcha. But I'll pave the way."

Several lean riders lounged around the south end of the first house, which end, Bruce grasped, was a store, such as all big cattlemen maintained on their ranges. He fell in behind his comrades, his faculties all keen. A tall Texan, leonine in build, and striking with his sun-bronzed stern face under a crop of white hair, surely had to be Melrose, and he advanced to the edge of the porch to boom out: "Howdy, riders. Get down an' come in."

Bruce felt that voice as though he had heard it but yesterday. It went through him like a blade. Beside the rancher there appeared a wiry rangy man, past middle age, with the features of a hawk. The seconds swept by. No other man came out of the store, whereupon Bruce relaxed, and slowly prepared to come forward.

"Reckon you're Mr. Melrose," said Tex leisurely, as he swung a long leg and in one step was off.

"Yes, an' heah's my foreman, Luke Slaughter. An' who may you be?"

"Wal, I'm Tex Serks, an' this is my brother Jim."

"Serks. Any relation to Jed Serks, down Waco way?"

"Jed's my uncle. . . . This is Peg Simpson an' Juan Vasquez, whove rode with us for years. . . . Lee, come out heah. . . . This heah is Lee Jones, who hails from Uvalde."

"Howdy, boys. I'm shore glad to meet you all. Reckon yore ridin' in is due to my call for men?"

"It shore is, Mr. Melrose," replied Tex heartily. "Sort of a Texas call, my uncle Jed said. He's answerin' thet himself if I send good word back home."

"Wal, we'll see thet you do. I hope there'll be more."

"Bescos of Red River is on his way heah with his herd. About three thousand haid, I reckon. Thet's only a start, Mr. Melrose. You'll have good company before long."

"Thet's good news, Serks," replied Melrose, his somber face lighting. It appeared plain to Bruce that he was a harassed man. Bruce liked his looks and warmed to him. "Luke, I'd like you to talk to these boys an' hire them pronto."

It had not been lost upon Bruce how the little foreman's hawk eyes had been studying them, and it dawned upon him that he had come in for most of the scrutiny. And he bethought himself of how Jesse Evans would meet this ordeal.

After Slaughter had sized up the other four he fastened his penetrating eyes upon Bruce, from head to toe and back again. If Bruce could have read the scrutiny of westerners he need not have been concerned about Slaughter's.

"You from the Jones breed, eh? The Big Bend Joneses?"

"Yes, boss."

"Which family, the good or the bad?"

"Wal, I'm sorry to say I come from the bad side. But I wasn't asked to choose."

"Right. I've had some bad relatives myself . . . . Jest fall in with Serks on yore way?"

"Yes, sir. I came by the brakes."

"You did? We'll talk about thet later . . . . Where'd you get thet bay hawse?"

"Wal, I didn't steal him," drawled Bruce coolly. "You savvy he's not Texas bred. I traded him from a New Mexico cowboy, down Uvalde way."

85

"Didn't mean to be overinquisitive," returned the foreman. "Grand-lookin' hawse. Can he run?"

"Wal, there ain't no rustler in Texas could get away from him."

"You want a job?"

"Yes, sir. I'd like you to throw me in with Serks' outfit."

"What can you do?" queried Luke dubiously.

"Wal, I can cook an' wash dishes, an' chop wood, an' dig—postholes—things like that," drawled Bruce.

"You look it, I don't think," said Slaughter, with a broad smile.

"Boss, don't hold my looks against me," appealed Bruce plaintively. "I jest ain't the kind to blow my own horn."

"Air you on the square?" asked the foreman deliberately.

Bruce met that hawk gaze unflinchingly, sure of himself and his honesty.

"Absolutely. But I don't see no call to confess my life history," he retorted.

"Shore not. Excuse me, Jones," replied Slaughter hastily. "You jest interest me, thet's all. You're no ordinary cowboy."

"Hell no. Who said I was?"

"Wal, yore getup—somethin' about you makes me see you as a cowboy who's had a tough deal. Shore I know a little about the Jones families. Good an' bad blood. Ruined by the war. . . . You ain't denyin' thet."

"No, sir. I'm all right, if you don't rub me the wrong way."

"I won't, Jones, you can rely on thet. . . . But any Texan who's seen the range life I have couldn't miss yore bein' a gunman."

"I take thet as a compliment," replied Bruce, entirely unruffled. "Is it any reason why I cain't fit in heah?"

"Not by a damn sight," declared Slaughter forcefully. "Jones, I don't have to tell you this job will be hard. Not manual labor. But hard ridin', hard shootin'. You savvy?"

"Suits me fine. Thet's why I'm heah."

"All right. What pay you want?"

"Not particular, so long's I get grub, some ridin' boots, an' jeans when I need 'em."

"Yo're on, Lee Jones, an' fer wages too. But I see you need the boots right now. Where'd you track up thet red mud?"

"Must have been the Red River, boss."

"Wal, you new hands, how do you want to bunk?" Slaughter rose from his kneeling posture.

"Boss, if you don't mind, we'd like to stick together," replied Tex Serks.

"Had thet figgered. An' it falls in with my idee of makin' you a special outfit."

"What you mean by special?"

"We're runnin' several outfits. An' I don't aim to throw you in with any of them. I want a small outfit thet can be heah today an' somewhere else tomorrow. Hard riders, trackers, an' handy with guns."

"Uh-huh. Not much herdin' stock for us, eh?"

"Is this Vasquez a tracker?"

"Best in Texas," was the laconic reply.

"Any of you cook?"

"Simpson can, in a pinch."

"I cain't wuth a damn. But I'll take my turn."

"Settle thet among yoreselves. Take two of the bunkhouse rooms between you, get grub at the store, kill yore own meat, an' be ready for orders."

The foreman went into the store, which Bruce saw contained an office. Melrose had already gone in.

"Wal, pards, it's all over but the fireworks," said Tex heartily. "Throw saddles, an' let's get settled."

The rooms were quite large, contained four bunks each, two on opposite walls, one above the other, a table, chair, lamp, open fireplace, wash-bench with utensils, and mirror.

Bruce went out to carry his saddle and pack into the room he would share with Peg. While he unpacked his belongings Peg staggered in under a heavy load which he dropped on the floor with a sigh. Bruce grinned and, picking up two buckets from the bench, sallied forth to get water, more than satisfied with the propitious way the situation had developed. His cue was to be wary and see every man first, as surely as that was possible. To that end he carried the buckets in his left hand and walked off the porch to pass the store.

Suddenly he saw Trinity in the doorway. He dropped the buckets as his mouth fell open, her name on his lips. Trinity heard the buckets fall and saw Bruce at the same instant that he put his fingers to his mouth to signal silence. She stifled a cry just in time, and managed to keep herself from running as she came toward him. Struggling to maintain his composure and play his part, Bruce removed his hat in an elaborate gesture and said in a loud voice, "Howdy, mam, I'm Lee Jones from Uvalde, one of Mr. Melrose's new hands."

"Bruce," whispered Trinity fiercely, fighting to keep back the tears and joy at finding him. "What are you doing here?"

"I might ask you the same, Trinity," he replied in a low voice. "But I can't talk now. Meet me at the canyon north of here tonight. And my name is Lee Jones."

"I'm pleased to meet you, Lee," said Trinity loudly and prettily. And she managed a smile before she swept off.

Bruce delayed his return. He rinsed out the buckets and refilled them, then took a long drink. It was Brazos Head spring water. When he looked up again Trinity had entered the store and Peg Simpson, laden with bundles, was hurrying out as if pursued by something.

Upon entering their cabin, Bruce found Peg on his knees before a pile of bags, which obviously he had dropped, rapt and spellbound.

"Lee, did you see that bootiful apparishun?" he asked eloquently.

"See what?"

"Hell, man. Thet gurl. The boss's dotter."

"Oh, yes. I saw a girl standing there," returned Bruce, struggling with his own amazement, as he deposited the buckets.

"Is thet all?"

"All? Shore it's all."

"My Gawd! Now I know you're no range cowboy. All the same I'm glad you ain't no devil with the wimmen. . . . Lee, she smiled at me in the nicest way. An' Slaughter said: 'Trinity, meet one of my new hands, Peg Simpson.' Lee, I seen she was took with me."

"Gosh, you're a lucky cuss. Thet's the big boss's gurl, eh? Wonder if there's any more?"

Bruce left him with his thoughts in a turmoil. Why was Trinity here at Melrose ranch? And why did they call her the boss's daughter? Lord, but it was good to see her again! He could hardly wait till that night.

Stamping into the store Bruce inquired generally where he could find some firewood. Slaughter sat at a table with Melrose. The former laughed outright as he said something to the smiling rancher. Trinity, who stood behind him, with a hand on his shoulder, was smiling too.

"What'd I tell you?" queried the foreman. . . . "Aw, howdy, Jones. What'd you bust in for?—Firewood, eh? Wal, we don't keep thet in our store. But if you'll open the back door of yore bunkhouse you'll find a stack."

"Thanks, boss," rejoined Bruce, a little at a loss at the foreman's facetiousness, and he was about to turn away when Melrose motioned him to wait.

"Luke, let's get this over. . . . Trinity, this is Lee Jones, another of my new hands. . . . Jones, meet my daughter."

Trinity, from behind her father's and the foreman's backs, managed a ravishing smile that still held something of wistfulness and hope. She wanted these men to like him. She said, "I'm glad to meet you, Mr. Jones."

Bruce forgot his role in a gallant bow, sombrero trailing the floor. "Miss, the pleasure is mine." Then he backed out on the porch, to stalk on a few strides, then pause, motivated by dust clouds far down the road. Then he called in at his door: "Fellars, come out. Hawses down the line, from the other direction."

Simpson followed Tex Serks out on the porch. They all gazed to the north, eyes glued upon the newcomers.

"Five riders. Wal, it all depends on who they air."

"Ha! Tex, you said a lot," replied Bruce coolly. "You boys stay out heah. Mebbe they ain't nobody. Peg, I'll mix yore sourdough."

"Lee, I knowed you was one of them hombres who's lookin' for someone," said Serks seriously.

"Me too, Tex. Eyes never still. Ears cocked like a jack rabbit's," added Peg in the same tone.

Bruce recognized the moment. "I'm sorry, boys. You read me true. But I swear it's no reason we cain't be pards."

"Wal, thet's enough fer me," rejoined Peg stoutly. "How about you, Tex?"

"I reckon. I'm either for a man damn pronto or agin him the same. Go on in, Lee. We'll size up this bunch."

Bruce went inside, rolled up his sleeves, and set to work on Peg's unfinished task. He heard the cowboys walk slowly on to the store, where Serks called in: "Boss, thar's riders comin'." And Slaughter's testy reply: "Wal, what of it? Air you scoutin' Comanches fer us? Riders always comin'." And Melrose's: "Stay indoors, Trinity."

Bruce's hands were as active as his thoughts. This quintet of riders might be Rangers or some of Belton's men. Sooner or later they would ride in. And Bruce meant to let the exigencies of the moment decide the outcome.

Finishing the dough Bruce opened the back door and was agreeably surprised to find a narrow back porch, with shelves on one side and neatly stacked firewood on the other. He packed in wood and built a fire, and put water on to heat. Sound of thumping hoofs outside, the rattle of gravel, and then voices drew him to the window, tense and strung.

The five riders were lined up outside the hitching rail. One sweeping glance relieved Bruce. He did not know any of them. Slaughter had advanced to the edge of the porch to greet these callers. From Bruce's angle he could not see Melrose or the other Texan.

"Howdy, Stewart," the foreman was drawling, "air you gettin' down?"

A tall rider, with ragged, unshaved visage, and

91

piercing black eyes, not unhandsome, removed the stub of a cigarette hanging from his coarse lips, to say: "Not today, Slaughter. Just fetched word over from Blazes' Waterhole to Melrose."

"From who?" queried Slaughter curtly.

"Our boss. Barncastle. Who else?"

Barncastle! So he hadn't killed Belton when he shot him, thought Bruce, with amazement and disappointment.

"Wal, let's have it," replied Slaughter.

"I'm talkin' to Melrose."

Slaughter called to the rancher to come out. Heavy footfalls attested to Melrose's movement. Bruce heard through the chinks between the logs of the wall Trinity's low voice, warning but indistinguishable. In a moment the rancher stalked into view, to loom over the little foreman. He bore a cool exterior, but Bruce's sharp divination deduced a burning interior. Bad blood was brewing between Barncastle and Melrose. Why hadn't he finished him off in Mendle?

"All right, Stewart. Go ahaid an' talk, but make it short an' to the point," said the rancher. "But how do I know you're Barncastle's mouthpiece?"

"Melrose, you'll have to take my word. Also that I'm a good deal more than his mouthpiece."

Slaughter interposed caustically, "Cattle foreman, right-hand man, or jest what?"

Stewart glanced contemptuously at the little foreman and did not deign other reply. Bruce, used all his life to crooked men of evil force, saw through this one as if he were an inch of crystal. Here was a stronger man than Belton. Indeed, Melrose had fallen in with bad company.

"I don't care what you air to Barncastle. But get out

92

what you've got to say."

"Hold your horses," returned the other sardonically. "This is your funeral, not mine."

"It's most damn likely to be Barncastle's," retorted the rancher hotly.

"That's why the boss gave me this job—maybe to save a lot of funerals. . . . First off, Barncastle wants a final answer on the partnership proposition."

"No. I won't throw in with him on his terms. Where's the five thousand haid I gave him the money to buy?"

"That herd is on the way. It's a long trip."

"Why didn't you an' yore outfit stay over there to drive them heah?"

"That was Barncastle's orders. Linden, who sold to him, agreed to do the driving."

"Stewart," resumed the rancher, manifestly holding himself in check, "I don't want to be unreasonable. But I'm sore, an' I'm gettin' leary. At Dodge City where I last saw Barncastle I wanted the money I'd lent him. He said he had paid it out for the herd. I asked him to go to the bank an' borrow the money. He made excuses. Then I went to the bank myself. They didn't know Barncastle. I left Dodge, an' he followed me heah. You can tell him I won't listen to any propositions till he gets thet herd heah or pays me the money."

"Melrose, it strikes me you may lose both herd and money," rejoined Stewart bluntly.

"*What!*" yelled the rancher, growing purple from neck to brow.

"You heard me."

"So I did. An' I'm beginnin' to savvy thet thet might be cheapest in the long run!" Melrose stalked back into the store.

Stewart lighted another cigarette. He was unperturbed

93

and apparently acting upon orders. If Bruce knew Belton, he had greatly changed to allow this Stewart to be a mediator. The other four riders lounged in their saddles, smoking, yet keen with interest. They were not young cowboys and had something of the matured hardness Bruce had seen in some of Billy the Kid's outfit.

"Slaughter, does your boss cool off after ructions and come to his senses?" queried Stewart.

"Wal, he does at thet, most times," returned the foreman. "But I doubt it on this deal. It sticks in my craw too."

"Many an old rooster like you has swallowed a fishbone that got stuck in his gizzard. Can you talk sense into him?"

"Shore I can, if I get the hunch thet *is* sense."

"Here's the hunch, Texas," replied the other caustically. "Barncastle is no man to make an enemy of. It's my outfit with him, fourteen strong. Indian Territory and Missouri men who haven't a hell of a lot of use for Texans. Melrose is alone out here, running fifty thousand head of longhorns. At least he had that many till this rustler gang dug into him. They almost wiped out his Little Wichita outfit. Well, on a range as big and free as this he can lose all his cattle before it gets settled. He needs Barncastle and my outfit. If you're smart you'll persuade him to forget his difference with my boss and throw in with him. . . . Do I make myself clear, Slaughter?"

"You do. An' no Texan ever took a gauntlet like yore's in his face without slappin' it back. If you knew Texans you'd never throw a bluff like thet. Now slope pronto, Mr. Stewart, you an' yore outfit."

Certain it was to Bruce that Stewart ill concealed

gratification at the split he had brought about. Like as not, Bruce evolved from it, Belton's burly lieutenant was promulgating some plot in his own interest. Without more ado, Stewart motioned to his men, and off they loped their horses, in the direction from which they had come. Slaughter went back into the store. Tex Serks and Simpson returned to face Bruce, fire in their eyes.

"Lee, you heahed all thet?" queried Tex.

"I shore did."

"Wal, what the hell? Did we ride in heah lucky or onlucky?"

"Lucky for Melrose," answered Bruce, with certainty.

Bruce repaired to the window and saw Melrose and Trinity, arm in arm, with the gesticulating foreman beside them. They turned into the tree-lined driveway leading up to the ranch house. It seemed to Bruce that another great opportunity had been laid before him. Cudgeling his brain, he could not shake that idea. But dared he risk telling what he knew when it jeopardized his own safety? Cap Maggard would ride along there any day. And ride right into a hot situation! For Melrose's sake Bruce could not help but hope the Rangers would come soon. Was it Belton precipitating this raw deal or that crafty Stewart? Bruce leaned to the latter being the instigator. Belton was getting double-crossed the same as he was double-crossing Melrose.

"Come an' git it," called Simpson. Bruce turned to join his comrades at the table. His seat was a box. The meal was good and they were all hungry. But that, Bruce suspected, hardly accounted for an almost complete silence.

After they finished, Tex said, "Wal, Lee Jones, what did you mean by sayin' it's lucky for Melrose thet we rode in heah?"

95

CHAPTER 8

BRUCE ROLLED HIS CIGARETTE EASILY, TIPPED BACK his sombrero, and eyed the keen Texans with what must have appeared to them a sober and penetrating scrutiny.

"Tex, I reckon it's my call to ask questions first?" he said.

"Shore. But get at it."

"Wal, before I ask any I'll tell you I *know* Melrose is being swindled as well as rustled—thet like as not if we don't interfere he'll be shot in a fixed quarrel, or murdered from ambush."

His four listeners reacted to that in a sudden tense silence. Then Peg Simpson let out a gasp, the vaquero uttered a sibilant hiss, Jim Serks gazed open-mouthed at Tex, who vibrated like a compass needle.

"Hell you say! . . . Lee, can you prove thet?"

"Yes. Barncastle is not the real name of the cattleman Stewart says is his boss. If he *is* a cattleman he's become one only lately. He's an outlaw, as bad as the West makes 'em. But a yellow cheatin' hombre. He an' this Stewart outfit have rustled Melrose's Circle M stock. Up into the thousands! Never mind right now how I know this. . . . Now for Stewart. I reckon thet's no more his real name than Barncastle's is. I'll gamble we'll find out sooner or later thet Stewart is one of the big cattle thieves, from New Mexico or Colorado. Anyway, he's what no doubt you seen him to be—a cold hard mean proposition, capable of any kind of dirty work. He's the power behind Barncastle. What *he* says goes. It's a pretty shore guess thet he wants a split between Barncastle an' Melrose. Then they'll rustle small herds to the north an' west, an' make one great raid, then haid for the brakes. I figger Stewart aims to work fast. Clean up this ranch by next spring."

"Ha! Plain as print an' shore easy to follow," said Serks, as Bruce ended.

"Heah now," Bruce went on, "shall we take Melrose an' Slaughter into our confidence?"

"No. I wouldn't advise thet pronto," returned Serks decisively. "Let's wait an' see what turns up next. Mebbe we can work on Slaughter to fall in with us without knowin' everythin'. He's a range hawk, all right. Let's let him feel us out. Let's get the lay of the range. Mebbe Barncastle will storm in heah soon, an' thet, I figger, might be too bad for him."

The five men agreed, just as Melrose's young son, Jack, walked in. He proved to be a friendly youngster about sixteen years old, and it was manifest that he favored the cowboy garb. He was packing a gun rather prominently. Bruce cottoned to him right away and figured he might be useful in the days ahead. Sure enough, in a little while he was telling them: "Dad is worried sick over his deal with Barncastle. An' Luke is madder'n a wet hen. Dad is afraid he's been hasty and oversuspicious. He's scared and wants Luke to go slow. Luke wanted to send you boys out to get proof that Barncastle isn't what he cracks himself up to be. But Dad said wait."

"Ah-huh. Jack, you're goin' to be a big help," said Tex thoughtfully, and he shot a knowing look at Bruce. "Would you mind tellin' us what you think of Barncastle?"

"Mind?—Hell, I'm tickled to death. I hate the hombre," declared Jack, with a vigor that belied his years.

Darkness had gradually settled down, and Bruce was

97

anxious to go and meet Trinity. He got up casually and announced that he was going out for a while.

"I won't wait up for you, Lee," grinned Peg.

Bruce saddled up quietly and unseen and rode straight for the canyon, half afraid Trinity would not come and half afraid of his own emotions. But as he rode up between the canyon walls he heard Legs snort and whinny and get an answer back, and his heart leaped for joy. In a moment he saw Trinity standing by a tree, her horse's reins in her hand, and he leaped from Legs' back before the big horse had even stopped.

Then they were in each other's arms and nothing else mattered. It seemed to pay Bruce for all his unloved years, his terrible ordeal of flight to survive. Trinity buried her face on his shoulder and clung to him, giving herself to unrestrained weeping. But she did not cry for long. She leaned back in his arms, wiping her eyes and looking at him.

"Trinity. You certainly are flesh and blood. But explain before I know I'm loco. How in the world do I meet you here?"

"Oh, there's so much to tell. Come, let's sit down."

Trinity took Bruce by the hand and led him to a mossy ledge near the canyon wall.

"Trin, were you followed?"

"No! No one knows I'm here."

Bruce found himself pushed back to lean against the wall and, unbelievably, Trinity within the circle of his arms.

"Bruce, do you remember that day—by the river trail near Spencer's ranch—when you rode down on Barse, changed clothes with him, took his horse and—and that money?"

"Remember!" replied Bruce bitterly. "I wish I could forget."

"Bruce, I was hidden there in the brush and I saw and heard it all."

"You know then—the truth about Barse?"

"Yes, I know. He was the bandit, not you. He was one of Belton's robbers. You rode off across the river."

"Trinity, you certainly were there," said Bruce slowly, expelling a deep breath.

"You took Barse's burden on your shoulders and left him to marry me because you thought I loved him and my happiness was at stake."

"Yes, that was what I thought."

"And you loved him too."

"Yes!"

"And your mother—you did it for her too, because Barse was her favorite."

"I—I can't deny it, Trin," Bruce said.

"I was so stunned by what had happened I couldn't call to you," Trinity rejoined. "Then you were gone down the fugitive trail. And mostly all for nothing."

"What are you saying, Trin?"

"You were wrong about me, for one thing. I had already made up my mind it was you I loved. I decided to trail you and find you no matter where you went or what you did. I—I wanted to fetch you back. Tell the truth . . . make you force Barse to admit his crime. If you would not come, I meant to share your life with you, whatever it was."

"Plain madness, Trinity."

"Well, crazy or not, that's what I meant to do. I muffed the whole thing. I should have told them in Denison before I left . . . that you were innocent. Now it may be too late—if you would go back. I've bad news,

Bruce."

"Ahuh!"

"Barse went back to the same old drinking and gambling. He's dead, Bruce. Killed in a fight over a card game."

"My God!" whispered Bruce huskily.

Trinity raised herself to her knees and embraced Bruce tenderly.

"What—about Mother?" he asked from beneath his bowed head.

"I can't say I'm sorry about Barse. But your mother has failed," Trinity said tremulously. "For you to go back now, unless we could prove your innocence, might be too much for her. You could be killed before we accomplished that."

Bruce looked up at Trinity.

"I'll take a lot of killing," he said grimly.

"That's just the trouble. That's what I'm afraid of. These trigger-happy Rangers—and others you might meet. Anyway, there's one good thing. Your mother is being well cared for. The Spencers took her in with them."

"Aw, that's good.—It's a shock learning about Barse. An' Mother. I reckon it had to happen sooner or later."

"Bruce, the damage is done. You can't change things now. What we must do is plan—how, where, what to do."

"Trin, before we go any further tell me about you. Where you've been, how you got here, why you're here."

Trinity told him of her trip from Denison to the Melrose ranch, about Lige Tanner and Captain Maggard, and how she proved she was Steve Melrose's daughter.

"Aw, Trinity, that's wonderful. Thank God for you. That's the only happy news I've heard since I rode away."

"The *only* happy news, Bruce?" Trinity came close to him again, her hands on his arms.

He drew her to him. "No, Trin, I'd—forgotten. I'm bowled over."

Again she put her arms around his neck and Bruce held her slender throbbing body warm against his.

"Trin, we can't go on like this," he said, abruptly pushing her back to arm's length.

"And why not?"

"I'm a marked man. There's a price on my head. You're the daughter of a rich rancher. You've got a background. Roots down. I can't have you involved. I wouldn't even if you were still Trinity Texas Spencer."

"You won't have much to say about it if you love me—as you seem to."

In the pale light of the new moon Bruce's gaze was riveted upon her in fascination. He remembered so well the small fair head, the graceful yet strong figure, and the little feet now encased in moccasins, her wavy hair locked in a braid. She had grown more lovely with the passing of time. Her dark eyes looked up at him with wonder and joy and sadness too. Suddenly he was to realize that the love he had borne her had grown terribly in the recent months of privation and hardship.

"You don't deny it, Bruce." She smiled. "We must plan, how to get away, where to go. I'm full of ideas."

Bruce broke away from her and paced back and forth in the glade. Trinity seated herself on a rock to watch him. His thoughts dwelt upon the vastness of Texas, of the West, and yet how small it had become. Quade Belton, Barncastle, and Melrose, Trinity's father. One

101

thing reasserted itself in Bruce's mind. Belton would not live long after Bruce met him again. This he meant to do. Melrose's troubles would be over for a while at least. Then the trail again, alone. But this he must conceal from Trinity.

"Trin, tell me more about this Brazos Head ranch."

"Dad runs several outfits between the Brazos and the Big Wichita. It's the best range in Texas."

"What about rustlers?"

"Oh, there have been rumors of raids. Dad says it's nothing serious. Just part of the country growing."

"It may be more serious than he thinks. What about this man Barncastle?"

"Oh!—You know about him?" returned Trinity.

"More than you dream of. And I overheard Stewart with your dad and Slaughter."

"They were going to be partners. Now they'll never be," replied Trinity, with some heat.

"Who did Melrose think he was?"

"Barncastle claimed to be a big stockman, with a ranch in Kansas and another across the line in New Mexico."

"Haven't you ever *seen* him?"

"Not close, Bruce. But why all the interest in Mr. Barncastle?"

"Where is he now?"

"He left this range over a month ago. Took his riders. Several days ago a messenger came. Barncastle had been shot in Mendle. Badly wounded, but not mortally. But why—why?"

"Did this messenger say who shot Barncastle?"

"I'm sure not. Dad was hopping mad. He would have come out with anything if he'd heard."

"Trin, I guess we must get used to shocks," Bruce

said. "I shot Barncastle. I curse the conceit that made me believe I never need shoot twice at the same man. . . . Barncastle is Quade Belton."

"Oh, no," cried Trinity, jumping to her feet.

"Yes, and next time I won't miss."

Trinity went to Bruce and placed a hand on his arm.

"Must there be a next time?" she asked.

"I'm afraid so, Trin."

"What have you become, a bloody gunman? The old creed. Even break. See who's the fastest. Bitter because you failed to kill him last time. Oh, I know, you've plenty of provocation. But why can't we just leave here—together?"

"Unthinkable, Trin. We couldn't make it across the plains."

"You did! I'm as good a rider as any cowboy. I could smuggle a pack. We could go tonight—tomorrow."

"You'd be missed," Bruce pointed out. "They'd track you."

"Bruce, you could go back the way you came. I'd bring supplies. Then I'd meet you in New Mexico. I'd find a way. We could go to Arizona. No one would ever find us."

"I tried that, Trin. Besides, Barncastle—Belton and Stewart have got to be stopped. They are dangerous as rattlesnakes. Your dad, great as he is, needs help."

"Oh, you're stubborn—bullheaded, just like you used to be," Trinity shouted at him in fury.

Bruce ignored her. "It'll be the same old story," he said. "A few small drives, then some bigger, then one last big one, and Melrose will be ruined and Belton, or Stewart, if he's really double-crossing Belton, will disappear to pull the same stunt somewhere else."

"And you think you can stop it."

"I'll have to."

Trinity gazed at Bruce thoughtfully. "I'm sorry I lost my temper," she said. "I've been selfish. I was thinking of you—of me. You are right. But just how do you propose to stop Belton? You can't ride out after him. He was never proved to be connected with the holdup at Denison. He can go where he pleases. You can't."

"I don't know what to do," Bruce said. "Trin, if I promise to ride away later . . . meet you—when things are better, would you agree, about my staying on to help your dad?"

"Oh, yes, yes, yes!" Trinity cried, coming to him again. "But you promise. We'll both watch. If any Rangers come, or anyone else who knows you—we'll go. You will go, and I shall follow."

Bruce could never understand how he was able to face this indomitable girl and lie to her. "All right. It's settled."

With a sigh of relief Trinity settled back in Bruce's arms.

"You're such a wonderful girl."

"If I'm so wonderful, shouldn't I be rewarded?"

"Yes. But all the gold in all the mines wouldn't be enough."

"I don't want gold. I want to be loved. Forget you are Bruce Lockheart for a little. Darling, to be serious, it'll take a good many kisses added to those you gave me to make up for all I've missed—back in Denison when I didn't know my own mind, and since."

It was moonlight in the little oval. Bruce held her in his arms and thought of the incredible thing that had come to pass. And of what he meant to do. Deceive Trinity and leave her. But would he be big enough to carry it through?

104

"Bruce, I must leave now. It won't do for me to ride in very late."

He walked with her through the glen to the edge of the timber, where Trinity had left her horse. She turned to face him.

"Bruce, will you remember, whenever you see me look at you like this, that I am telling you I love you?"

"I'll remember," he replied gravely.

"*Mucho grande caballero*," she said, and lifting a gentle hand to his lips she melted into the shadows.

CHAPTER 9

NEXT MORNING THE FIVE WERE AT BREAKFAST IN Bruce's bunkhouse when Slaughter entered and asked Bruce to take Jack Melrose and go deer hunting along the brakes.

"Huntin' deer?" queried Bruce.

"Shore. But don't miss cattle, tracks, riders, or nothin'. Savvy? At thet, we need some venison."

This order necessitated walking to the pasture beyond the corrals. In the big fenced-in meadows there were a score and more of fine-looking horses. Young Jack appeared leading two clean-limbed mustangs. One was a pinto that surely took Bruce's eye.

"Mawnin', Lee. Heah's yore hawse for the day. Belongs to Trin. She wants him exercised."

"Gosh! He's a beauty. . . . How'd you work this hunt, son?" asked Bruce, as they made for the bunkhouse.

"Trin. She runs this ranch, an' don't you overlook thet. Said she wanted venison, an' persuaded Luke to have you look after me."

"Wal, we're lookin' for more than deer, Jack,"

returned Bruce.

"What, for instance?" asked the youth, his dark eyes flashing.

"Slaughter wants a line on cattle, tracks, riders, out along the brakes."

They saddled their mounts. Jack ran into the store for a rifle while Bruce got the lunches from Tex. "Lee," he said, "I told the boss I'd ride out to look you up after while, an' he said I'd stay set right heah. What's yore angle on thet?"

"Wants some of us heah all the time," rejoined Bruce significantly.

"Funny deal, eh? But I like it. Let's play his game as if Comanches were ambushin' the trail."

Presently they were astride. Young Melrose had the seat of a range rider and made a fine picture on his horse. They rode off toward the line of timber.

They entered the belt of timber and crossed the rushing stream of amber water to climb the far bank. They were not half a mile from the base of the bluff that sheered up green and then gray to the rim above. Clumps of brush and trees straggled down from the slope to fall down on the level.

"Jack, I'll hunt through this timber an' you take the line where it thins out. The sooner we hang up a deer the shorter distance we'll have to pack it. Go slow, see everythin', especially down toward the range, an' whistle once in a while, so we'll keep even with each other."

They parted, and soon Bruce was wending a slow way through the open glade, and under the trees. Rabbits ran ahead of him. In the distance he heard turkeys gobble. Once he sighted a doe and a fawn. There would be plenty of deer, and he chose to let Jack

106

do the killing.

It was an Indian summer day, growing sultry and smoky, melancholy with the notes of migrating robins and turtledoves, and full of the dreamy languor of the woodland in late autumn. Bruce felt it with strong emotion. He could hardly believe the facts of his existence at the moment. Trinity had waved to him. She had not been afraid to let this fiery brother of hers divine that she liked this new rider, lately come to Brazos Head. She loved him. She was building her dreams of the future around him. She was as clever and resourceful as she was sweet and lovable. She had already helped along the good opinion of father and brother, and of their old foreman. Bruce longed to give in to the glamour of the facts and dream with her, build their castle, but he dared not let himself go. If he could be free and safe this hour, what joy to yield to thought and plan of a future with this lovely girl, and a ranch in this ideal and rich upland of Texas.

His meditations were broken by a rifle shot, and then a whistle. Bruce headed the mustang down toward the open. He was some little time locating his comrade, but at last saw him, on foot, rifle in hand, bending over a fallen deer. Approaching the spot, Bruce found that Jack had shot a fine two-point buck.

"Good work, son. It didn't take you long. Get yore hawse an' rope while I gut this buck. . . . Then we'll hang him up."

"Shore hit him plumb center. Yore turn next, Lee. We can pack two in as well as one."

In short order they had the deer disemboweled and strung up to the branch of a tree. Then they rode on south, keeping inside the edge of timber. Bruce sighted a black bear up on the slope. It saw them and plunged away through the shaking brush. Perhaps ten miles from the ranch they reached the zone of rough brakes. Ravines as close together as the ruts on a washboard opened out of the slope, all black with timber. It was necessary to ride down toward the range to get around the wide mouths of these gorges. They grew wilder and bigger toward the south. Bruce judged that fifteen miles or more from the ranch there began the real brakes of this rim country, which for years had been notorious as a rendezvous for savages, renegades, buffalo hunters, and at the present time was a harbor for rustlers.

A hundred miles, approximately, to the south Bruce had hunted buffalo and between that locality and the farthest point he had reached there stretched some of the roughest and wildest country in Texas. Water and grass and game in abundance, and tangled jungles of timber, filling huge brakes in the rim, afforded hiding places for gangs of outlaws that never could be apprehended. The brakes of the Rio Grande, about which he had heard, could scarcely have been more inaccessible than some of this country.

"Jack, you've got a glass. Let's climb to thet high point an' take a look-see, as the Indians say," suggested Bruce.

They haltered their horses at the base of the slope and began the ascent. Broken masses of rock, fallen timber, thick chaparral hindered progress, but in due course they reached the objective, an outcropping ledge some five hundred feet up.

"Jack—what—a sight!"

"Don't you—love Texas—Lee?"

"I reckon I've—about arrived," panted Bruce.

Streams like threads had their sources in these brakes and united below to make a river, the dark line of which faded in purple immensity. Cattle that Jack claimed wore the Circle M brand clustered in league-square patches, far to the south of the Brazos.

"An' Dad never drove them over heah, you can bet on thet," added the boy sharply.

"Wal, they could drift over heah," observed Bruce thoughtfully. "Take a look with yore glass way down there where we cain't see with the naked eye."

After a long survey of the vague range Jack handed the glass to Bruce. Almost out of sight showed a patch of black, but whether or not it was cattle could not be ascertained.

"It's south we must look for stock—an' trouble. . . . Gosh, what a lookout! Boy, a scout stationed heah could watch these brakes for fifty miles."

The belt of green along this section of rim was miles wide, and that did not count the timber that ran up the gorges. The *Llano Estacado* bulged higher toward the south for farther than the eye could see, and the serrated and overgrown slope augmented its wildness. There was a rugged grandeur in this rampart, separating desert and range. But Bruce could not take time to gloat over the beauty and ruggedness of this scene. He fell to studying the mouths of the gorges and the gray stretches that opened from each one. Close at hand, within five miles, he sighted cattle in surprisingly large numbers, a few straggling buffalo, and two separate columns of smoke, one coming out of a gorge, the other located down on one of the many timber lines. Without comment he returned the glass to Jack, who began a long and thorough search. Bruce knew the lad had come across something that might as well be wrong as right.

"Lee, I'll bet two bits rustlers air drivin' cattle in small bunches south an' east toward the lower Brazos."

"Won't take you up, kid. Thet's an observation worthy of Slaughter or Serks."

"There are a good many cattlemen on the lower Brazos, so I've heahed."

"Would Texans buy cheap cattle an' ask no question?"

"I reckon—some of them. Lee, who could be makin' those smokes?"

"Gosh! Anybody. But we'll make it our job to find out. I've a hunch they're shady campfires."

"They're hid well enough. Lee, let's go down, eat our lunch, an' mosey for the ranch."

"I want to fetch Serks an' his outfit up heah, before we go farther."

They retraced their steps to the level and after a short rest were homeward bound. Bruce passed by a number of opportunities to shoot a deer, as he did not want to burden the mustang with additional weight so far from the ranch. Jack did most of the talking. He was a dynamic, voluble personality, and therefore most likable. About midafternoon, within five miles of the ranch, they separated, though keeping within sight of each other, and kept that position until they reached the point where they had hung up the deer. Bruce helped Jack tie the carcass behind Jack's saddle. Some distance beyond this place Bruce flushed a flock of wild turkeys and, getting off with his rifle, shot two running gobblers.

"Gee, you cain't shoot thet rifle atall!" declared Jack, when they met again. "I never hit a runnin' turkey yet."

"Easy, Jack, if you pick out the right one. Never try to hit one runnin' crossways. . . . Hello! Look. Someone heard those shots."

"Where?"

110

"Boy, it's yore sister, shore as I'm born. An' she's ridin' thet hawse."

"Trin can ride to beat hell. But, Lee, she doesn't ride like thet for fun. Somethin's wrong!"

"Hope not, but as it must come, why, let it. Let's go."

In short order the speeding mustangs closed the gap between them. They met in the open, half a mile down from the edge of the timber, and not far north of the stream. Bruce searched the girl's face for confirmation of his fears. His heart sank like lead in his breast. But it was her strained eyes that betrayed her. Bruce was mute, while Jack burst out: "Trin, is somethin' terrible wrong?"

"No. I just wanted to ride out—meet you—and talk to Lee," she replied, almost out of breath.

"Lee?" ejaculated Jack. "So soon?"

"Soon nothing. Lee is an old—friend I met in Waco—when I visited there—with Dad."

"What you givin' me?"

"Jack, I haven't time to—explain now. But I will—when I get home. Will you ride ahead—and—"

"Shore, Trin. Don't worry about me. Lee an' I are pards," replied Jack soberly, and rode on ahead.

Trinity transfixed Bruce with tragic eyes.

"Four Rangers rode in today—on the—lookout for news of Bruce Lockheart!"

Although prepared for that very thing, Bruce sustained a terrific shock. A clammy dew spread even to the palms of his hands. Then in a flood, hot and tempestuous, the blood waved all over him, burning with the passion of self-preservation. In one instant he was back in that frightful state of a hunted fugitive who had a thousand times more at stake than life—the dream of love this girl had inspired, despite all his will and

111

reason! These faded in the fierce fire of the instincts to fight, to kill, to flee. Ride the man down! Creed of the Texas Rangers! Ride the poor miserable fugitive to his doom! Destroy the hope of regeneration! All that uplifting thought had to go for naught. And, what the hard years had made Bruce surged relentlessly to the fore.

In the madness of the storm he scarcely felt the girl's clinging hand on his. But presently he was forced to face her, and then again shock conflicted with all this tide of emotion. She loved him. She was horribly frightened. She could not speak. She read his mind.

"Ride over—here—dear," he whispered huskily, and crushed her bare hand in his. They rode out of sight under some trees. Jack walked his horse leisurely, not gazing back. "Now—tell me. . . . Who?"

"Sergeant Blight—one of Captain Maggard's Rangers," she said, with difficulty. "I knew Blight— months ago, at Waco. He made up to me. The other Rangers—three of them—I've never seen."

"They're after *me*?" queried Bruce, as she paused.

"All of Maggard's men—are after you," she went on, gaining voice with effort. "They split at Mendle. Blight trailed a horse along the foothills—just on a chance, admittedly. Maggard went to Dodge with three men. The others stayed at Mendle."

"How'd you find this out?"

"Dad told us at dinner, quite casually. 'Bruce Lockheart? Where'd I hear thet name?' Then he called Maggard a damned old bloody grudge tracker. 'Why the hell,' said Dad, 'doesn't he trail these rustlers thet live off Texas cattlemen?' . . . Bruce, it'll be as we thought. Maggard will come here. Blight has orders to await him."

"Aw! . . . it wouldn't be so bad if I could only have run into Belton."

"Shot him and rode away?"

"Yes. Now I'll never. . . . You'll be left—"

"Let's talk of these Rangers," she interrupted, strengthening in voice and courage. "Your first fierce thought is to meet them—at their own game—to kill."

"Yes, Trinity. That's a man's instinct. They've hunted me like a dog. I'm tired of running and hiding. They'll ride me down in the end. . . . Why not?"

"This is what terrifies me!" she cried passionately. "I feared it—I knew it. . . . But, Bruce, your promise?"

"It can't be kept."

"Oh, darling!"

"Girl, can't you be reasonable?" he demanded. "I can't keep it, unless I surrender. How *can* I do that?"

"It'd save you—and me. . . . Bruce, I love you—with all my heart and soul. . . . It's my life. That's why I beg of you to think—*think* away this hate—this passion to kill."

"Trinity, are you asking me to give up to these Rangers?" he asked strangely.

"No! Neither that nor betray yourself by gunplay. Bruce, I've got more sense than you have." She urged her mustang closer, until they pressed together, and then she clasped his hands like steel. But it was not an act to embrace—to give way to love. Driven to extremity, a woman's courage and intuition rose in her, stronger, he felt, than all the primitive passions of men. "Sergeant Blight doesn't know you from Adam. None of them do. I made you promise to leave, but it's not the time. If you *did* go now, it'd betray you. You stay, and if we can't fool them—and Cap Maggard with all his damned stubbornness—then we don't deserve happiness. But we can do it, Bruce."

"All right. If you say it like that—look as you do—I'll believe anything. I'll do anything."

"Can you change from your easy, cool, watchful way—your reserve—say, to a happy cowboy, just made up with a sweetheart he'd lost and regained?"

"Lord help me!" ejaculated Bruce.

"Let's help each other. Perhaps if we'd kiss each other it might seem different."

"It might. Come—Trinity," he rejoined falteringly, and whether with desperation or remorse or unutterable gratitude, he loved her so unreservedly that when she sat back in her saddle, red as a rose, shining of eye and disheveled of hair, she did not appear the same girl.

"How do I look?" she asked hastily.

"Beautiful. No Ranger on earth would ever take you for the sweetheart of an outlaw."

"Let's rustle, then. Don't forget your part. Call Dad 'Colonel.' Play up to me, Bruce."

"Just what are you going to do?" Bruce asked her.

"Never mind! Just follow my lead. Play up!" Trinity said, and with that she wheeled her horse and spurred away.

Trinity led the way across the open, and down into the gully. On the other bank Jack waited for them, apparently seeing or thinking nothing. Bruce caught up with them, his keen eyes roving around the ranch premises. There were saddled horses at the hitching rail in front of the store and lounging riders. Tex Serks stood up when he spied them and strode forward to lean against a post. He was interested. Two big supply wagons were being unloaded. Melrose and Slaughter were grouped with strangers on the porch. Bruce beat down the reaction of the gunman. He staked all on the

114

presence, the charm, the cleverness of his sweetheart.

Most striking of all at that crucial moment for Bruce was to see Tex Serks and Peg Simpson amble out to meet him, to be beside him when he dismounted. No significance perhaps to the others present, but to Bruce tremendous!

CHAPTER 10

BUT IT CAME ABOUT THAT BRUCE, SUITING HIS ACTION to Jack and Trinity, did not on the moment dismount.

"Dad, we had a dandy hunt," declared the lad vociferously. "Got my deer plumb center. An' you ought to see this Jones cowboy shoot turkeys on the run!"

That focused all attention on the arrivals. Bruce's glance long since had assured him that he had never seen these Rangers, which augured well for their not having ever seen him. Still under his easy exterior he was taut.

"Howdy, Sergeant Blight!" was Trinity's friendly greeting, and she bent over to offer her hand to the Ranger. "Welcome to Brazos Head ranch."

"Miss Melrose, this is a pleasure," declared Blight, shaking her hand warmly. "I'd have known you, of course. But my! What a few months can do for a girl!"

"Thanks, if that's a compliment. . . . Sergeant, let me introduce my fiancé, Lee Jones, from Uvalde."

"Ah! . . . Yes? Your fiancé? . . . Well, hod do, Lee Jones. Glad to meet you—and congratulate you," returned the Ranger, genuinely surprised and plainly taken aback, as he proffered his hand.

With the impact of Trinity's words, Bruce almost fell

off his horse. So this was her game. And what would happen now? It was too late for any recall. He had to go along.

Then Melrose, who had stood there utterly astounded, his jaw dropping, burst out.

"Wh-at! . . . What's this? *Yore finacé?*"

Trinity's vivid blush and confusion were certainly natural, and most becoming and effective.

"Now, Dad," she cried, "Please don't embarrass Lee before our visitors."

"But good heavens, girl! *You* engaged?—To Jones. Why, he just got here!"

"Very modest short romance, Dad dear," she replied demurely. "Lee and I met when you took me to Waco. We saw each other a little—had an understanding. Then we quarreled. It, was my fault. But Lee really rode here to see *me*. We made it upand I'm very happy."

"I'll be da-doggoned! You deceitful little—aw, I don't know what! I'll look into this. . . . Jones, I hope you can give a thumpin' good account of yoreself."

"Colonel, I just cain't reach up to yore expectations," said Bruce, in distress. "I begged Trinity to—to let me see you before she told it."

"Wal, Jones, I didn't mean any offense," replied the rancher, somewhat mollified. "But I'll talk turkey to you."

Trinity's face then was wonderful to behold. To those who saw her, except Bruce, there could be only one reason for her glowing radiance.

"Dad, ask Sergeant Blight to supper," she said, gathering up her reins. "Lee, I'll expect you. . . . I'll run along or it will be very late."

Certain it was that Bruce, when he leisurely dismounted, absolutely could not face Peg and Tex. But he felt their eyes upon him. Fortunately young Jack came to his rescue.

"Lee, you shore can handle a knife," he said. "S'pose you cut out a haunch of this deer for you fellars, an' I'll pack the rest up to the house."

Then Sergeant Blight spoke up. "Won't you give me a piece? We're out of meat."

"Shore thing. . . . Lee, cut it without untyin' my rope."

Meanwhile Bruce had slipped saddle and bridle off the mustang, which without taking time to roll, bolted for the corrals. Melrose resumed conversation with the Rangers. The situation had passed off without a single one of Bruce's misgivings being justified. He could not believe in the actuality of the facts. He seemed in a seventh heaven and the bottomless pit of despair at one and the same moment. Supper at the ranch house, with Trinity! Could he stand such an ordeal? The very thought made him quake inwardly. Still how impossible to avoid it! Trinity's wit and forcefulness quite took his breath, and the girl's resistless determination to save him, and stand by him, affected Bruce as nothing else could have done.

Dusk had settled down when he re-entered the cabin. Lamplight and firelight made the big room bright. When Bruce faced his comrades, accusing as they looked, he realized that his status had changed, and vastly for the better.

"Say, am I a low-down hombre to look at like thet?" ejaculated Bruce.

"Lee, it's shore An amazin' thing to find out, an' makes us solid heah at Brazos Haid," declared Tex Serks. Jim nodded approval of his brother's deduction, Peg winked at him, and Juan's dark still visage broke to a huge smile.

"Lee, we're mighty glad for yore sake, an' I'll bet my last peso thet Trinity is lucky too," added Peg.

"Thanks, Peg. I feel better. . . . Tex, listen to this," said Bruce, and proceeded to tell what he and Jack had seen down at the edge of the brakes.

"Wal, fellars, the plot thickens," returned Serks. "No more'n I expected. . . . Lee, here's our story. Peg an' Juan couldn't locate a camp out at Blazes' Waterhole. An' they didn't pick up a single steer down on thet range. Damn queer, for they said thet range was as big as all outdoors. So they rode back heah to take up Stewart's trail. Juan tracked thet hombre an' his outfit down to the road, an' along thet road, across the bridge where you waited for us thet day, an' farther on a few miles to where the tracks cut off the road, takin' a line southwest toward the brakes. What you make of thet?"

"A lot thet looks bad."

"Bad? Say, it couldn't look no wuss. I'll report to Slaughter an' in the mawnin' Peg an' Jack can light out thirty or forty miles north toward where Melrose's cowboy outfits air supposed to be. You an' me will take Juan an' track Stewart down."

"Right. But not so far thet Stewart can get a line on us."

"Shore not. It's a good bet thet one of them smokes you seen, mebbe both of them, came from Stewart's camps. Soon as we locate them again, we'll hole up till night, an' then sneak up on foot."

"Thet means layin' out all night," said Bruce seriously. "It's pretty far over there. Over twenty miles."

"Wal, boy," drawled Tex, "you do yore courtin' tonight to last fer a spell. We may be gone a couple of

118

days."

"Supposin' we locate Stewart's outfit. What then?"

"The boss will want us to watch them. Sooner or later we'll find out why they make camp in the brakes over sixty miles from Melrose's main cattle runs."

"Tex, there's no guessin' how many riders Stewart an' Barncastle have."

"No, an' thet's what we must find out."

A footfall and a knock on the wall near the open door preceded Melrose's voice: "Come along, Jones. We might as well rustle up to the house."

Bruce bent over Tex and whispered in his ear for him to listen to the Rangers' talk, if he could do so without detection. Then Bruce went out, to find the rancher with the sergeant and foreman waiting on the porch. He led off into the gathering darkness toward the ranch house, evidently resuming a conversation with Slaughter and Blight about cattle rustlers. Bruce listened attentively. The Ranger was rather slow to believe cattle stealing had become anything to be concerned about, at such a distant point from markets.

Presently the road wound between lines of trees into a parklike space where the ranch house stood with lights shining from many windows. Melrose went across the wide porch, opened a huge door, and ushered them into a great colorful hall-like living room. A long massive table occupied the center. Beyond it, in the midddle of the wall, a fire blazed in a large open fireplace. Rugs and skins and blankets on floor and walls lent vividness and color. Comfortable armchairs, a blanket-covered window seat, a shelf of books, lamps, and tables further added to the comfort, if not luxury, of Melrose's living room. Bruce counted eight doors leading out of the room, two at the south and north ends and four on the wide left of the great fireplace. One of these opened into a bustling fragrant kitchen. A gunrack stacked full of rifles drew his particular attention.

"Sit down, friends, while I mix some juleps," said the rancher cheerily. "Supper will be on pronto, from the smell out heah."

Later they were called to supper. If Bruce ever had sat down to such a sumptuous repast he had forgotten it. Trinity, radiant in white, was beside him, and they had scarcely made themselves comfortable when the sly girl sought and found his hand under cover of the table. She squeezed it, too, as if to bring him out of his trance and to say, "Didn't I tell you so?"

"Jones, you've been so surrounded by my admirin' family," spoke up Melrose, "thet we saved our drinks. Will you give us a toast?"

Trinity gave Bruce's hand an inspiring pressure, upon which he acted as if all his life he had been used to such situations. He reached for the glass and stood up.

"Colonel, I've not been a drinking man. I've had to cultivate a steady hand. But on this occasion—sure the most uplifting of my life: To the prosperity and happiness of the Melroses of Brazos Head ranch."

The rancher ended the merry response with the bang of his glass on the table.

"Well said! . . . Trinity, thet from yore Texas cowboy!"

Bruce sat down with mingled feelings, into which edged the sudden shocking realization that he had totally forgotten his role as cowboy. He felt like a straw in a swift current. What would Melrose and his Ranger guest think? Trinity whispered something indistinguishable in his ear, but it was sweet. And as a man under a spell, which did not wholly eradicate appetite,

Bruce went through that supper.

Slaughter and Sergeant Blight left soon afterward.

"Dad, I'm ridin' out with Lee in the mawnin'," announced Jack.

Melrose threw up his hands in resignation. "Son, if Jones an' the Serks boys want you, it's all right with me."

"I'll vouch for him, boss," said Bruce quietly.

"Any orders from Luke?"

"No. Haven't reported to him yet. Heah's what Jack an' I saw on our hunt today." And Bruce briefly recounted their discoveries on the ride to the brakes.

"Ha! Fits in with what Serks told Luke tonight," observed Melrose thoughtfully. "Some hot times comin'. Wal, to tell you boys the truth, I've long expected this. An' I've been lucky to have it hold off so long."

"Melrose, where does Barncastle fit in?" queried Bruce significantly.

"I've about given up, Lee," declared the rancher wearily. "I'll give him a few more days of grace, then—"

"Aw, Dad, give thet hombre nothin'," interrupted Jack.

"Son, don't rush me," replied Melrose impatiently. "All in good time. I'll never again judge any man hastily. Lee, I had a younger brother—a wild fellow who was ruined by the war. But if I had been tolerant an' kind, instead of violent an' distrustin', he might have been saved, if not reclaimed. He went to the bad . . . an' the Rangers killed him."

Bruce nodded understandingly. "Someday I'll tell you my story. An' what made me a lone rider, hard an' . . . ."

Trinity intervened by putting a hand on her father's

121

shoulder and facing Bruce, such a lovely picture of youth and beauty, and something compellingly womanly, that Bruce came back to the present with a sharp pang.

"Who's a lone rider—hard, and what?" she asked sweetly, but with a deep and thoughtful look.

"I am," burst out Bruce, almost passionately. "An' hard? My God, you know I am!"

Jack took advantage of the momentary silence to clap a hand on Bruce. "Shore. If you hadn't been you wouldn't be heah to help us out of a hole. . . . Dad, don't believe this cowboy if he says bad things about himself. An' give him a little time alone with Trin. Thet may make him forget a lot. . . . Good night, pard."

"Son-of-a-gun!" ejaculated Melrose. "Jack is like my brother—only steadier—smarter. He'll never go to the bad. . . . Lee, suppose we get it over."

"You'd better, if I'm to be any good on this job," replied Bruce despondently.

"Trinity, leave us alone a moment."

"No, Dad. What you say to Lee means everything to me. Life or death!" said Trinity, very low, and she grew as white as her dress.

"Child! You look—why, you are yore mother come back! Perhaps thet is good. If I remember myself when I ran away with yore mother I'll be kinder to Jones."

"Then, Dad, can I stay?" she asked tremulously.

"Trinity, you know my bark is worse than my bite. . . . See heah, Lee Jones. Who'n hell air you?"

"I'm willin' to let it go whatever way you think."

"But, man, I've always been a sucker who believes everybody is fine an' honest until it's proved otherwise, which it shore is a lot."

"Boss, you mean I'm not just what I seem?"

122

"Hell no. Air you?"

"I can answer that truthfully both ways."

"Thet toast tonight to us—to the prosperity an' happiness of the Melroses. You didn't speak thet like a lone-ridin' hard cowboy."

"But I am one!"

"Then you've been somebody else once. You have breedin' an' class. From thet angle you're good enough for her. Now what have you to say?"

"Melrose, if you'll give me a little time I'll tell you everythin' about myself."

"Yeah? A little time. What for?"

"Because if I tell you now like as not you'll hawsewhip me or shoot my laig off."

"Wal, you 'pear to be a fellow who could stand thet for Trinity."

"I could. Either or both. But in thet case I cain't help you as I know I can if you trust me."

"I'm trustin' you, Lee, else we wouldn't be talkin' this over. All the same, I don't like to be kept in the dark."

"Boss, you're a grand Texan," burst out Bruce. "By heaven, I'll keep nothin' from you!"

Trinity left her father's side to embrace Bruce. She was, in that moment, a woman whose love gave her command of the situation.

"No. You have told Dad enough. Wait. This is not the time. If Dad beat you—disgraced you here at Brazos Head—drove you away, I'd go with you!"

Melrose stroked his chin in perplexity. "Trinity, what kind of talk is thet? I don't want you to leave heah."

"Then, Dad darling, see it my way for a little."

"Easy enough. I like this queer cowboy of yore's. . . . But if as you say I might beat him an'. disgrace him

123

heah an' now if he confessed, why wouldn't I do the same later?"

"I'll risk that. But the important thing is you need Lee now. You could hire other cowboys, some of them hard riders and dead shots. But no one who can see through Barncastle and his outfit."

Melrose started up, his dark face lighting, his stalwart form vibrating.

"Lee, you knew this heah Barncastle before?"

"Yes, I did. I shore did."

"He's not what he pretends to be?"

"Absolutely not."

A sudden relief chased the somberness from Melrose's face.

"Lee, we'll let it go at thet," he said feelingly. "I take you on Trinity's trust. . . . Now, you young folks forget me an' the whole mess I've made of it heah, an' spend a little while alone."

He strode out, stamped off the porch, and left, evidently for the store and office. While Bruce bowed to the astounding circumstances, Trinity turned out several of the lamps, left a shaded one burning. Then she shoved a huge armchair closer to the ruddy fire and bade Bruce come. And when he sat down in that chair she slid over the arm, into his lap. Presently her head was on his breast and she was crying softly.

"Don't cry, darling," he whispered, with deep feeling. "You were wonderful. I'm sorry I almost failed in my part."

"Bruce . . . but I'd better—call you Lee," she returned. "You were—just perfect. They all liked you. And Dad? . . . I never saw him so—so serious. You struck him right. . . . I'm just crying be-because it's over. You're accepted—as my—my friend. You're not

124

on trial. . . . And if you can help Dad, he'll overlook whatever you were—and we can be happy."

Bruce succumbed to the hour. And the fact that he was a hunted outlaw failed to enter his consciousness.

"Br—Lee, I've a wonderful idea," she whispered in his ear. "Do you want to hear it? You'll be crazy about it!"

"I'm afraid to heah. I cain't be any crazier than I am."

"Well, darling, here it is. . . . I'm going to homestead the oval where we met last night—up by the spring."

"Homestead! What for?" he returned thickly.

"So we can build a cabin and live there. It'll be protected from the northers. And do they blow? You wait. There are two more fine big springs, rich grass, as you know. Oh, yes, Lee, I made friends with Legs today. Not one horse we have can compare to him. . . . And plenty of wood."

"Just where do you aim to build this cabin of dreams?"

"Where do you say?"

"By the big spring—Brazos Head—where we met. I'd want something like that to remind me always of how good Heaven has been to me."

"Bruce, you can say the sweetest things. For a man who swears he never—"

"Hush! Don't ever tease me about other girls. Thank God, you're the only one who ever was or ever will be."

When Bruce left her on the porch, white and slim in the starlight, the night was cold with frost in the air and the coyotes were howling. He walked from the big gate to the bunkhouse without one single lucid thought. A light in his room brought him back to earth. Peg and Tex Serks were still up, smoking before a bed of red coals.

"Listen, Lee," said Tex, beckoning him closer. "We

heahed some things tonight. Melrose an' Sergeant Blight had a hell of an argument in the store there. To piece things together, these Rangers are heah on orders from Cap Maggard to find trace of one Bruce Lockheart, bank robber, gunman, an' Lord only knows what else. Wal, it seems our boss hasn't a hell of a lot of use for Rangers, especially Maggard. Melrose cussed him proper, an' said if the Texas Rangers wanted to be welcome heah they'd shift trails to these rustlers. After thet the Rangers left the store for their place, a few doors down from us. Then the boss an' Slaughter had a long powwow, spoke too low for us to heah much. But we heahed some. Melrose is for hirin' more riders. But Slaughter is agin thet. Luke swore this heah Serks outfit was big enough. Shore a compliment to us, Lee. About thet time I strolled into the store an' told Luke what we wanted to do in the mawnin'. He was for it. Melrose wanted to know what we'd do in case of a fight with a big outfit. An' Luke said: 'No open fight with any bunch, if we can avoid it.' An' I put my ante in. 'Boss, soon as we locate this outfit thet's been rustlin' heah we'll take to night attack. If they're throwin' up a cabin we'll burn it over their haids. No outfit can elude us with Vasquez trackin'. He's a hound on the scent.' An' Melrose agreed, only he wanted us to make sartin shore who air the thieves. Last thing he said was thet he just couldn't believe Barncastle was a rustler."

"Funny!" mused Bruce. "The man is hipped on believin' a word bad against anybody. Still he explained thet to me." And Bruce related what Melrose had told about his fateful judgment of his brother.

"Huh. Mebbe thet's good for us, hey, Lee," rejoined Tex sagely. "Let's turn in. It's late."

126

CHAPTER 11

BEFORE SUNRISE NEXT MORNING, WHILE BRUCE AND his comrades were at breakfast, Juan Vasquez suddenly held up a warning hand to enjoin silence. The cabin door was wide open. They all listened.

"Hawse comin' lickety cut," said Tex Serks, and leaping over the bench he strode to the door.

Then Bruce heard a rhythmic beat of rapid hoofs on the hard road.

"Rider," spoke up Tex. "Hawse all lathered. Somethin' up, fellars."

Tex went out to the porch, followed by Peg and Jack. From inside Bruce looked over Juan's shoulder to see a dusty, foam-flecked horse and rider come in from the north. As he neared the end of the bunkhouse Bruce descried a slim cowboy, whose complexion was hidden by dust and lather. As he hauled on the bridle, to bring his mount short up, it was evident that he could use only one arm. The other hung limp. As he stepped out of the saddle Bruce saw that one hand was a dirty red from blood and caked dust.

"Call Slaughter an' Melrose," he said.

"Not heah yet. We're Slaughter's new riders. Who're you?"

"Buster Wells from the Little Wichita outfit."

"Hell to pay?" queried Tex sharply.

"You said it, cowboy," replied the other grimly.

"Come in. . . . See you're crippled. . . . Juan, look after his hawse. Peg, get hot water an' clean bandages. . . . Lee, help me off with his coat. . . . Jim, run up after the boss."

Tex was swift, decisive, and efficient. He slit the

127

rider's shirt sleeve, exposing a bloody forearm. "You can set down, cowboy. . . . Peg, give him a drink." Tex washed off the dried blood, to expose a clotted bullet hole that went clear through the arm. "No bones broke," he said cheerily, after feeling and flexing the arm. "Nothin' atall, this bullet hole. Clean as a whistle. Looks like you lost some blood."

"I reckoned I'd bleed to death," returned Wells.

Peg wiped the rider's lean face with a wet towel, which office showed the visitor to be pale despite his bronze skin. He was a towheaded, blue-eyed Texan under twenty years.

"Don't talk no more now," said Tex, as he bandaged the injured member. "Some strong coffee might help."

"Reckon it would. I been since yesterday sunup without nothin' but water." While he gulped the coffee Peg handed him, quick steps sounded outside, then Slaughter looked in at the door, stern and fire-eyed.

"Buster Wells!" exclaimed the foreman. "An' shot!— Say, cowboy, yo're not bad hurt?"

"Not bad. But I bled a lot an' rode some."

"Boss," interrupted Tex, "if I know anythin', he rode darn fast, if not far."

"All right, Buster. I needn't say how glad I am yo're heah safe. . . . Where's yore gun?"

"It got shot out of my hand."

"Aw, hell!" swore Luke, and he sat down heavily on the bench. "Somebody give me a cup of coffee, an' a bite. I must be growin' old. . . . . Go ahaid, Buster. Talk."

At that moment Sergeant Blight and one of his Rangers edged in. They betrayed a keen curiosity.

"Wal, about this time yestiddy mawnin'," began young Wells, "we was haidin' south with the herd of

128

longhorns—accordin' to orders, all we could round up—and was drivin' them across the Little Wichita when we was attacked from the timber on the far bank. Most of the shootin' was below me. I seen hawses an' riders go under. Three or four of the boys got back to the bank an' began shootin' from among the trees. But the cattle kept swimmin' right along over. I was about to haid back when bullets began to spatter close. As I'd got out of the deep water I spurred into the brush an' cut up the bank to my right. I came out on top in the timber. I seen riders along the edge in the open. An' I figgered I'd have to be quick gettin' away or be trapped. So I broke right out into the open. Two riders chased me, shootin' fast. I shot one off his hawse—saw him roll over the bank. The other fellar shot my gun out of my hand pronto. I couldn't get my rifle out, so I made a run for it, an' got away. . . . Wal, I was lucky. Them rustlers must have figgered I'd keep on goin' upriver, an' cross to join what was left of our outfit. But soon as I was out of sight I haided south. I reckoned I was all of forty miles from heah, an' ought to make it by late afternoon. I got dizzy an' lost my haid. Fust cover I come to I hid an' stopped my arm bleedin'. Thet was long after dark. I had some bad spells when I walked my hawse, an' jest managed to hang on. Fact is I went to sleep or passed out, I don't know which. Anyway, when daylight came I braced up an' rode on in."

"Buster, you say you saw some of yore outfit hit—an' go underwater?" queried Luke.

"Yes, I did. I wish to Gawd I hadn't seen so clear," returned Wells, with passion. "I was several hundred yards upstream from the main herd. There came a couple of shots—then a whole volley. I seen hawses an' riders go under—an' not come up. One boy was Art

Semper. His hawse plunged right up, hard hit, an' I seen Art slide off. I think, but cain't be shore, thet I recognized another boy, Jeff Stevens. He jest fell forward over his pommel an' sank with the hawse. The rest I didn't have time to recognize."

"How many boys got away?" asked Slaughter, evidently profoundly shocked.

"Three or four, no more."

"What'll they do, Buster?"

"I reckon after shootin' back some they'll ride hell-bent for our other outfit on the Big Wichita, fifty miles, mebbe, across."

"How many cattle did you round up to drive down heah?"

"We didn't count. But it was a big herd."

"Shore thet rustler bunch will take up yore cattle drive? Where?"

"Lord only knows. These rustlers have plenty markets. An' not all regular cattle buyers!"

"I hate to believe thet, but I do," rejoined the foreman, with finality. "Serks, make Buster comfortable heah. You've an extra bunk. An' you an' yore outfit stay heah till further orders."

"Boss," replied Tex earnestly, "if you don't mind me sayin' it, cattle herdin' for the present should be given up for rustler huntin'!"

"Shore. But make Melrose see thet. Up till lately cattle stealin' was jest a fleabite to him. We're losin' stock in herds. It's a d— critical time. I'll confer with Melrose."

"Slaughter, I'll go with you," declared Sergeant Blight impressively. "I think I can tell him what to do."

"Wal, at least you can back me up," replied Luke dryly.

Serks put Wells into the unoccupied bunk, where he dropped to sleep at once. Presently Jack Melrose presented himself in Bruce's room.

"Why aren't we ridin' to the brakes?" he demanded. "Luke is havin' an argument with Dad, an' thet damn Ranger who sided with Dad. They fired Trin out an' wouldn't let me go in."

Bruce briefly told Jack what had happened to change their plans.

"All the more reason we should ride to the brakes," he said tersely. "What you say, Lee?"

"Shore, if you want to fight."

"An' you, Tex, what you think?"

"I believe we've somethin' to find out over there," agreed Tex.

"Let's go anyway."

"We better wait, lad."

"All right. Come in the store, an' I'll treat. Candy an' smokes."

"Not me, Jack," replied Bruce. "I'm going to feed my hoss."

Whereupon Bruce took up his bridle and a nosebag of grain and sauntered off pastureward, his mind full of the menace of the morning's news. The big horse came quickly, keen and whinnying, his fine head jerking up and down, his eyes alight. He ate greedily while Bruce stroked his nose. When he had finished, Bruce slapped his rump and started back to the bunkhouse. Suddenly he saw dust devils on the road near the ranch and presently made out three riders and a buckboard. A moment later he noticed dust coming along the edge of the brakes.

Puzzled and apprehensive as to what these two groups of riders meant, he started for the bunkhouse, keeping low. When he reached the lower corral the first group swept by and up to the main building. Bruce peered cautiously through the fence, and his heart went cold. Quade Belton was getting out of the buckboard and walking up the steps to the house. Bruce grabbed his gun and then stopped. Belton was too far off for a good shot, and he had three armed men with him. Nor could Bruce go into the house and shoot Belton down before Trinity and her dad. He would wait, face Belton when he came out, and settle with him once and for all.

The time dragged interminably while Bruce waited, his trigger finger itchy, his nerves taut. Belton's riders slouched on their horses near the buckboard, smoking and joking.

Suddenly the front door burst open and Belton stormed out, red-faced, followed closely by Melrose. They exchanged angry words. "Good," thought Bruce. "Melrose has told him off." Then the noise of riders coming in distracted them. From his hiding place Bruce could not see who it was, and then to his dismay he saw Belton start off in the direction of the store and out of his line of fire. Bruce sheathed his gun, and ran away from the corral, through the trees and shrubbery, to the slope of the hill, and from there to the pasture fence. He found that from this point he could get near the bunkhouse closely without being observed, by keeping behind a clump of tamarack. This he gained and, crawling to the edge, lay there, panting, and keen to see and hear.

The incoming riders had reached their objective, and several of them had dismounted. But the three riders who had accompanied Belton up the road still sat their horses. Tex Serks' lofty stature and tawny head showed plainly above the other cowboys and Rangers. Slaughter appeared to be pushing his men back on the porch. He succeeded to some extent, which left Belton standing in the open space between them and the riders facing a tall man whom Bruce immediately recognized as Stewart. Sight of him seemed to have surprised and infuriated Belton, who yelled, his voice pitched high in anger, "What are you doing here?"

"I might ask you the same," replied Stewart, and Bruce even at that distance could detect the insolence in his tone.

"I came to pay Melrose the money and accept his deal—and split with you, by God!" Belton retorted.

"Wal, it's kinda late in the day."

"You were going to drive a herd of Circle M cattle south. I heahed you make thet deal with Vic Henderson."

"Shore I made thet. But Vic had ten riders. He didn't need us. So I rode over heah to block yore deal with Melrose."

"You'd already done thet, you— — —rustler!"

"Wal, Quade, I ain't denyin' thet," said Stewart, his voice still cool but his posture becoming more menacing. To Bruce it was unmistakable.

"You gave me away to Melrose."

"No, I didn't. But I meant to. An' I'm goin' to."

"You're a rotten liar. All you've done is lie to me. Double-cross me! Melrose told me you said you were more than my mouthpiece, thet it was his funeral, not yours, that I wouldn't have the deal, an' that he'd lose both his money an' cattle. Do you deny that?"

"Hell, no. I'm only tellin' you thet I haven't given you away yet, but I'm goin' to. We've split an' it's good riddance. An' a little more of yore gab will get hard bullets, not words, from me!"

"You cheatin' cow rustler," screeched Belton, and Bruce could see him shaking all over like a man with the ague.

"You four-flush bank robber," replied Stewart, cold as ice.

Bruce could see that the bystanders had moved out of line with Stewart. There was a tense moment, then Stewart drawled tauntingly: "Come on, lady-killer. I'll land another Bruce Lockheart trade-mark right there. . . ."

Bruce's shock at hearing his own name was immediately disrupted by two gun reports, one a second after the other. Belton stood upright, staggered, and fell in a heap. Stewart drew another gun, and evidently stood off the onlookers, though none of them appeared to make a move, while one of his men searched the fallen man, and stood up with money belt and huge wallet in plain sight. Stewart backed away from the crowd, his deep voice booming out. He was the last to mount his horse. Then all the riders, himself in the rear, still with two guns leveled, got into motion on the road. Presently Stewart wheeled to spur his horse and yell, which was a signal for his gang to ride. In a few moments they were out of sight down the dust-clouded road.

CHAPTER 12

HAD BRUCE ACTUALLY KILLED BELTON HIMSELF, AS he had sworn, he would not have sunk so prostrate under the released emotions that had possessed him during and after Belton's fatal duel with Stewart.

Relaxing on the grass under cover of the thick

tamaracks, Bruce lay, eyes shut, heart pounding, sweat pouring, succumbing to wave on wave of feeling. The first had been a stinging shameful sense that Stewart had beaten him to the job; the last, after running a gamut of useless hate, regretful elation, bitter accusation, was the realization of the relief Trinity would experience. Game Texan though she was, she did not want him to kill even an old enemy unless driven to it.

Trinity made all the difference. Bruce sat up with the strength of renewed energy. He could not have asked for a luckier break. Almost surely Belton had been the only man there who could identify Bruce Lockheart. That significance grew so great that it overwhelmed him. How things had worked out! What amazing perspicuity and vision Trinity had evinced! A rush of reverence and tenderness for her drove out the morbid and deadly sensations that had beset him.

Sight of Melrose with his son and daughter emerging from the yard gate brought Bruce to his feet. Keeping the clump of tamaracks at his back he crossed to the bunkhouse, and hurrying down the long porch he came up behind the Rangers and Serks boys just when the Melroses arrived on the scene.

Bruce pushed ahead between Tex and Peg. "Where'n hell have you been?" queried the former gruffly. And Peg said: "Big doin's, Lee. Saved us the job, an' shore opened our eyes."

Belton lay on his back, his hair and beard matted with blood and dust, his face a death mask hiding all except stern tragedy. His gun was beside his limp hand.

Trinity's eyes met Bruce's as he stepped out beside Slaughter. She had not looked at the dead man. Bruce read a good deal in her gaze. She was composed and walked aside to the porch, where Sergeant Blight accosted her kindly. Jack appeared bursting with excitement and elation. Melrose made a dark picture as he bent a pondering gaze upon the prostrate man.

"Even break, I reckon?" asked the rancher.

"Yes. Even enough. But Barncastle was slow," replied Slaughter.

"Stewart beat him to a gun, of course."

"Shore, it was thet hombre who called himself Bill Stewart. But it wasn't his real name."

"Small matter. The thing is, he killed Barncastle, cleaned him of my money, an' rode away."

"Wal, he shore got money aplenty," returned the foreman, in disgust. "A big fat wallet an' money belt. Our Ranger guests representin' the law shore didn't do much representin'.."

"Cut that kind of talk," interposed Sergeant Blight curtly. "We had no idea what we were up against, until too late. An' at that, eight men to three."

"Wal, I reckon you wouldn't count my outfit much help," rejoined Slaughter, with sarcasm.

"Boss," cut in Tex Serks, "as far as we're concerned we wanted to see just what happened."

"Melrose, when you heah who this Stewart is you'll be glad we avoided a fight," said Slaughter forcefully.

"I'm glad without heahin'. All the time I'd have liked my money. . . . An' who in the hell is this Stewart hombre you're fussed about?"

"No less than Bruce Lockheart," replied Slaughter profoundly.

"*Wha-at?* . . . Thet outlaw Cap Maggard has been ridin' after so long?"

"Thet same, boss!"

A strange sensation as of being walled in assailed Bruce, riveting him to the spot.

"Who found thet out?" demanded the rancher.

"Wal, it struck me thet Stewart gave thet away himself. He called Barncastle a name thet shore wasn't Barncastle, an' jest before he shot him he said he was goin' to give him another Bruce Lockheart trade-mark. Besides, Sergeant Blight said he recognized Stewart."

"I did, sir," spoke up the Ranger. "From a description given me by a man at Mendle who saw Lockheart shoot Barncastle there. What Stewart meant by trade-mark was another bullet mark like that one made at Mendle. And look for yourself."

Melrose moved to bend over, then straightened up. He saw what Bruce had already noticed—a round blue bullet hole, almost bloodless, beside that raw and livid scar.

"Bruce Lockheart!" ejaculated the rancher. "Another Texas outlaw an' gunslinger! . . . It means thet outfit of Stewart's air just what they looked like—not cowboys, but a hard-bitten bunch of rustlers."

"Shore you hit it plumb center, boss," agreed Slaughter. "An' it's a tough blow. . . . . I reckon I need a drink."

"Me too. Somebody cover this pore devil over till I decide what to do with him."

"Dad, we'll start a cemetery," put in Jack, not without humor.

"Wal make it way off somewhere. . . . Trinity, you would come down heah with us. Won't you please go home now? Mother was upset, you know."

"I'll go, Dad. I just wanted to make sure . . . ." she returned, and did not end her speech.

Melrose and Slaughter entered the store, followed by the Rangers, who were certainly curious and probably thirsty.

"Jack," spoke up Tex Serks, "let that job go for a little. Then we'll help. . . . Come on in, Lee."

"Jack, please take her home," said Bruce earnestly, tinglingly aware of Trinity's clinging cold hands and eyes that said so much.

"He needn't leave. I'm—all right," faltered Trinity. "I heard the shots—and thought you . . ."

Jack led her away, despite her feeble protests, and Bruce hurried into the cabin. The Serks boys were there, Jim still and silent as usual, Tex pacing the floor. Juan was packing in firewood. Peg was busy with his cooking and was humming a cowboy's song.

"Where were you, Lee?" asked Tex.

"I went to the pasture. Saw dust clouds, and presently riders. I got as far as thet bunch of tamarack in time to see the fight."

"Ahuh. As it turned out you wasn't needed, but you might have been. It was a bad mess. We come out lucky, but there'll be serious consequences."

"Do you think thet Bill Stewart really is—Bruce Lockheart?" Bruce's feelings when he asked this question were a strange mixture.

"Hell! Why not? I shore hope not. But you know yore Texas. He's a bad hombre, believe me. Reckon these Rangers air hipped on the fellar they're after. They see what they're looking for. But as we've thought of him as Stewart we'll call him Stewart."

At this point Peg Simpson sang cheerily, "Come an' get it 'fore I throw it out."

Before the hungry five had finished their meal Slaughter entered, far less gloomy in appearance. "Boys, keep on eatin' an' don't mind my talk," he said, and closed the door behind him. "Melrose doesn't know it yet, but today's doin' has been good instead of bad fer

138

us. What you think, Tex?"

"I should smile. We know what we're up against."

"An' you, Lee, give me yore slant."

"Wal, I feel a hell of a lot easier in mind," declared Bruce, absolutely sure of his own sincerity.

"Do you all agree with me an' the boss thet this hombre's outfit has been stealin' our cattle?" asked Slaughter.

"I'm shore, but cain't see any proof thet'd hold in court," said Tex.

"We're settin' in court right heah," declared Peg Simpson.

"I know Barncastle drove Melrose's Circle M stock, an' I can prove it," added Bruce.

"How can you prove thet?" demanded Slaughter.

"Will you take my word for it an' wait till I get ready to tell all I know?"

"Certainly. Certainly, Jones," replied Luke hastily. "No offense. I was jest curious. I believe you an' can appreciate you may hev reasons. . . . Melrose has given me a free hand. He advises callin' in all the boys off the Wichita range an' let the cattle herdin' rest till we clean out this Stewart outfit. What you-all think about thet?"

No ready reply from the cowboys augured that the question raised was a serious one.

"Like throwin' good money after lost money in a poker game jest to get even," pondered Serks. "Say Melrose's lost ten thousand haid—"

"But, Tex, thet's all out of reason," interrupted Slaughter. "A couple of months ago by rough count he had fifty thousand haid. It'd hev taken a hundred rustlers to drive ten thousand, an' we're pretty shore Stewart's outfit numbers fifteen. We got thet from him."

"Shore I'm exaggeratin'. . . . But for the sake of

figgerin' deep let's say ten thousand haid stole. All right. Thet leaves forty thousand. A lot of longhorns. Too many in these swift-changin' days. Melrose cain't hardly get no richer. These cattle in Dodge would sell for fifteen dollars each on the hoof. Figger thet out."

"Tex, yo're arguin' for us to keep what we got instead of riskin' to lose more?"

"I am thet."

"It's sound sense. But what the hell to do about this Stewart, or whoever he is? He'll rustle all our cattle."

"We won't let him, boss."

"But, Tex, with this little outfit of yore's—what'd you do?"

"Mebbe better than with a bigger one. Boss, we four, not countin' Jones, hev seen some rustler fightin' down on the Colorado. We cleaned out two bunches of rustlers in the river bottoms, an' did it clever. No posse work, no ridin' up an' fightin' in the open. We tracked these rustlers, slipped up on their camps at night, ambushed them, made runnin' attacks on fast hawses. We killed some of them an' chased the rest out of the country."

"Humph. How many of you?"

"Six one summer, an' eight the second."

"Who was in charge of yore outfit?"

"Wal, we didn't have any boss, onless it was me. We jest worked together."

"An' you want to take this job on yore hands?"

"Shore. We told you thet before."

"Serks, I hev to hand it to you for bein' a nervy bunch. I can talk Melrose into seein' it yore way. But these damn Rangers—they want to run things. Blight, he's already makin' suggestions. This Stewart bein' Lockheart—why, these Rangers swallowed thet—has

140

upset them. Cap Maggard will be heah pretty soon, an' they'll go loco after Stewart."

"All the better. But if possible we'd rather go it by ourselves."

"Shore. You must know, though, thet a Ranger Captain can swear in any Texans as deputies an' order them around."

"Yes, I know thet. An' it's a drawback. But he isn't heah yet. He might be days or weeks comin'."

"Meanwhile Sergeant Blight aims to rule this roost. I reckon you-all wouldn't want him to give you orders?"

"Not much, boss. You see I've been out with a company of Rangers. They're more soldiers than cowboys. I shore admire thet Ranger Service an' I know what Texas owes them. If Maggard gets heah pronto, we'll fall in line. Anythin' to clean up this rustler outfit. But I say action—action no later than tomorrow mawnin'."

"Suits me fine. Tex, I like yore idee. I'll go right up to see Melrose. What'll you want?"

"Fast hawses. We know thet Melrose has them. How about it?"

"I reckon no faster in Texas. Thet's a hobby of the boss's. The best of our stock air in the big pasture. What else?"

"Three rifles, at least—more if you have them."

"Got some new forty-four Winchesters in the store. Jest came last load. Plenty of shells. . . . Come to think of it, Tex, the rustler outfit didn't pack rifles on their saddles."

"Did I notice thet? Wal, you bet. But Stewart had one, all right. As a matter of fact, boss, those riders with Stewart didn't impress me much. Lee, what's yore angle on them?"

"Not a hard-ridin' outfit. You know what I mean, from a cowboy's point of view," replied Bruce. "They were mean-lookin' men. Bad eggs, shore. But they haven't been chased thin. Cow thieves, fat an' rollin' in greenbacks, an' pretty hard an' cocky. They'll be hell on fightin' but not much on runnin' an' hidin'. . . . I've seen somethin' of hunted men."

"What's yore idee, Tex?"

"I'll take my outfit an' young Wells, in the other bunkhouse there. He's rested an' his arm's healed. He knows this range. Struck me keen, thet boy. An' don't overlook Jack, boss. There's another boy to tie to."

"Hell, yes. . . . Okay, men. I'll rustle up to see the boss. Come along, Lee."

"I'll go later, boss. There's a little job out heah thet I wouldn't miss for a bushel of pesos."

"Plantin' our handsome Barncastle. Jones, I just wonder if you ever knowed him once."

"Wonder away, boss. It won't get you nowhere."

It was sunset when Jack and Bruce, assisted by Juan, were ready to lower the canvas-wrapped Barncastle into a lonely grave they had dug out on the prairie. Belton's grave! Bruce had helped dig it. The man had indeed a cowboy's last resting place, out on the lone prairie, where the coyote wailed at night and the wind waved the grass by day—too good a grave for that traitor. They drove back to the ranch in the buckboard that Belton had left there.

"Funny how things can happen," mused Jack. "Thet yellow hombre drove up heah this mawnin' in this rig, an' we used it to pack his carcass out here to bury."

Tex Serks and his five riders crossed the South Fork of the Brazos near sunset next day, and made dry camp under Flat Top Mountain, a good fifty miles from Melrose's ranch. The promise of fast and enduring horses had been justified. Two lightly packed mustangs kept up with them. The only incident of the day was a short stop at a cattleman's newly located ranch. He had a small herd on the South Fork, too small, he said, for the rustlers to bother with. He confirmed Serks' suspicion that a bunch of riders, driving a big herd, had passed that point early in the morning of the day before. Tex's outfit sat up round a campfire considering what to do when they caught up with the thieves.

"Camp Cooper is a short day's ride from heah," said Buster Wells.

"What's Camp Cooper?" asked Bruce.

"Old military post built by Mackenzie in 1871. Abandoned years ago, but there's a settlement sprung up. Stores an' saloon. Mackenzie road from Santone runs through Cooper. Pretty much traveled in summer."

"Road crosses Chisum Trail at Fort Worth," added Serks. "Crosses a railroad before thet, couple of days' drive. But rustlers would be more liable to dispose of cattle to some trail herder."

Bruce was not sure of his ground, but he believed that he had ridden through this country somewhere between the Chisholm Trail and Camp Cooper. This part of Texas had opened up to cattle raising since that time, which saw the end of the buffalo-hide hunting.

Next day, after careful study of the tracks they were following, Tex held his eager comrades to a walk. Sharp-eyed rustlers could detect pursuers miles away. After a slow day's travel, Serks' outfit arrived at Camp Cooper after dark. They made camp on the outskirts while Tex and Bruce rode past the crumbling adobe walls of the old fort into town. A few buildings, a few dim lights hardly seemed enough to justify the life of the place. Serks halted in front of a ramshackle clapboard building adorned with a crude sign.

"Lee, I'll mosey in heah an' you go across the road to take a look in thet saloon."

"An' what'll I do?" asked Bruce.

"Buy a drink. Size up the place. If thet outfit air camped near heah, you can gamble some of them will be there."

Bruce strolled into the big barnlike low-roofed saloon, keen as a whip for more than Serks' reason. Half a dozen uncouth men stood at a rude bar; others sat at tables, evidently gambling; and a group of booted and spurred riders, dusty and travel-worn stood around a stove, where a fire was crackling. As Bruce asked for liquor he watched this group out of the corner of his eye. They alone of the occupants of the saloon paid any attention to him. Facing about with the drink in his grasp, he gazed at them from under the wide brim of his sombrero. A moment's survey convinced him that these men might be of the rustler type. A tall dark-garbed man had his back to Bruce, until one of his companions touched him, saying quite distinctly, "Vic," when he turned to stare. So this striking individual bold of eye, hard-lipped and scantily bearded, was Stewart's right-hand man, Vic Henderson. Bruce, with a curious heat in his veins, shifted his gaze to Henderson's companions, long enough to recognize them again. Then he turned back, made a pretense of drinking his liquor, and sauntered outdoors. Crossing the road, he waited in front of the hotel for Tex. That worthy did not appear for some minutes.

"Come on. We're ridin'. See anybody?" said Serks brusquely.

144

"Henderson an' five of his outfit."

"Yes, they're heah, camped about a mile north on the creek. How'd you know?"

"One of them poked Henderson, whose back was turned, an' sayin', 'Vic,' he indicated me. I sized them all up an' rustled. Bold outfit, Tex. Had their own way too long. Never been shot up bad."

"Wal, they will be, pronto. Fork yore hawse," replied Tex, mounting. "We'll go slow out of town—but we're ridin', Lee, jest you an' me. I knowed the hotelman in there. He told me Henderson just sold two thousand longhorns at four pesos a haid. To Jerry McMillan. Big cattleman an' trail driver out of Waco. Few of these drivers will pass up a good buy. . . . We'll ketch Jerry less than ten miles out, at the Brazos crossin'."

Once out of town, Serks led off at a swinging pace. The road was good and the stars bright. No more was said until the red light of a campfire gleamed in the distance. It turned out to be a mile off the road. Tex explained that the black line of trees marked the course of the Brazos. Soon they rode into the lighted circle of two campfires, where cowboys sat, eating, around a spread tarpaulin and a Negro cook was bustling about.

"Howdy, trail drivers," called out Serks.

"Howdy, riders. Get down. You're jest in time," replied a tall man, rising to expose a lean red face and narrow eyes that gleamed in the firelight.

"Thanks. No time. . . . McMillan, you shore ought to remember me."

The cattle driver strode closer to peer up at Serks. "Wal, doggone me, if it ain't Tex Serks," he burst out cordially, and extended his hand.

"Howdy, Jerry. I'm damn glad it's someone who does know me. . . . Late today you bought about two

145

thousand steers from Vic Henderson, didn't you?"

"I didn't know who the hell he was," rasped out McMillan.

"Jerry, those steers wore a Circle M brand."

"Shore, a lot of them did. Some unbranded, though."

"Didn't you figger the deal off color?"

"I cain't say I did—much. But Henry there, my foreman, he wasn't so keen. I'm sorry, Tex. But you know this business."

"Shore. I reckon it's lucky we know each other. This herd belonged to Melrose. It was rustled. Some of our Little Wichita outfit got killed. Buster Wells is with me, back in camp. He was in it, an' got shot. . . . This hombre you bought from, Henderson, Vic Henderson, is right-hand man to Bill Stewart. Have you heahed of him?"

"Hell, yes!" declared McMillan.

"We're on his trail. . . . Now, Jerry, what're we goin' to do about these cattle?"

"Shore, I'll give them up. But, by cracky, I'll go after Henderson."

"Yes, an' git all shot up fer yore pains," interposed a cowboy who evidently was the foreman. "If we go after Henderson, what's to become of the rest of this bunch of cattle? Jerry, better drive on. If we git to Dodge, you won't lose any money."

"Sound advice, Mac," added Tex. "Listen. Heah's a deal. You take Melrose's cattle along with yore's. An' say, what can you sell for at Dodge?"

"Fifteen dollars minimum. Pretty shore for more."

"Thet's fine. You sell for fifteen. Take out what you paid Henderson, an' say three dollars a haid for drivin', then send the rest to Melrose. Will you do thet, Jerry?"

"Cowboy, I'll jump at it," declared McMillan eagerly.

"But say, you must be sorta keen yoreself to take this Stewart on?"

"Thet's our job, McMillan," replied Tex grimly. "Spread it along the trail, will you?"

"You bet. Melrose's riders on the warpath for rustlers, particular Henderson, Stewart, an' company."

"Thet's the ticket. So long, Jerry. You'll heah about what comes off, on yore way back."

"Hold on. Jest a minnit. I've heahed rumors about this West Texas range, beyond the headwaters of the Brazos. How about it, Tex?"

"Finest range in Texas. Room for a million cattle. Melrose will welcome neighbors. The more we have the tougher it'll be on the rustlers."

"Hell! I'll come myself. Our range is about wore out. Tex, tell yore boss thet I'll fetch my family an' drive the rest of my cattle up Brazos way this very fall, if the weather holds."

"Plumb fine, Jerry. So long. Good luck, cowboys."

Bruce turned with Tex and they picked their way between brush and rocks. Tex held forth on how lucky they had been to make such a deal for Melrose. Bruce's reply had to do with Vic Henderson. And Tex's curt reply to that was: "Ride an' think!"

Their horses, noses toward camp, made short work of that ten miles to Cooper. But they did not go through town. Making a detour, they rode through some thick grass toward the camp, to be hailed by Jack Melrose, rifle in hand: "Who goes there?"

"Don't shoot, Jack. You'll need yore lead," replied Tex.

Supper had been kept hot for them. "Been ridin', huh? Fellars, look at their hawses," complained Peg, round-eyed and curious.

147

"Blanket the hawses for a little, Juan," said Tex, dismounting. "Wal, pards, we found our stock an' got it back on a fair deal for the boss. The rustlers air heah. Thet is, they was an hour ago, Henderson an' five of his outfit in the saloon, an' the rest in camp, on the other side of town. I seen one campfire. . . . Lee, grab a bite an' a swaller of coffee."

Sober silence fell upon the group while Tex and Bruce hurriedly partook of food and drink. Presently Tex faced Bruce with intent glance and caustic query. "Lee, what you think's our game?"

"No time like right now," replied Bruce decisively.

"I figgered thet, too. Our luck's in. Any idee how to proceed?"

"You fellars lay onto thet camp, an' I'll break in on Henderson an' his bunch. They'll be drinkin' an gamblin', almost shore. There was a back door to thet saloon. I'll bust in on them, make shore of Henderson, an' maybe a couple more, an' slope quick in the smoke."

"Lone hand, eh? I had you figgered, Lee Jones, or whoever the hell you air. But not much. Jim an' I will go along, back you up. Peg, you take Jack Melrose, Juan, an' Buster, locate thet camp on the other side of town, sneak up as close as possible with yore rifles, an' bust 'em."

"Lovely. How'n hell will we know they're rustlers?" asked Peg.

"There's only one camp out of town, besides ours. An' thet's Henderson's. They might all be there right now, though probably not. No matter how many! Sneak up close, if you have to crawl. Make a plan. But shore thet bunch will be movin' after you yell."

"Yell? Hell, we oughta pot-shot them. Didn't they

murder Buster's pards in cold blood?"

"Yes. But you yell: 'Hey, rustlers, hands up!' . . . . They'll duck an' go for their guns. Then give it to 'em. . . . Jack, if you miss yore chance, I'll beat hell out of you."

"Miss? Say, I can shoot the ears off runnin' jack rabbits," replied the lad.

"Yeah? But these ain't rabbits. They're tough hombres thet will shoot back. . . . All right, let's go." Tex looked at his big silver watch. "About nine o'clock. Peg, if Henderson an' pards air in the saloon, we'll start our party in, say, fifteen minutes. Leave the hawses heah an' rustle."

Tex stalked off toward town with Bruce on one side and Jim on the other. Bruce had long since suspected that this Tex Serks was one of the Texas breed of gunfighters, and now he was sure of it. Bruce felt no doubt of the outcome, backed by these Serks brothers and counting on the element of surprise. To be sure, gunmen like Buck Duane, King Fisher, Billy the Kid, and others of like ilk, could not be surprised, but Henderson was not of that deadly stripe or he would have been better known. Bruce's thoughts gradually set in the one direction, and before they reached town he was cold and ready for lightning action. Tex uttered hardly another word. Once on the wide road he led his comrades down on the left side. Presently Bruce recognized the saloon and whispered to Tex. There was no one in sight, but it was by no means a silent town. Two dark buildings stood between the lighted saloon and the three stealthy men. Bruce drew Tex and Jack off the road into an open lot next to the dark buildings. They stole around back of these, and soon located the yellow lights of the saloon. They crept up close to the wall, and left to the window, where Bruce halted his allies and cautiously raised himself to peep in. For a moment the light blinded him. Then he made out objects. As luck would have it, Henderson and his men sat at a round table right in the middle of this back part of the saloon. No table between the door and the gamblers! There were bottles in front of them. On the moment Henderson said gruffly, "Boost you fifty."

Bruce drew both the guns he was now carrying and leaning his head close to Tex and Jim he whispered: "Set up for us!—Throw the door wide open! Come after me. I'll talk. When they go for their guns, shoot. Then duck out."

Stealthy as Indians the three rose to the left of the door. Serks stepped back to face it, his stiff fingers slipping into the crack, opening the rickety door an inch. Bruce stood quivering. Wide swept the door.

Bruce bounded far over the threshold.

"*Set tight!*" he yelled.

Jingling thuds of spurred boots ceased on each side of him. Instantly all other sounds faded. The inmates of the saloon froze in their seats and on their feet.

Henderson, with a man to both right and left, faced Bruce and his companions. The other three had their backs turned. A nervous cough, a shuffle of moving feet, broke that tense silence.

"Wal, we're settin' tight," snarled Henderson. "What's the deal?"

Bruce's answer was momentarily checked by a distant rifle shot, then a rapid volley of shots. Henderson heard them. So did his men. Their heads cocked like the ears of startled jack rabbits.

"Holdup, huh?" continued the rustler leader. "Strangers, you don't get our money without a fight."

"No holdup, Henderson. Just a roundup of two-bit rustlers!"

Sinister intake of whistling breaths attested to the different reactions following Bruce's taunt. He grasped instantly that these men would not have to be shot in cold blood.

"Show your proof as well as them four guns," flashed Henderson, his dark bold eyes rolling.

"We just had that from McMillan."

"Then I reckon you're waitin' on us," returned the rustler sarcastically. He knew he was trapped, but was yet uncertain by whom. No doubt three cowboys, even with guns extended low, caused him no great concern.

By this time every other inmate of that saloon had vanished as if by magic.

"Where's Bill Stewart, who hands out Bruce Lockheart trade-marks?" spat out Bruce.

"He ain't here. An' who the hell might you be?"

That manifestly meant more to Henderson than the menacing guns. His dark visage paled. A divining suspicion needed little confirmation. The mention of Bruce Lockheart at that moment had had exactly the effect upon them which Bruce had calculated.

"I might be Buck Duane, only I ain't," retorted Bruce mockingly.

"*You're* Lockheart!" hissed the rustler. "By Gawd! . . . Fellars, I *told* Stewart not to hide under thet name."

It was the bitter protest of a desperate man who saw no way out of this trap. Like a steel spring released, he leaped up, overturning chair and table and jerking for his gun. Bruce's shot might have been a battering ram solid against him. With wild yells Henderson's men plunged into frenzied action. Bruce shot Henderson again as he swayed, and then the man next to him whose

151

gun was bursting red. Booms to Bruce's left and right deafened him. Through the smoke Bruce emptied the right-hand gun at the disintegrating group. He felt a thud that whirled him halfway round. He bounded through the door, falling over Jim Serks, who was ahead of him. As Bruce picked himself up he saw Tex taking a last shot from behind the doorpost. Bruce changed hands on his guns and leaped to Tex's side. He peered through the obscuring smoke, to see a blaze of fire, then another, men running, one staggering, others on the floor.

Tex jerked him back. "Let well enough—alone," he panted. "We busted 'em. . . . Jim, how air you?"

"Hit, but not bad, I guess," replied his brother.

"I got burned. How about you, Lee?"

"Bored. But high up. Nothin' to stop for. Let's finish it."

"Hell, it is finished. Them who ain't daid air shore shot up. Come, let's mosey. What luck! We're smothered with it."

"But I don't want to go yet," protested Bruce, reloading his empty gun.

Tex dragged him away from the wall and into the darkness. "Hell, what you want? I seen you bore Henderson an' thet little hombre next to him. An' me an' Jim wasn't loafin'. . . . Where you hit?"

"Shoulder cut. . . . Gosh, I'm bleeding," replied Bruce, and sheathing his gun he felt inside his shirt, and pressed his scarf against the wet hot wound.

"Listen!" whispered Tex suddenly. "Hawses. Down the road—out of town."

Bruce heard a rhythmic beat of swift hoofs that attested to the escape of some of the rustlers.

"You heah, Jim. How many hawses?"

"Three shore. Mebbe four."

"Bet they all haven't got whole skins. We'll go to camp, tie up yore hurts, an' wait for Peg's outfit. Then we'll see."

Arriving at camp they found it empty, the fire still smoldering. Tex threw on fresh wood, which promptly blazed up. Then he dug into saddle bags for salve and linen. Jim's wound was a bullet hole through the fleshy part of his thigh, of which he made light. Bruce's turned out to be a painful but not serious cut through the top of his left shoulder. It hurt and burned so that it effectually subdued other sickening sensations.

"Somebody comin'," warned Jim Serks.

Tex seized a rifle and fronted toward several dim forms approaching in the starlight. Then he relaxed. Jack's voice, high-pitched and strange, came clearly in the cold air. Tex counted the figures. "Wal, doggone! All there an' none staggerin'."

In a couple of moments Jack bolted into the campfire circle, followed by Peg and the other two. Except for Jack, who was white and rapt, the others were manifestly downcast.

"Hey, anybody hurt?" queried Tex, sharply.

"Not a scratch. Jack has a hole in his hat. Thet's all our injuries."

"Look there," cried the youth, holding out his sombrero and sticking a finger through a hole in the crown. "Bullet hole! I tell you thet hombre'd spattered my brains about if I hadn't ducked."

"Spattered nothin'," said Peg. "Whatever you got in yore haid, kid, is shore not brains."

Bruce was quick to see that Peg was disgruntled, no doubt over the failure of their sortie, while Jack was laboring under extreme emotion.

"Wal, spill it," rejoined Tex cheerfully. "Yo're back

153

safe. An' no matter if you fellars fell down altogether, we busted Henderson an' his pards. We shore did."

"Hell, you say!" ejaculated Peg, coming out of his gloom like the moon from under a dark cloud. And he gazed from one to the other of Tex's comrades. "By damn! Lee, you got bored! . . . An' Jim too. Aw, thet's hell. I hope to heaven neither of you is hurted bad."

"Peg, I'm 'hurted' bad, for the moment," replied Bruce. "But only a scratch. Jim, though, will have a stiff leg for a while."

"I gotta heah all about it pronto," declared Peg. He squatted before the fire and extended his open hands, which were far from steady. Tex, too, saw that Peg was off color somehow, and with Buster silent and Juan back in the shadow it looked none too favorable for the quartet. Whereupon Tex told in detail what he and his two companions had done. Peg sat there, his round eyes popping and his mouth agape.

"Holy shivers! Why didn't you say somethin'! Tex, let's go in town an' see how many of them hombres you did bore."

"You bet, presently, after we heah yore story."

"Let me tell it," demanded Jack. He was ghastly of face and shaking like a leaf, conditions which had succeeded his rapt elation.

"Hold yore hawses, kid," returned Peg. "Tex, I gotta hand it to you fellars. . . . Lee, thet was a slick idee of yore's lettin' 'em think you was Bruce Lockheart. Jest balanced thet even break in yore favor! Strikes me you shouldn't have taken thet risk. You could have done as wal, mebbe better, by stayin' outside an' shootin'. . . . Aw, I know, we don't shoot anybody, even murderin' rustlers, in the back, but by thunder we ought to, when we get the chanst."

154

"Suppose you tell us what happened to you?" demanded Tex.

"Aw, hell! A lot happened. We let two of them get away. Jack balled it up for us."

"But I bored one!" shouted Jack, divided between mortification and rage.

"You what?" queried Bruce.

"Lee, I—I shot one . . . k-killed him. . . . . Heah's his gun an' money to prove it."

Bruce, in consternation, though he could not see why he should feel so, stared at Peg for confirmation.

"For creepin' criminy's sake!" yelled that worthy. "He did. He showed us up. He had more nerve, or else he was crazy. He wouldn't do what I ordered him to."

"Ah-huh. Wal, Peg Simpson, suppose you tell us what come off," returned Tex, at once fascinated and incredulous.

"All right. By gosh, you won't believe me, but it's so. . . . We found thet camp right out in the open, two hundred yards or more from any cover atall, except some little bushes a rabbit couldn't hide behind. There was four hombres at thet campfire, one of them cookin', an' the other three arguin, trackin' up an' down, watchin' for somebody to come. Shore they was expectin' Henderson, an' I reckon their share of the swag. An' sore as a lot of pups thet'd been smacked. Made it damned hard for us. We wasted time talkin'. I was for shootin' at thet long range. Juan said no good. Buster agreed with me we oughtn't risk crawlin' closer. Hell, it was suicide. Thet white-faced kid there, thet Melrose who's born to be Billy the Kid Second listened a little, then he lit into us for a lot of yellow dawgs thet couldn't even bark, let alone bite. He said we had orders. I took trouble to try to explain to Jack thet there

155

was turrible danger. We didn't want him in particular to get bored. He gave me the hawse laugh. 'Wal, I'm goin' alone,' he said, an' before I could grab him there he was on all fours crawlin' right out in the starlight. Hell, I could of seen a grasshopper out there. What in the devil to do? There we stuck. Jack crawled flatter an' flatter. I swear he made a good Comanche job of it. We knelt there behind some bushes, rifles cocked, ready to blaze into them when they seen him. But he made the first tuft of sage, went on to the second, an' then we could see him like a black worm halfway across that flat, with only one more bit of cover between him an' them rustlers. They'd got into a hot argument, shore, but they was lookin' toward town, an' how in the hell they didn't spot him I'll never understand.

"Buster says, 'The idgit won't go any farther than thet last little bush.' I reckoned the same, but I was cold with fright. He was crazy, Jack Melrose was. But I said: 'Boys, wait a minute longer.' . . . Jack got to the last cover safe, an' we damn near dropped daid from relief. He lay flat a minute while our gun fingers itched. I was figgerin' thet I could of bored one of them rustlers in the daylight, but at night I wasn't atall shore. . . . All of a sudden Jack got up on one knee, drew a bead on thet outfit an' bawls at the top of his, lungs: *'Hands up, rustlers!'* . . . You should of seen them! One of them spotted Jack an' threw his gun. But Jack bored him because thet hombre took too much time aimin'. He fell all over the place. An' the others looked like scramblin' ants. They got out with guns bustin' fire, an' grabbin' up things they rustled for their hawses. Course by this time we was shootin', an' Jack got in ten shots more— we figgered thet from his empty rifle. But so far as we could see none of us even winged one of them. They

156

just vamoosed in the dark. We heahed yore shootin' in town an' shore hoped you was havin' more luck than us. All quiet for a little with us watchin'. Then we heahed hawses beatin' it to town. They rode through, haided west. . . . Wal, we made for their camp. Jack got there ahaid of us, an' he was searchin' thet hombre he'd shot, for all the world like a Ranger. An' he yapped at us: 'See what I did? If you hadn't shown yellow, we'd got all them rustlers. I hit one of the others, you bet. Saw him fall, get up an' run stiff-laigged.' . . . I reckon what I said to Jack oughtn't be told. An' thet's about all. We left their camp as we found it."

Bruce sat mute, watching this brother of Trinity's as he reacted to the story of his sheer recklessness. Bruce did not know which he felt more deeply, grief for Jack at his first blood spilling or admiration for the lad's courage. Tex Serks probably experienced the same conflict, for he shook his head and eyed Jack as if reluctant to speak. Finally he said: "Jack, it was a great trick. But you was wrong. Peg was right. If you'd done thet to save life, supposin' one of us was prisoner in their camp, I'd have patted you on the back. As it is, I gotta call you a wild hair-raisin' crazy kid, an' if you don't make me feel shore you'll never take such chances again, I'll fire you."

Jack bowed his head in shame. "Tex, I know now it was wrong. I was out of my haid. If you don't tell Dad, I'll swear never to be such a fool again."

"Tex, you'll track the three rustlers who got away?" asked Bruce.

"You bet. Shore they'll ride for Stewart's hole, which we shore want to locate. But with half of us crippled, I don't want to tackle Stewart's outfit till we're mended. Course we might trail them to their camp, an' let Jack

157

wade in alone to clean them out."

"Aw, stop it," cried the lad poignantly.

CHAPTER 13

TWO WEARY DAYS LATER THE RIDERS DISMOUNTED AT
Brazos Head to throw saddles. Juan gathered up the
bridles to lead away the tired horses, snorting at the
smell of water. Jim limped to the porch. Then he waited.

"What you see?" whispered Peg, as Jim made a
significant move with his hand. Then Bruce spied a
strange buckboard and a wagon in the shadow of the
store wall. They had not been there several days before.

"Who'n'll could thet be?" growled Peg. "Somebody
always comin' heah."

Bruce smothered an imprecation and moved on to the
door of their bunkhouse. They went in. Peg lighted the
lamp. "Gosh! it's good to get home. These heah quarters
will spoil us. Set down, you fellars. I'll have a fire an'
hot water in a jiffy."

"Peg, you're right. We are spoiled!" said Bruce. "Hot
water, shavin' your bristly chin, an' clean shirts."

"Wal, you shore owe thet much to yore girl. I'll bet
you two-bits she'll be heah before you can scrub yore
dirty face."

But Peg for once was mistaken. Bruce achieved the
agreeable change in quick time, but Trinity did not
appear. Nor did anyone else. For Bruce something
oppressive hung over the bunkhouse. While Peg cooked
supper Bruce redressed Jim's injury, glad to proclaim it
was healing and not so inflamed.

Presently heavy steps sounded on the porch from the
north end. Sergeant Blight appeared in the doorway,

158

framed in the firelight. He looked curious and none too civil.

"How'd you make out, cowboys?" he inquired.

"Not any too damn good," replied Peg, after it seemed apparent that neither Bruce nor Jim meant to answer.

"Well, I advised Melrose not to let you go on thet wild-goose chase."

"Yeah? He let us go, all right. An' it wasn't so wild."

Juan shoved past Blight, carrying a water pail and an armload of firewood. The sergeant, no doubt feeling that even if there was anything to learn these cowboys would not tell it, stamped back to his own quarters.

"Why doesn't Tex come?" complained Peg, for the second time. "Supper's most ready."

"Maybe he's eatin' up there," suggested Jim.

"Shore, he'd grab the chanst, same as I would. . . . Let's pitch in, fellars. We haven't had a square meal for three days, an' this is good."

They needed no second invitation. And they cleaned the platter, as Peg put it. Jim went to bed, while Juan helped Peg with the chores. Bruce smoked a cigarette, waiting, growing more on edge. Nevertheless, nervous as he was, he did not hear voices until the keen vaquero held up an arresting hand. Bruce started toward the door. He listened before he peered out. Footfalls and deep voices of men sounded out there in the darkness. He saw the red lights of cigars. Melrose's sonorous voice boomed above Slaughter's quick high-pitched one, and then that of Tex Serks cut in. Besides these men, Bruce recognized there were others, talking low, tramping along.

"Heah's Tex all right," said Peg, over Bruce's shoulder. "An' our boss. But thet ain't all. Lee,

159

somebody's come. I wonder now—if—"

Trinity's sweet laugh, slightly unnatural to Bruce's familiar ear, checked Peg's cogitations, and rang the gamut of sensations through Bruce's being. He stepped back into the bunkhouse, stiff outwardly, and inside all riot, while Peg kept on looking.

Bruce heard Jack's quick and jingling steps bound upon the porch and into the store. He struck a match. Other footfalls jarred the porch, to Bruce's strained ears forceful and pregnant. Several men were talking at once, evidently not to each other. Melrose's familiar step led others into the store. A swifter tread, surely known to Bruce—surely Tex's—

"Oh, Tex—please wait!" called Trinity, and in her sweet high-pitched tone Bruce caught the significance that he had in her laugh.

But Tex strode in. He drawled something casual about being late, but his appearance was such that Bruce did not distinguish what he said. Tex was pale under his tan. His tawny eyes gleamed like agates through a blaze. If ever Bruce had been put on his guard by a singular and lightning flash of intelligence, this was the time.

Bruce had divined what Tex's gaze portended. He stepped into the center of the room and stood hands down, fighting a desperate sense between what Tex warned him to be and what Trinity expected of him.

She entered the door, drawing with her a stalwart bareheaded man, whose stem and lined face, darkly bronzed, consummated the shock of certainty for Bruce.

Trinity hung with both hands to this Texan's right arm. She was lovely, with a strange radiant flash of face and magnificent eyes, now dark as midnight, unfathomable to all men save Bruce, who felt that moment the most wonderful and terrible of his life. This

160

Texan sweetheart of his held this strange man's right arm naturally, casually, perhaps, but to Bruce it had an awful significance.

"Heah you air," she pealed out, indicating Bruce. "Heah's the lucky cowboy, my fiancé, Lee Jones, from down Uvalde way. . . . Lee, meet Captain Maggard of the Texas Rangers."

In that poorly lighted room Bruce had an advantage which perhaps he did not need. Courage and intelligence would surely have failed him, leaving only the terrific instinct to kill rather than surrender, but for sight of Trinity and the look in her wide dark eyes.

"Wal, Lee Jones, I'm shore mighty glad to meet you," said Maggard warmly, extending a big hand to the arm of which Trinity still clung. "And to congratulate you on being the luckiest cowboy in this heah Texas."

"How-do, Captain," rejoined Bruce, huskily, as he met that proffered hand, feeling the panic loosen around his heart. "Thanks—thanks. . . . I shore am—a lucky hombre."

Captain Maggard indeed did not know him from Adam. The narrowed gray eyes regarded Bruce with the shrewd scrutiny that he must have accorded to any stranger, but in it there was nothing inimical or doubting; merely the sizing up of a man who had won a girl of whom he was surely fond.

"Jones, eh? One of the Big Bend Joneses. Wal, I never knew any of the good outfit. Hope you belong to thet," went on the Ranger.

"Heah, Captain Maggard," ejaculated Bruce, making pretense of protest, "Melrose asked me thet."

"Wal, son, from the Texas look of you—and what I heah—I'd be mighty careful about askin' you sudden questions," drawled Maggard, in friendly significance.

Trinity left the Ranger's side and clutched Bruce's shoulders with hands that he knew needed support. "Lee, I—I'm glad—you're back," she said unsteadily. Bruce could not keep from wincing as she pressed down on his wound. *"Lee!* . . . You're wounded!—I—I felt . . . Jack lied to—me!"

"Trinity, it's nothin'—only a scratch," Bruce assured her as she sagged against him. But she did not rally. Her weight full upon Bruce attested to complete loss of muscular control. In alarm he moved her, speaking he knew not what, and when he saw her face he realized she had fainted.

"Clean out, poor kid," spoke up Maggard sympathetically. "Lay her down, Jones. Somebody get water."

Bruce laid her upon a lower bunk and knelt beside her, while Maggard leaned over them and Peg came running with a pan of water. Wetting his scarf, Bruce bathed her face, aware of his trembling fingers and thumping heart. Trinity came out of it quickly, just as her father and Jack entered the cabin.

"Trinity. . . . Lee, Cap, what the hell's this?" boomed the rancher.

"Boss, it's nothin'. She just fainted," replied Bruce.

"What? Trinity fainted? Wal, that's a lot. Bet it's the first time in her life."

"Steve," interposed the Ranger, "she was over-wrought, I reckon. Felt her sink heavy on my arm as we came in."

Meanwhile Trinity stared at Bruce, at the others, then back at him with wide eyes, from which the fear slowly disappeared. She clung to Bruce a moment, then recovered and sat up.

"Lee—Dad! What, happened?" she asked, with a wan

smile.

"Trinity, you fainted," replied Bruce.

"You shore keeled over," added the Ranger, patting her head.

"Me faint?—Well, how funny! I don't remember a thing."

Jack interposed by putting an arm around Trinity. "Sis, I'll bet a hawse Lee made me out a liar an' thet's what knocked you."

"Oh!—Yes—yes. That was it," cried Trinity, and if she was not sincere she was a most consummate little actress. "I felt that big lump on Lee's shoulder, all hot and moist. And he just slid out from under me, like a lame horse. . . . Lee, you—you—"

"Trinity, I didn't even stop a bullet," protested Bruce. "Just got nicked. I'm sorry I scared you."

"Lee, take her up to the house an' don't stay too long," interrupted Melrose.

Presently Bruce, as one in a dream, found himself outside in the dark, with Trinity pressed close to his side and clinging to him with both little hands. Away from the lighted doors and windows Bruce slowed their pace, and put an arm tight around her.

"Darling—y-you're safe!" she whispered, and leaned her head on his breast.

"My God—Trinity—it was terrible!" replied Bruce, panting at the mere mention.

"Oh, I knew that," she murmured, in agitation. "But, Bruce darling, I was all right till I saw you. That settled me. Oh, but you were beautiful to see."

"Wal, my love, I shore didn't feel beautiful," drawled Bruce. "Meeting Maggard after these endless two years of his tracking me—of my being haunted day and night—was simply worse than I had dreamed of. It'd

163

have been bad if you hadn't been there—but that made it terrible."

"Bruce, it was. I didn't *know* he wouldn't recognize you. It was the supreme test. I had to see it. Now, thank God, we're safe."

"Are we? Will I ever be? . . . Trinity, you were hanging on to that Ranger captain's arm. I understood it. You can't fool me, even if you try."

"Darling, I don't want to fool you," she returned entreatingly. "I had thought out the best possible course to pursue. I didn't dream it'd be so hard. If he had recognized you—and tried to arrest you—I'd have hung on to him. All I thought of was to help you get away."

"Trinity, if Maggard had known me—had called me to surrender I—I'd have shot him!"

"Oh, I understood that the instant I laid eyes on you. And just then I'd not have cared one single damn. But now I see how wrong that was. Now I see that my prayers have been answered."

"Trinity, do you know, I like Maggard. You wouldn't think it possible. But he's fine—a real true Texan, like Sam Houston must have been, and McNeely, one of the first Ranger Captains."

"Bruce, the Captain is all for Texas," rejoined Trinity. "That's what you and I are up against. The State versus Bruce Lockheart!"

"Hush! Don't even whisper that," replied Bruce. "It's you, Trinity, who give me hope and life. This situation here is critical. But I've the nerve to face it. I'm accepted here—your dad's rider—your Texas cowboy beau! It's unbelievable."

"Yes. But it's all true," she replied tenderly. "Maggard came today with two of his men, driving from Fort Griffin. He asked me if I'd ever heard more of

Bruce Lockheart. I told him no. Lee Jones had caught up with me first. He called me fickle. He doesn't suspect. I think he was glad I hadn't found you, Bruce."

"Sooner or later someone will show up who really knows me," Bruce interrupted. "Then I'll have to fight or hit the trail again. The country will get more settled. This luck can't last."

"Hush, Bruce, and listen. The other three came yesterday, with horses and packs from New Mexico. That makes nine in all. These last are the ones you want to look out for. If they brace you—accuse you—get perfectly furious and bluff them. You can do it now. But don't *kill* one of them, except in self-defense. This is all unlikely and farfetched, but we must be ready for anything. If the unexpected happens—oh, Heaven, I pray it won't!—come to my window at night and wake me. I'll plan with you or hide you or go with you or meet you later. But one thing you must swear: not to desert me. Good night!"

Bruce took it very slowly across the flat toward the bunkhouse, trying to control emotion Trinity had roused in him in order to apply himself sternly to the problem at hand. At the moment he did not have to do anything save await developments. At the cabin he found Tex and Peg Simpson deep in what appeared a serious discussion.

"What's it all about, boys?" asked Bruce.

"Wal, I say we've got hell on our hands," was Tex's pregnant reply.

"Ahuh. Wal, talk, you close-mouthed cowhand," retorted Bruce, and he was not in fun.

"Lee, this heah Cap Maggard is an all-fired conscientious man," went on Tex. "Stern hard Texas Ranger, an' duty is his passion. He's goin' to swear us into his company as deputies."

"What? He is like hell."

"Thet's what I thought. But he doesn't know it. But after you listen to him a little you'll like him."

"I did that already, Tex. Sort of strange about Melrose an' Jack havin' no use for him. He just loves Trinity same as if she was his own. He hasn't any family. An' Trinity doesn't return it, believe me."

"Tragedy in the family, Lee. Rangers strung up a relation once. Wal, Maggard's on the track of this Bruce Lockheart outlaw again. He said he'd never been off it in two years. An' Bruce Lockheart is Bill Stewart, sartin an' shore, accordin' to Maggard. So it suits him fine to get his man, an' clean out these rustlers who're stealin' Melrose pore. . . . Lee, it's a safe bet thet Melrose will send us with the Rangers, whether we want to go or not."

"Yeah, I figgered thet myself. It might be a good idee."

"Shore, between our two outfits we could wipe them rustlers off the slate. Credit for thet means as little to me as I'm shore it does to you."

"But I don't like bein' bossed."

Peg Simpson intervened: "An' I ain't gonna be! If Maggard gives us a free hand, I'll go."

"Boys, the thing i. Maggard won't order you out. He'll want you to help him, an' you'll find yoreself likin' it. Honest, I'm glad he drifted along. You know damn well one or two of us would get bored in a fight with Stewart's outfit. Might be me, or you, Peg, an', Lee, it might be you. Think of Trinity, an' be glad we won't have to risk so much."

"Aw, Tex, it's good sense," said Peg.

"Reckon I'm glad, too."

166

Bruce found sleep something as remote as this situation was incredible. Here he was about to go out with his mortal enemy, Captain Maggard, to ride down himself, Bruce Lockheart. It seemed like a story told round a campfire by some romance-loving cowboy. What should become of the real Bruce Lockheart if the fictitious one was killed? And he would surely be. For this Stewart rustler was no man to surrender. Bruce could not marry Trinity under the name of Lee Jones. It was a conundrum. Yet withal it kept Bruce awake for hours with its sheer drama. And it was the cause of his sleeping late the next morning.

"Air you daid?" broke into his dull ears in Tex's impatient voice.

"Aw, he's in love," said Peg. "A fellar gets thet way."

Bruce meekly admitted that that must have been the reason for his laziness. He felt but little discomfort from his wound. Jim and Buster, the other cripples, were up and about.

"Fellars, what's all the noise outside?" asked Bruce, as he splashed over the basin.

"It's a wagon train. Rolled in late last night."

"Big train?" went on Bruce, thinking that this was not so good.

"Tolerable. Twenty wagons. I know the trail boss, Seever. Rode for him when I was a kid."

Jack ambled in at that junction. "Gee, what a sleepy outfit! Had my breakfast long ago. Tex, Dad wants you an' Lee to come up pronto."

"What's on, Jack?" asked Bruce.

"I don't know. But I think, by thunder! I oughta be let into these confabs. Anybody, for instance like Seever, the trail boss, would take me for a kid."

Bruce strode off alone toward the pasture. He did not

care to meet any of the caravan members at close range. Nobody could ever tell! The vast world of Texas was growing small. There were not, however, any of the white canvas-covered wagons closer than the flat along the stream. Horses grazing, men around campfires, columns of blue smoke—against a colorful background of autumn foliage, all this made a picturesque scene. From the pasture Bruce cut into the trees.

He approached the store from the rear, seeing the dozen or more men on the porch and bench, and others packing out bundles. At that moment Captain Maggard emerged from the door, in the act of lighting a cigar. Tex Serks lounged against the porch rail. Peg Simpson was on his knees before the door of their cabin, and Juan was stacking supplies. That move, Bruce thought, argue, for a departure of the Rangers before this day was out.

Bruce had come to within a few steps of the porch when the posture and look of a stranger caught his ever-watchful eye. Suddenly this man called out in deliberate ringing voice:

"*There*! That's the man!"

He stepped out to point at Bruce; voice and action were so marked that the attention of all suddenly focused upon Bruce, who stiffened in his tracks.

"What man, you?" demanded Captain Maggard gruffly, stepping off the porch. Tex Serks vaulted the porch rail to take a couple of lumps and stop. Melrose appeared, followed by Slaughter.

It had come! Bruce caught it quick as a lightning flash. This man knew him. And as his mind accepted it all, his internal muscular force united in a terrible intensity.

"Here! This man. I know him," sang out the accuser.

168

"I saw his bay horse today in the pasture. I never forget horses. He was forkin' that horse when I saw him."

"Wal, who is he?" queried the Ranger slowly.

"Bruce Lockheart! The outlaw you're after. I saw him shoot Barncastle—and kill Whistler."

"Man, you're drunk!" rasped out Maggard, in anger and contempt. Yet he had sustained a shock. All eyes swept from this gray-clad, dusty-booted teamster to Bruce, who stood motionless, crouching a little, his quivering right hand low.

"Hold on, pard!" yelled Serks, coming round to Bruce's side, but not close.

"Captain Maggard, he's your—man," said the stranger haltingly, growing ashen of face now that he realized the peril his impulse had perpetrated. "I just came—on this wagon train. I was in Mendle that day— Saturday, October fifth. I stood in front of the Elk Hotel—heard Barncastle call him Bruce Lockheart. . . saw him draw and shoot."

"Hey, stranger, if you're not drunk you're crazy," interrupted Melrose stridently. "My God—you're in Texas! For less than that you could be shot."

Melrose shouldered his way out. "Steady, heah," he ordered, in his sonorous voice. "Hold yore hand, Lee!"

"Far enough, boss—an' you, Captain. This is my mix!" retorted Bruce, his tone like ice.

"But, cowboy, the man's mistaken," protested Melrose. "Anybody can make a mistake."

"Not with me."

"Seever, who is this man?" interposed Maggard impatiently. "He's in your train."

"Name's Clark. Reliable man, so far's I know. But shore he's no Texan," replied the wagon boss.

Bruce silenced them. "You all had yore say. It's my

169

turn. . . . Clark, take it back or go for yore gun."

Maggard roared: "I'm in authority here. Listen—"

"Not over me. . . . Mr. Clark, if you ain't shore you made a mistake—throw yore gun."

Clark gulped and swallowed hard, realizing too late what he had brought upon himself. "I must—be wrong. I take it back."

Bruce relaxed, then strode forward along the porch rail toward his bunkhouse. Tex followed him and shut the door.

Maggard could be heard roundly cursing the man who had caused the upset. Melrose added his tirade: "Clark, thet fellow you braced is Lee Jones. One of the gunslingin' Texans. He's a cowhand of mine. An' engaged to marry my daughter Trinity. Get the hell back to yore wagon an' thank God for the luck you had. It might not be so good the next time."

Voices mingled then in a general commentary on the incident. Tex sidled up to Bruce, to put an arm round his shoulder. "Close shave, pard. Thet man *knew* you!"

"*Tex*! . . . My Gawd—he did!" groaned Bruce, and sinking on the bench he bowed his head, overcome by this last significant revelation of Serks' knowledge and loyalty.

"Don't weaken. We got all the cairds," whispered Tex. "An' with Trinity we'll be too cunnin' for the old fox."

The door burst open to admit Jack, pale and wild-eyed, with Peg hanging onto him, and the other boys behind.

"Lee, I lost my nerve I was so scared," declared Jack. "Thet— — — locoed fool! Takin' *you* for Bruce Lockheart. You oughta have bored him."

"Thanks, Jack. I guess I saw red because of Trinity,"

170

replied Bruce quietly.

"My word! Lee, we gotta keep this from her."

"Right. See thet you don't loosen up, Jack. . . . Tex, what's the deal, if there is any yet?"

"Plenty deal. Listen to this one. It'll make you hop. Seever saw a herd of Circle M longhorns, driven by four riders across the road not ten miles below thet Brazos bridge."

"No!"

"Yes, an' you should have heahed Melrose roar."

"If that isn't the limit!" exclaimed Bruce, throwing up his hands. "Four more added to four we know of, with Stewart and eight other rustlers make sixteen, if I can count."

"Correct, Lee. Move up in class. There might be more. We're in for a hells-beltin' scrap. Slaughter wants to send for his Big Wichita outfit. Maggard's orders air to pack for a long chase an' not to forget to load down with gun shells."

"Jack, I cain't help but like that Ranger," said Bruce.

"Wal, I ain't crazy about him myself," replied Jack. "But I feel softer toward the flinty old bastard since he persuaded Dad to let me go."

CHAPTER 14

BY LATE AFTERNOON NEXT DAY A CAMP OF THE Rangers had been reached under the butte ten miles west of Flat Top Mountain. Captain Maggard, with Sergeant Blight and two other men, rode on to Cooper on a scouting expedition. This left four Rangers in camp, and eight of the cowboys, Tex's group having been augmented by the addition of Lester, who had

171

ridden in the night before from the Big Wichita. He had reported to Melrose that nineteen Circle M riders had pushed the rancher's thirty-odd thousand head into Sycamore Valley and were holding them there.

Maggard's camp was well hidden from every point except the top of the butte. It was the intention of the Captain to hold his force there only until plans could be formulated. One of the features of Ranger efficiency was its mobility. They packed light and rode hard. But Bruce agreed with Tex that the Rangers would have done better to be less open in pursuit and attack. Invested with authority, their habit was far removed from cowboy or savage stealth.

Before supper Bruce suggested that he take Jack, make a quick ascent of the butte, and reconnoiter for sight of campfires. Tex thought it a good idea. Accordingly, they zigzagged up the steep slope, gaining the summit after night. A careful search of the brakes and the long slant of ground down to the prairie, using the glasses, discovered five campfires, three of them mere pinpoints, one good-sized and not far distant, and the fifth a large blaze. When Bruce and Jack returned to camp Tex received their report with neither surprise nor perturbation.

"Wal, there's been movement of riders an' stock south ever since we hit Brazos Haid," he remarked ponderingly. "An' I agreed with Luke Slaughter thet we'll find the Circle M cattle south of the river."

"Mebbe this Stewart hombre is an old rustler from the ranges north," added Peg Simpson. "He'd have to be orful bold or careless to sell all his raids in one place."

"My idee is if he's an old hand he'll concentrate as big a herd as he can drive over heah somewheres, an' then make for the Chisum Trail to drive north to get the

172

big price. Then not come back."

Bruce thought that a clever deduction. "Shore thet's what I'd do, if I put myself in his place."

"I'll tell you what, fellars," spoke up Jack. "After we lick the daylights out of Stewart, let's turn rustlers an' clean up the range from Waco to the Canadian."

All those sitting round the campfire, except Tex, got a laugh out of this. "Now ain't thet a bright crack?" burst out Tex. "Ain't you a fine son of Steve Melrose, an' brother to Trinity?"

"Aw, course I wouldn't, Tex. But it'd be fun, an' shore a whoppin' adventure."

"Listen, leather-pants, you'll get all the whoppin' adventure you want before you get back home."

Conversation lagged after that. The Rangers were the first to seek their blankets, then the cowboys, one by one. Bruce was not the last, but after he turned in only Tex took a look at the horses and around camp before he went to bed.

Next morning they were all up bright and early, anticipating the return of Maggard and the action sure to follow. But as the Captain did not come nor show up down the prairie, Tex took it upon himself to send Juan out on a scouting trip while he and Bruce again climbed the butte. From this vantage point they would be able to see Captain Maggard and his Rangers long before they drew near camp. Nothing of importance, however, rewarded half the day's vigilance from the butte top. Maggard did not return that afternoon, and he had not put in an appearance when the cowboys went to bed. Next morning, after a late breakfast, Tex sighted a single horseman some miles down on the prairie.

Using the glasses, he promptly said: "It's Cap Maggard. Nobody else in sight. Hawse tuckered out.

He's been pushin' leather."

"Mebbe somebody oughta meet him," suggested Peg.

"Not any of us," rejoined Tex, and strode across the space between the two camps.

Two of the Rangers hurriedly saddled horses and galloped down to meet their captain. Tex and Peg made random conjectures as to what had happened and what more to expect.

"Wal, reckon we're goin' to see some Rangers in action," said Tex finally, and the way he said it was a tribute to their fame.

Maggard and his men rode into Tex's camp, and he dismounted while the others hurried over to their quarters, stern business in their demeanor. Maggard was dusty and hot.

"Look after my hoss," he said. "We run some. . . . Tex, what's your report?"

"Wal, we sighted five campfires over heah where we saw the smokes thet day. But nothin' movin'. Juan took a careful scout up the draw. No tracks workin' this way."

"I rode out before sunup. Get me some breakfast. . . . Last night we struck Flat Top after dark. We were goin' round headed for camp when we heard cattle bawlin' over the ridge. So we got down an' worked around to where we could see a campfire, men eatin' supper, and more guardin' a good big herd. That was the herd Seever told us he'd seen bein' driven south. Plenty steers wearin' Circle M brands. We watched long enough to know those cattle were not bein' driven by cowboys. Then we went back and up the creek bottom to hide in the brush. This mornin' I left before dawn. Blight is to watch thet drive till I send more men, and then break it up and join us here or at the haidquarters of

174

this rustlin' outfit."

"Who'll you send?" queried Tex shortly.

"Blight should have four or five more men, and one who knows the country."

"Send one of yore Rangers an'—"

"Yes, Horton said he'd go."

"Wal, Buster Wells an' Lester an' Jim Serks an' Peg. How about it, Peg?"

"Fine an' dandy. Reckon Jim would do better hawseback than climbin' about them brakes, as I've a hunch you fellars will have to."

"Saddle up. Pack some grub and water. Rustle," were Maggard's terse commands.

"Right. May I ask what we'll do, so Peg an' the others will have a line on it?"

"Serks, it's up to you. Show me this Stewart-Lockheart camp, and then I'll tell you."

No more was said. Peg served Captain Maggard with breakfast while Juan brought in the horses. Jack sat down, bending a dark frowning brow over his weapons while he cleaned and reloaded them. Bruce filled a canvas water bottle and tied it on his saddle. He stuffed his coat pockets with strips of salted meat and several biscuits and apples.

In short order Horton and his riders were ready to leave.

"Any more orders, Captain?" he asked.

"Yes. Subject to your good judgment. Ride to the east and south of that bunch of rustlers. Drive them toward the brakes over heah, where we'll be on the lookout. Don't kill any man you can take prisoner."

They rode away down the slope, keeping to the north of the creek bottom, where brush and trees would hide them for miles.

"Captain Maggard, what did you find out in Cooper?" drawled Bruce, concealing his bursting curiosity. Tex and Jack left off their tasks to listen.

"I hate to say so, but it was better than a Ranger job," admitted the Captain. "I didn't get to see the bodies, because that Cooper bunch buried them. Some friendly relation about that saloon. But it's always so. Rustlers with money to spend always have influence. This Stewart-Lockheart outfit shore made friends. Boys, when I make my report, I won't mention cowboys. Pretty low-down of me, shore, but you've no idea how many enemies the Ranger Service has. Politics. Hope you don't care about it."

"Hell no," replied Tex.

"I'd be glad not to have any credit," added Bruce grimly.

"Damn you boys, anyhow. Yore just Texans after my own heart. Lord, but I'd like to make Rangers of you for keeps! Why, boys, there are a thousand outlaws hidin' down the brakes of the Rio Grande. When badmen hide in there, we have to wait till they come out. They have to eat and gamble and drink. Then we nail them. But this Bruce Lockheart! He's a different hombre. Never could get actual track of his gamblin' and drinkin', or chasin' dancehall girls, or wuss."

"Captain, speakin' of this Lockheart," replied Tex earnestly, "I know this country through heah, better than you or any of yore Rangers. I know the Panhandle an' the two Chisum Trails. Dodge an' Abilene, too. An' I've got an idee some of the jobs this Bruce Lockheart is blamed for he never did."

Maggard slapped his leg so soundly that the dust flew from his trousers. His eagle eyes narrowed and gleamed like fire back of yellow amber.

"Serks, I'm afraid of that very damn thing," he declared, stridently. "It *might* be true. I've been told so. But I *don't* believe it. I've spent nearly two years in the saddle tryin' to ride the man down. I've tracked him, hounded him from Mercer to Santone, from the old cattle trails to New Mexico. And all I can actually pin on Bruce Lockheart is his part in a holdup of a bank. He was with one Belton. That gang got a hundred and fifty thousand dollars out of that holdup. We recovered most of it. Pell, one of my rangers who was killed, knew Lockheart had some of that money, hidden somewhere. I know for shore that Lockheart took all his money when he left Denison. I always wondered why Lockheart rode away instead of stickin' it out. But so far as I know, he never threw a gun on a ranger. Funny deal. I'll get to the bottom of it someday, and I'll be glad if Lockheart does turn out to be an hombre like Stewart. . . . Wal, to the job at hand," added Captain Maggard, sobering. "Serks, can we ride up on this bluff?"

"Shore, easy gradin' up."

"All right. Leave camp, packs, and extra hawses heah. It's a good place. The hawses will stick. You-all want to pack a little grub."

An hour later Maggard and his three Rangers and the cowboys were climbing the butte on horseback, grading up the steep slope. Tex, who was leading, cut back near the top and came out close to the spot where he and Bruce had done their scouting. Here Maggard ordered his followers to dismount and search the country.

"Never saw the beat of that," he said, pointing, and it was significant to Bruce and Tex that he picked the very region in which they had located the smokes and fires.

"Tough country to crack," remarked one of

Maggard's Rangers, who was using a field glass.

"Beats the Big Bend and Rio Grande brakes to a frazzle," replied the Captain gruffly. "We've got a job cut out for us."

Jack, who was using his father's large glasses, was the first to locate something. "Dust risin' this side of Flat Top. Cattle movin'," he said laconically, like an old scout.

"Where?" demanded Maggard, turning away from the brakes. Tex directed him and Jack gave him the glass. "Ha, big dust area that. Like buffalo travelin'. But I can't see any stock movin'. My eyes aren't what they used to be."

Tex and Ranger Weatherby, concentrating on the Flat Top country with glasses, finally decided cattle were moving up the prairie slope to the west toward the brakes.

"That's strange," said Maggard, puzzled. "Why would rustlers drive away from their markets?"

"Captain, my idee for some time has been thet this outfit is collectin' a big herd to drive north."

"Looks like it. Good move for us. Horton and Blight will haid them off, I'll bet. And if they don't we'll be over there somewhere waitin'. But where? Looks like I see a million places."

"Take the glass an' follow thet longest an' widest open grassy flat. . . . There. Up to where it narrows an' meets the black of the brakes. Look careful from there up till you see peeled logs shinin' bright."

Presently Maggard boomed out that he had sighted Tex's objective, and added that it looked like cabin building on a big scale. He shook his head dubiously.

"This heah is the only point in the whole country where thet pile of logs can be seen," said Tex impressively.

"Wal, I shore hope we don't have to find it. Those brakes in there stand on end and look thick with chaparral and timber."

"Beats the Braseda all hollow," put in Bruce. "Any outfit could hide in there."

"Juan can track them," said Tex. "No worry about thet. But—"

Weatherby interrupted by calling attention to smoke rising at the edge of timber where it met the prairie. This gray triangle showed straggling bunches of cattle, the same stock, no doubt, that the cowboys had located previously. No one, however, could sight anything else down there until Jack took the glass and after a long survey called out: "Hawses grazin'. Old cabin roof. An' thet smoke we seen. Outfit there."

But no other of the company could make out what Jack asserted was there, plain as a jack rabbit's ears.

"Jack, maybe you're like that boy who swore he saw a whole field full of deer, which finally worked out to be a single black stump," drawled Maggard.

"Captain, I cain't help it if you-all air blind as bats. I always could see better'n anybody, except Trinity."

"Kid, lemme have the glasses," said Tex, taking the boy seriously. "Tell me where to look." Then he sat down so that he could rest his elbows on his knees to steady the binoculars. Time and again he changed the focus. At length he froze on one spot.

"Wal, Serks, if it takes you thet long there cain't be anythin' to see," complained Maggard.

"There is. Jack's right. The kid can see," replied Tex, standing erect again, his hawk eyes flashing. "I saw thet cabin roof more'n once. Reckoned it to be a rock. . . . Big outfit there, shore."

179

"Jack, I take it back" returned Maggard conscientiously. "Serks, you're boss till we get there. Rustle!"

"Reckon I'll take one more look at thet Flat Top country," said Tex.

"Dust settled. I can see thet without the glass," rejoined Jack, as he handed it to Tex.

"Right again, Jack," announced Tex presently. "Captain, thet herd is not movin'."

"Wal, Horton has had time to haid those drivers off. If there's a chase, as I reckon, we want to get between this outfit over heah at the cabin, and the rustlers Horton is after."

Bruce thought that good logic and expressed himself so to Serks.

"We got time unless thet outfit down there didn't show no fight atall," he said. "We're off, fellars. Jack, you stick close to me. Juan, you pick out a trail. Ride now, but don't cripple a hawse."

Two hours later Bruce calculated they had traveled fifteen miles through and around exceedingly rough country to make a third of that distance in a straight line from the butte. That wide-mouthed gorge opening under the steep escarpment was rocky and bushy, the stream bed choked with huge boulders and driftwood from the brakes. By noonday they had crossed it, working upstream all the time, and then began a slow ascent of the south bank up to the timber. Here they struck flat country and easy going, except that the tall grass hid fallen trees and snags. Heavy grass and thick brush and timber gradually thinned out toward open country. In the swales buffalo wallows showed signs of recent use. No doubt the thick willow bottoms and clumps of tamarack hid plenty of the shaggy beasts. Deer were numerous and tame. Flock after flock of wild turkeys and pigeons made way for the line of horses. Coming to a deep ravine, choked with green foliage and black thickets, Tex rode down into it and, finding an open plot with running water, decided here was the place to leave the horses. That scarcely pleased Captain Maggard, who was a heavy man and not used to traveling on foot.

"How much farther?" he queried.

"I cain't be shore. Juan says two kilometers. But it's not thet far to the open. I could see through the trees."

"All right. We can come back heah to camp, if necessary. . . . Slower now, Serks, so I won't miss gettin' the lay of the land."

More open, level, and beautiful country extended south from the bank of that ravine. The grass grew knee-high and rustled under tread; the clumps of brush stood few and far between; trees were smaller in size and farther apart—all of which indicated an approach to the prairie.

"Better wait till the deer an' turkeys wander off without bein' scared," advised Tex, sitting down on a log to take off spurs and chaps.

"Ahuh. Look over yore haid," said Jack, and pointed to a flock of circling buzzards high above the green foliage. "Wonder whose carcasses they savvy."

It was not a reassuring and comfortable thought. The blue sky and white clouds, the hot sun and golden lights varying with patches of shade, the faint breeze in the treetops, the stir of the waving grass and flowers, the purple haze of Indian summer in the distance, the serenity and peace of the woodland—these seemed at immense variance to the extreme probability of sudden fire and smoke and fierce yell and tragic death. But that was exactly what Bruce sensed. He did not appear to be the only one with such somber thoughts.

But the irrepressible Jack broke into this austere quiet: "Cap, let's find out where we're at and what we're doin'."

"Lot of sense in that, son" was the reply.

Without more ado Tex picked up his rifle and glided up the low bank to the level. The others followed in single file. Tex took a long look and listened. Evidently they were still far from their objective, wherever it was. Then the cowboy led off again, walking stealthily and silently, peering ahead in a half circle. At the end of a hundred steps or so he halted for a long cautious moment.

The cowboy was like an Indian, Bruce thought. Walking behind Maggard, fourth in that line, Bruce exercised all his own keen faculties. The Rangers, in heavy boots, cracking twigs occasionally, annoyed Bruce, and caused Tex to caution them with forceful whisper.

All the features Bruce had noted before appeared to grow more marked. At length sight of the open prairie, with bunches of cattle, and an occasional buffalo, warned Serks that he had better sheer away from the edge of the timber belt.

The ring of an ax smote Bruce's ears, clear as a bell. All the men heard it, and stiffened. At Maggard's gesture and action they all sank into the grass to crawl like huge snakes. The order of travel now changed. Instead of single file, they spread out in a line close together and looked to the Ranger chief for orders. Bruce seemed divided between hate for this ruthless Texan and admiration for his devotion to law and duty. Such militant warriors were needed to keep Texas from being overrun and overruled by evil men.

Maggard would crawl a few yards, then pause to listen and look, and regain his breath. A keen ear could have detected his panting several rods away. The ring of the ax ceased. Grasshoppers and bees arose in front of the stalkers; the buzzards circled lower; horses could now be seen out in the open; a faint sound of running water struck Bruce's ears. During another and longer lull in the approach, Bruce raised himself somewhat to get the lay of the land.

The apex of the prairie triangle appeared to head into a notch of the black slope, which bulged out in vine-covered cliffs, mossy green, flower spangled, with long ferns and scarlet and orange leaves. The murmuring water Bruce heard did not come from the thin veillike cascade that poured like smoke from off the cliff. There was a stream of some volume emerging from that notch. The silver-grassed prairie ran level to the cliffs that formed part of an amphitheater, out from which, far enough to be in the sunlight, stood an old log cabin falling into ruin. A pale-blue column of smoke issued from somewhere beyond the cabin. The spot was the loveliest Bruce had ever seen, excelling the oval where he and Trinity had dreamed. What a location for a ranch! Then on the instant, cold and sickening, came the thought that this spot might be his grave. If so, Bruce thought bitterly, it would be the closest to paradise that he would ever get.

Finally, after what seemed a long interval, Maggard whispered to Tex to send someone closer for the purpose of taking stock of the rustlers in camp.

"Let me go," whispered Jack eagerly. "I'm the smallest. I can wiggle like a snake through the grass. We used to play Injun. No one ever caught me."

Tex nodded. "Kid, use yore haid."

In a few seconds Jack was out of sight, and it took a sharp eye to detect the ripple of the grass that indicated his direction.

Captain Maggard apparently did not list patience among his virtues. He appeared restless, and actuated by a sense of need to hurry which did not manifest itself in the others. Bruce saw no occasion to be swifter, at least not until Jack returned; but he appreciated that the Ranger must know vastly more about such stalks. Jack was gone so long that Bruce grew extremely worried. Certain it was that Maggard would not wait much longer. But presently the grass quivered and split in front of Maggard, Bruce, and Tex, to admit the lad into their presence. He was pale; his dark eyes glowed; his breast heaved.

"I had to go clear—around the cabin," he whispered, panting. "Way outside. . . . One guard watchin'—down the prairie. He's expectin' someone. . . . Eight hawses saddled. . . . Five rustlers gamblin'. One on the ground—haid on a pack—asleep. I heahed the guard answer somebody: 'Cain't see any riders, but shootin' way off down-country. Call Stewart!' "

"Wal, son, you shore belong with my Rangers," said Maggard, in smiling praise. Then he suddenly grew tense. "They're expectin' the rest of their outfit. We must hurry. Spread out in pairs. Surround the cabin. Shoot when I shoot! Lee, you come with me."

Bruce crawled to Maggard's side just as a halloo came from the other side of the cabin, evidently a hail for the leader, Stewart. If there was an answer, Bruce did not catch it. Maggard now worked his way with remarkable stealth and agility for so big a man. He held a gun in each hand. Bruce carried his rifle and used his

184

free hand to facilitate his progress. He would almost catch up with Maggard, when off the man would crawl again. Bruce felt that there was too much hurry, unless Tex and the others used a like celerity. Bruce hoped and believed Tex could take care of Jack. Still that lad, after his stern lesson, might well account for himself.

They crawled a few yards, then lay quiet listening and resting, after which they cautiously peeped up out of the grass. Back toward the cliff the grass began to grow less high and thick. Bruce saw a corner of roof porch supported by a pole, then a neatly stacked pile of firewood, and an ax stuck in a chopping block. On the second rest after that one Maggard prepared him for something by nudging him with his foot. Then Bruce sighted the eight saddled horses and the guard, standing on a stump, facing down the prairie. His posture was one of tense attention. Maggard crawled on, more slowly now, stifling his labored breaths. The murmur of running water grew louder. Voices reached Bruce, but were indistinguishable. Bruce calculated that fifty feet more would bring him and Maggard within sight of all the rustlers. Their position now was precariously close, no more than sixty steps from the end of the cabin. Any man looking out that way could see their moving backs. Yet the Captain crawled on. He had nerve. He knew what he wanted. He would get it, too, unless some totally unforeseen contingency arose. He drew ahead of Bruce and farther over toward the cliff, which appeared to loom above them. The stream ran at the base of the cliff, evidently leaping over rocks to the left and softly splashing beyond out of sight.

A fringe of grass and fern obstructed Bruce's view of the ground ahead. Maggard, ten feet to the right toward the cliff, started on again, with a precipitancy that was impossible for Bruce to emulate. He whispered for the Ranger to wait. A tremendously acute damming up of all Bruce's faculties seemed to impede his progress. Danger with him was a sum of all his senses magnified into a sixth one.

Spreading the fringe of ferns, he peeped out. A wide well-worn trail ran along in front of him. Maggard had crawled nearly to the middle of it, a grim figure, ponderous and forbidding, gun extended in each hand.

Suddenly a slight sound, potent and arresting, and not unlike a knock of an antler upon hard wood, startled Bruce and sent a gush of fire along his veins. Maggard heard it, for he flattened himself in the middle of the trail. For a second Bruce quivered all over. No deer! The air was charged with the peril he had felt a thousand times. Again the strange sound smote his ear, different this time, more like a stealthy step of boot. Someone was coming. He dared not raise his head above the ferns. But he laid his ear to the ground.

No step, but a rhythmic beat of swift hoofs on hard ground! That had not been the sound which had flattened him and Maggard to the earth. The Ranger had turned his face away from the cliff, toward the cabin, and his grim expression meant that he would open the fight the instant he located the imminent peril he sensed and which Bruce absolutely knew was close.

The pregnant silence split to the guard's peal of alarm. Sharp voices, thud of boots, ring of coins and guns on wood attested to the action of the rustlers. The guard's shrill call elicited no other response. Rustlers and stalkers alike seemed to fall into suspense. Tex and his allies no doubt were waiting for the Captain's signal. Maggard lay flat, knowing that death, from some source still unseen, was close at hand.

At this juncture, Bruce saw, out of the corner of his eye, a movement of something above him toward the looming cliff. No bird! It was dark—blotted out light. He looked up.

And his swift glance took in a stairway of cut poles that zigzagged up and around a corner of cliff. In another instant the gliding form of a man came in sight, to lean over with malignant dark visage and set bold eyes aflame. He leaned over holding his breath, strung with passion, behind a cocked gun pointing down! Maggard, still listening, was not aware of this impending peril.

Swift as a flash Bruce took a shot upward. This gave the rustler a violent start, even as he pulled the trigger. As Bruce fired he saw flame and smoke belch from the rustler's gun, then he heard the thud of lead striking ground to whine away. The shooter let out a hoarse bawl of agony and pitched sheer off the stairway, falling headlong into the stream.

Maggard rolled back into the ferns, out of Bruce's sight. Thundering bang of rifles, wild yells from the cowboys, brought Bruce erect, to leap behind a tree.

Poking his rifle round the tree Bruce peeped out. On the instant he could not spy any rustler that he could get a bead on. But evidently Maggard did, for Bruce felt the concussion of shots amid the volleys farther off, and he smelled burned powder. Another and larger tree offered better cover and possibly better command of the situation. Bruce checked the impulse to leap, and got down to crawl swiftly to this vantage point.

From this he saw that pandemonium had broken loose. Clouds of smoke, bursts of red, boom and bang above the sharp crack of rifles, plunging shrieking horses, figures of men darting into the cabin, other figures whirling round with whirling horses—all this confusion distracted Bruce's sight from one objective, at which he might have shot.

Out of the melee three horses lunged with riders hanging low, legs over the saddles. Bruce took one hurried shot, then another at the bobbing figures. He missed. But one of the cowboys hit a rustler, for Bruce saw him fall head down, to be dragged by his foot caught in a stirrup. All three horses gained the woods.

The shooting lessened in volume. Maggard, too, was evidently unable to find any more targets. "Look sharp, Lee!" he called. "In the cabin!" But Bruce could not even see any smoke puffing from the dark doorway or the blank shadow under the porch. Gunshots, though, proved rustlers were inside.

Bruce took time to look at the scene. Not one of the cowboys or Rangers was in sight. But a moment's survey of the front discovered puffs of smoke rising from the grass, from behind a log over to the right, from rocks on the left. Bullets thudded into the logs of the cabin, inside the door and under the porch roof. Prone figures of two rustlers in the foreground attested to deadly aim. Two horses were down. Three other horses, bridles flying, riderless, were slowing down a hundred yards or more out in the open.

Presently shooting from outside the cabin grew intermittent and then ceased. It lessened, too, from the inside.

"Hey, you rustlers in there!" bawled Captain Maggard. "Surrender and save your lives!"

"Come in an' get us!" yelled someone in answer.

"We'll burn you out!"

"Who're 'we'?" came the hoarse reply.

"Captain Maggard's Texas Rangers."

"Aw, you're a liar. We seen cowboys. An' they ain't so many as they was. Haw! Haw!"

That coarse intimation sent the blood back to Bruce's heart. It might well be, probably was true. That reckless boy Jack! He might be one of the victims.

"I'll burn you out!" shouted Maggard, in a voice that brooked no doubt.

"Aw, go to hell!"

"Surrender, or you'll burn or hang!"

Gunshots answered that. Heavy bullets from a buffalo gun spanged and whistled over Bruce's head.

"Cap, you better shut up," he warned.

"Sounds like Maggard fellars," called a different voice. "Maggard, you bloody old hound, we prefer to burn rather than risk surrenderin' to you."

"Give you one minute!" yelled the Captain, in strident anger.

"Bah!" came the taunting reply.

Bruce heard Maggard cursing to himself. The old Ranger never shirked battle nor was he averse to shedding blood, but it seemed he had a hankering to capture criminals.

Suddenly Jack's youthful voice pealed out, highpitched and wild: *"Hey! Hey!* . . . Tex, look out! Riders comin'!"

Apparently Jack was alive indeed and hidden somewhere, at an elevation, where he could see more than was possible for Bruce. But Bruce heard faint gunshots down over the gray slope of the prairie.

"Lee, you heah guns off there?" called Maggard.

"Shore do. Down the open country."

"Can you see any riders yet?"

"No. I'm too low to see far."

The heavy buffalo gun boomed inside the cabin and a

murderous slug ripped through the side of the tree that sheltered Maggard, then droned away into the woods.

"He burned me, Lee," said Maggard, grim and apprehensive.

"Stand sideways. Keep yore haid in, Cap. Thet hombre cain't shoot atall!"

Again Jack's piercing yell rent the air. The boy must have been in a leafy tree to Bruce's right. It was his rendering of the Comanche war cry and left little to be desired. Jack was a help with his keen eyes and unquenchable spirit. After the long concatenated yell, which echoed through the woods, came his warning: "Fightin' riders heah. Look out!"

Everybody in and out of that cabin heard the boy's warning. It clamped them silent. Bruce could not see a moving thing, and he calculated that no one else could.

"Lee," called Maggard, from behind his tree.

"Yes, Cap, I heah you."

"That Texas lad kind of tickles me."

"Me, too. An' he scares the hell out of me, too."

"Reckon it's Horton and Blight chasin' thet outfit up from Flat Top."

"Cain't be anyone else. . . . There, I heah gunshots clear now. . . . Cap, it'll be hotter'n hell heah pronto."

"Wal, I reckon, for that outfit, anyhow."

Bruce risked peeping out from the right side of his tree. He saw three riderless horses tearing up the prairie toward the camp. *Zip!* A bullet stung his forehead with flying bits of bark. Boom of the heavy buffalo gun accompanied that close call. Bruce jerked his head back, feeling the cold sweat come out upon his tingling flesh. Almost simultaneously with that boom rang out the biting report of a .44 Winchester. The bullet struck somewhere in that cabin, and not upon wood. A harsh cry of fury and pain added conviction to Bruce's thought. Jack Melrose had proved himself again.

Intermittent gunshots sounded clearly out on the prairie. Cautiously Bruce again peeped out from his covert. The three riderless horses, with bridles and manes flying, were on a dead run for the camp. Behind them, half a mile, came five-six horsemen, spread wide, approaching as fast as spent horses could gallop. As Bruce looked he saw a puff of smoke, then another, followed by dull reports. These horsemen, facing back in their saddles, were firing at another line of riders, six in number, and unmistakably cowboys. It appeared to Bruce that they could have closed that gap between them and the rustlers had they wanted to incur the risk. They knew what a surprise sooner or later awaited the fleeing rustlers.

"What you see, Jones?" asked Maggard impatiently.

Bruce told him briefly, and elicited a grunt of satisfaction from the Ranger.

"Workin' out fine," he replied. "But those hawses may run over some of our men."

"Their lookout. Jack has warned us. They heahed it too. . . . Doggone! So did the rustler hombres inside. They're makin' it bad for Tex an' the others out there in the grass."

Incessant shots from inside the cabin proved that the rustlers corralled in there had anticipated and perhaps seen the besiegers in the grass attempt to shift their positions. Meanwhile the riderless horses ran into camp, wet and wild-eyed, plunging to a halt. And on came the two lines of horsemen, one fleeing and the other pursuing.

"Lee, wait till they run right in heah," ordered Maggard, sharply.

Bruce had put his hat on the end of his rifle, to stick it out from behind the tree—a ruse to draw the fire of that rustler with the heavy buffalo gun. But no shot! Either that one of the besieged had been stopped or more likely had joined forces with his comrades, to open fire upon the cowboys out there in a precarious position.

"Lee, hasn't that hombre with the needle gun let up?" queried Maggard.

"Yes, or gone forward in the cabin."

"I'm makin' for that back door."

"Don't risk it, Captain. The fight's goin' our way."

"Too good a chance to miss. . . . Watch close!"

The Ranger ran to another tree, hid there a moment, then on to the left for fifty feet, and from there gained the back wall of the cabin. He had a rifle in his left hand, a gun in his right, and he looked formidable as he reached the dilapidated open door. Bruce knew his action had been motivated by keen judgment backed by marvelous nerve. Peering in the dark doorway, Maggard evidently could not locate any rustler to shoot at.

Bruce could no longer watch the Captain, for the climax of culminating action out in front forced his attention there. Scarcely a hundred yards away the approaching rustlers were yelling, manifestly to bring their comrades out to their rescue. The six pursuers came on, guns swung high, a confident and menacing posse.

Bruce had never experienced a fighting moment in any way similar, or in any part as nerve-racking. On galloped the spent horses, their riders' dark visages beginning to gleam in Bruce's sight. He found it hard to get a sure aim on one of the bobbing horsemen. But any instant he expected bursting flame and smoke from the grass, and, a volley right in the faces of the oncoming and doomed rustlers.

Still the firing from inside the cabin kept up, three guns working almost in unison. Suddenly hollow shots banged, closer to Bruce, and of earsplitting detonation. Maggard, screened by the doorjamb, except his right arm and half of his head, was shooting with deliberate aim into the cabin.

While Bruce saw this, a dozen guns burst to the right and left of the galloping horses. One of the leaders of the riders pitched headlong out of his saddle. Another, hard hit, slumped low and swerved away, riding right over cowboys on that side into the woods. A riderless horse pounded into the space before the cabin, snorting, lunging among the other riderless horses. Bruce took a flash-shot at a rustler sweeping by to the left, and made sure that he hit him. The other two riders, one crippled, turned off to scatter the cowboys and race under the trees.

Then the rapid shots ceased. The rifle hidden in the tree to the left, evidently manned by Jack, barked two more times. Bruce saw the pursuing riders split, two spurring to left and two to right, in pursuit of the escaping rustlers. The center two riders came on, hauling in their mounts.

A hoarse shout brought Bruce's attention to a staggering rustler, who came out of the cabin with his hands up. Maggard appeared then, his gun leveled upon this man, and he strode out in front of the cabin.

"Ride them down!" he thundered. "Serks— Weatherby—all you men—run back for your hawses. *Ride them down!*"

Bruce saw Jack running across to Tex and Juan who appeared to rise out of the ground. They all joined Weatherby to run off through the woods to where the horses had been left. From behind the cabin then appeared a Ranger, manifestly wounded, as he slumped forward, almost unable to walk.

"Bates!—You hurt?" shouted Maggard.

"Not too bad—I reckon. . . . But Miller is done for. I heard him get hit," replied the Ranger.

The bloody-visaged rustler, not able to stand, sank down, his back to a pack. He appeared to be weaponless and far gone. Bruce approached slowly, his gun still in hand, not sure that the engagement was ended. But he had seen enough of Captain Maggard to be certain that worthy had accounted for the rustlers in the cabin.

"We'll make it a clean haul yet," said Maggard somberly, as he sheathed his guns and laid hold of the staggering Bates.

"Where you shot?"

"Heah, under my arm."

"Lay down. . . . Let me see. . . . Bates, that gunshot won't kill you . . . Where's your scarf? . . . Jones, let me have yours, too."

Bruce, loading his rifle, gradually relaxed his vigilance. He listened for shots, but none came. He gazed into the woods and out on the prairie. Riderless horses in sight, but no men. Those escaping, rustlers, slipping into the woods, would have to be tracked. Bruce calculated that if he had hit the rider he shot at there would be three crippled, one badly. Another might have escaped unscathed. Bruce approached the wounded rustler and asked him how he fared.

"Wal, I'm wuth two daid men," he grinned.

"Where is Stewart?"

"Aw, Bill wasn't heah."

Bruce went back to Maggard and laid down his rifle, offering to help. But before he could stoop he heard a faint sound, apparently from the cliff.

194

"What's that?" queried the alert Maggard, sitting back on his haunches, his bloody hands suddenly still. Bruce did not answer. "Behind the cabin!" whispered the Ranger.

"No!" but he wheeled instinctively at Maggard's suggestion. A magnetic sense pulled Bruce back, to glance up the zigzag stairway that led to a lookout platform on top. This he had not seen before. He faced clear around. The cliff corner ended thirty steps away and the stream turned that way. Bruce's wary gaze worked farther to the left.

"Reckon it wasn't anythin'," said the Captain, again bending to his task. He persuaded all but Bruce's instinct.

Then a faint hollow hoof crack on stone startled Bruce. Ranger or cowboy riding across the stream! But his flying consciousness repudiated that. Maggard stiffened, one bloody hand with scarf outstretched. A splash, a snort, a thud!

Bruce wheeled to see horse and rider halted at the edge of the stream and a riderless horse emerging from the wall of green foliage. To Bruce's right a man of supple and powerful frame appeared, straightening up from a leap across the stream.

"*Bill*!" shrieked the rider, in tone of terrific alarm and warning.

CHAPTER 15

TREMENDOUS SURPRISE STUNNED BRUCE. AS HE recognized Stewart, his next reaction of fury toward Maggard was as stultifying as the surprise.

"What—who?" asked the Ranger haltingly.

"Stewart—you blockhead! Don't move!" hissed Bruce.

Then Bruce came out of his stupefaction. But Stewart held the advantage. If he had drawn then he could have killed Bruce. That, apparently, did not strike him. Amazement and uncertainty clamped him momentarily, though his instinctive action was to stand stiff, feet spread, right hand low.

Bruce's mind, swift as his sight, grasped the facts. The horseman apparently was not armed, except for a rifle in his saddle sheath. The carcass of a deer lay across the pommel and his knees. Thirty short paces separated Bruce from the transfixed rustler. Bruce's supreme need was to distract Stewart, retard or break his control at the critical instant.

"Moze," rasped out Stewart, his dark visage turned red, "I *told* you I heard shots."

Then the wounded rustler to Bruce's left raised his head.

"Boss, you're late—fer us. . . . We're cleaned."

"*Who*?"

"Rangers under Maggard—thar. . . . An' cowboys."

"Where—rest of them?"

"Chasin' cripples—all over."

With gleaming eyes on Bruce and Maggard the rustler chief had jerked out those queries.

"Aha! . . . Ride-the-man-down Maggard!" he said coldly and bitterly. "Your last ride, Cap!"

Maggard knelt motionless and mute, expecting a murderous slug through his back, but his quivering raised hand, the compass-needle oscillation of his eyes argued a move to help Bruce.

"Same for you, Ranger!" hissed Stewart, indicating Bruce.

"I'm not a Ranger," said Bruce steadily.

"You're no cowboy."

"Who said I was?" taunted Bruce.

Stewart vibrated perceptibly to that, his dark gaze speculative.

"Gunslinger, eh?" in slow derision.

"Yes! The man whose name you stole," flashed Bruce furiously.

"Hellsfire! . . . Who?" bellowed Stewart, his visage working.

"Bruce Lockheart! But you couldn't steal his hand!" sang out Bruce, in fierce passion.

Supreme test for Bruce—an instant's wait—the flicker—the break! Then he drew and fired in one swift action. Stewart's gun flew high as that hot lead tore through his heart. He had time to let out a mortal scream before Bruce's second bullet cracked his skull, knocking him flat as if struck by a battering ram.

Hard on that followed Maggard's whirling round, gun in hand. It clicked twice on empty chambers, then boomed. And Stewart's rider, jerking his rifle out of its sheath while spurring the horse, fell backward, arms and rifle aloft, to slide one way while the deer carcass slid another. His horse bolted down the stream, while the other animal, evidently Stewart's, lunged and snorted wildly, but did not run.

"Reckon they won't come to life, but you better take a look," spoke up the Captain, breathing hard.

Guardedly Bruce obeyed the order, so far as the horseman was concerned. The man lay face down in the shallow water, which had a red tinge to mar its crystal clearness. Retracing his steps, Bruce had no power to avert his somber gaze from the rustler who had added degradation to the name of the outlaw Lockheart. The rustler chief lay stripped of his potentiality, but what he had been gleamed coldly on his set features. Beyond him some few rods up the stream lay the half-submerged figure of the rustler who had fallen from the cliff stairway.

Bruce, deathly sick from several causes, returned to Maggard, to give him a silent report. The Ranger stared up at Bruce, cool and collected, yet behind the inscrutable bronze mask and the glint of gray eagle eyes there worked something no man could read.

"Listen, son," he drawled. "My life has been saved before a number of times, but never from so tight a fix, and never twice by one man. . . . It embarrasses me . . . what the hell to do about it."

"My Gawd, Cap!" burst out Bates rapturously. "He was quicker'n chain lightnin'!"

"Reckon he had to be, Bates. I shore almost felt bored through the back. . . . Lee, your pretendin' to be Bruce Lockheart was about as slick a trick to throw off a gunner as I ever saw."

For a moment Bruce could not believe his ears. A trick—pretending to be Bruce Lockheart—did Maggard really think that? Faced with extermination for both Maggard and himself, he had again revealed his identity, instinctively realizing that the name of Bruce Lockheart was as powerful and surprising a weapon as his gun. That Maggard had not grasped his sincerity, had believed that he resorted to a trick, seemed almost incredible, so powerfully had Bruce been obsessed by all that his name implied.

He pulled himself together as best he could to reply to Maggard. "But for thet, Captain, he might have beat me to it," he said slowly. "But I tried it before, an' it worked."

198

"Lee, how'd you guess Stewart wasn't *really* Lockheart?" queried Maggard curiously.

"Wal, I reckon Tex helped me come to thet conclusion," returned Bruce ponderingly. "But if he had been Lockheart I could have told it pronto."

"Damnation blazes!" exploded the Ranger, as if suddenly realizing. "All this bloody mess for nothing . . . . Lockheart still at large! . . . Where in the hell is he?"

"Captain, you can hardly call this raid on rustlers all for nothin'," retorted Bruce, curt in his amazement at the passion of the man.

"No, certainly not. But I was after Lockheart. If the Ranger Service had to take care of rustlers, what'd become of Texas? It'd become a stampin' ground for all the criminals in the West."

"So—you make a distinction between rustlers and outlaws?" asked Bruce bitterly.

"Yes. You cowboys and cattlemen naturally regard the rustler as the great evil of Texas. But you're wrong. What are a few cattle—or a thousand haid—to a cattleman like Melrose? Why, he doesn't even know how much stock he owns. On the other hand, take the stagecoach bandit, the bank and train robber—that is to say, the killer—the outlaw—he's the bad hombre for Texas."

"I see. It's the cash loss—the blood spilt," rejoined Bruce moodily.

"Lee, take your rifle and go get up on that stump. And watch."

Bruce was glad to escape from the proximity of Captain Maggard, for whom, on the moment, he felt almost a baffled hate and helpless rage. But he could not escape from his own thoughts, which were dark and somber indeed. Standing on the stump Bruce had command of the approaches to the camp. Beyond a fringe of green brush he saw more parklike country, well wooded, climbing to the black brakes.

In due time he saw riders coming in two directions. They proved to be the Ranger contingent, bringing in a crippled prisoner, and Tex, with his cowboys, who reported the escape of the two rustlers, one of whom was injured. Bruce kept to his stand on the stump, though he sat down to rest. Jack had led in two riderless horses. Now that the fight was over, the boy appeared cracking under the strain. He did not approach Bruce, which was indication enough of the lad's perturbation. Finally Peg Simpson rode in with two more riderless horses. Bruce watched them hold a powwow around Captain Maggard. At length Tex Serks strolled over to Bruce, to fix him with gimlet eyes. But there was something warm and almost reverent in the strong brown hand that clutched Bruce's knee. Peg followed him.

"Peg, where's Jim?" queried Bruce, reminded that he had not counted Tex's brother.

"Shot up bad. But was able to ride home. He an' Blight got shot fust off when we jumped the rustlers. Blight had it plumb center. He was daid when I reached him. . . . Wal, we had a runnin' fight then—a slow one, after the fust few miles, when we dropped three of the outfit. My idee was to chase the rustlers up heah, for two reasons. To find out where their camp was, an' probably drive them right into you fellars. It worked good an' luck was with us."

"Luck! Was it with *me*? I reckon."

"So I heahed," replied Tex dryly. "Maggard is a fishy old cuss. Not any feelin' atall. Blight an' Miller daid.

Cole shot bad, an' Weymouth hurt. All in service to Texas an' the Rangers—thet old geezer said, proud as hell. . . . He told us how you saved his life twice. Laid it on thick, Lee. But I reckon thet was a job fer the likes of you, pard. . . . Maggard thought your ruse to fool Stewart—about yore bein' Lockheart—was slicker'n a whistle. Fact is they all reckoned thet way. . . . Neither Cap nor nary damn one of them guess you *air*—"

"Cut thet, pard, Tex—for now anyway," interrupted Bruce, a spasm strangling his speech. "Shore I feel deep an' strong—for you—Tex Serks."

"Same heah. We're two of a kind."

"What's the old buzzard up to next?"

"Don't know. I'll go see. Anyway, we've a job on hand. If only Jim made it home safe!"

Tex left Bruce divided between somber and grateful thoughts. It was too soon for anything to dispel the sinister mood of killing, not even the incredible fact of having saved his great enemy's life. What would Trinity say? And with thought of her, Bruce's emotion began its powerful sweep against the darker forces. He felt that he might have killed a hundred men, to be locked in the callous stupor of the slayer of his kind, yet gladness for Trinity, the hope that raised its head for her sake, and the succeeding irresistible flood of love would in some spiritual transformation even change human life.

CHAPTER 16

AS HE RODE ALONE TOWARD THE RANCH, BRUCE'S mood gradually assumed terrific proportions. For a while, at intervals, emotion got sidetracked in the return of living over recent action, the facts of incredible happenings, the usual sensations following death dealt by his hands. But the overwhelming emotion that began to take shape was one of disgust and despair at still having to hide under the name of Lee Jones. Gradually the realization of that damnable fact overcame the stress of tremendous battle consciousness, with its aftermath, and wholly possessed his mind.

It fixed his mood, and every mile he rode added to the insupportable tragedy of the thing, for him and for Trinity. When passion reached its uttermost, Bruce faced an astounding and deadly impulse to betray his identity and kill Maggard.

"I'd like to do it!" thought Bruce. "I ought to do it! . . . Not for hate, but to put an end to this hopeless situation. With Maggard dead I could get away for good."

Trinity was the sole heartbreaking barrier to his grim thought. It loomed before his consciousness, presented itself in profound and terrible clarity, then went out in darkness as a candle snuffed by the wind.

"Then what?" he groaned.

It seemed all his life consisted of dark and hateful and miserable rides to escape justice, enemies, bloodshed, imprisonment, or death. He now seemed to be riding to escape himself. Not Maggard, but his own conscience was on his trail!

He arrived at the ranch not far ahead of Jack, and the line of riders stretched out behind. Bruce slipped his saddle, gave his horse a drink at the trough, and led him away to the pasture, purposely delaying his return.

Lamplight blinked out of the bunkhouse windows and doors as he lagged back, weary and beaten. In his room he found Peg bustling about, Juan starting a fire, Tex bending over his brother Jim. That reminded Bruce. He,

202

too, bent over to peer at the younger Serks.

"Jim! . . . Gosh, yo're alive an' thet's something. I hope yo're not in bad shape."

"Yes, I am, Lee—but most from the ride."

"You didn't have much more blood to spare. Packin' any lead?"

"Nope, but the weight on me feels like a ton."

"Who fixed you up?"

"Slaughter, an' he didn't 'pear worried. So I'm not."

Bruce busied himself with washing and shaving, not that he was inclined to such duty but to keep moving and avoid the talk that had to come sooner or later. After supper Bruce lay down in the shadow of his bunk, fully dressed, for he well knew sleep would not visit him that night. Jim fell asleep. Tex and Peg smoked incessantly. Juan came in to settle down quietly beside the fire, upon which he laid small billets of wood. After what seemed a long time Bruce heard light quick footsteps outside, on the gravel, then up on the porch. A sharp rap sounded on the door.

"Who's there?" called Tex.

"Trinity. Open the door," came the peremptory reply.

Tex gazed at Bruce, who shook his head, and at Peg, who dropped his eyes.

"Let me in!" came in Trinity's high-pitched voice.

"But, Trinity, Lee's asleep—an' Jim bad hurt. . . ."

"Sleep!—Wake him up." And Trinity beat a tattoo upon the door with some solid article, perhaps a whip handle.

"I've gone to bed, Trinity. Wait till tomorrow," Bruce called out, with a feeling of helplessness.

"Ump-umm, darling," replied Trinity. "I'm going to see you now if I have to break in or climb through the window."

Whereupon Bruce arose to open the door. The light flooded out upon the girl, muffled in a big coat, but with her white face and flashing eyes exposed.

"Humph! You dressed pronto," she said.

"I didn't say I was undressed," expostulated Bruce. "But—but—"

"There are no buts, honey. Get your coat. It's cold as blue blazes."

Tex brought the coat, and said in an earnest way: "Trinity, if it's only you wanta heah about the fight, let Lee off. I'll tell you."

"Thanks, Tex. But I want him."

She must have nettled Tex, or he was irritated and upset anyhow, for he retorted: "Girl, he cain't go spoonin' with you—after shootin' up a lot of men!"

"Idiot! I don't want to spoon," cried Trinity hotly. "And I don't give a damn if he's shot a dozen rustlers, and got shot himself. I *want* him!"

Bruce intervened, divining that Trinity was unalterable in this temper. "I'm sorry," he said hastily. "I just wanted to shirk it, Trinity."

He slipped into his fleece-lined coat, even with Trinity clinging to him, and let her lead him out into the gloom. The night was dark, no stars showed, a cold wind swept in off the prairie. Coyotes were wailing dismally. The loneliness and melancholy of the range struck Bruce with ruthless significance. Trinity clung to his arm with both hands, and appeared to be leading him toward the dark line of trees that marked the yard.

"I had to see—you—darling," she said.

"Yes, of course. It's just as well. I wanted to talk to you sometime. Now's as good as any."

They stooped through the bars of the fence and groping their way under the trees in the pitch blackness

204

found their bench. They were sheltered there, but the wind moaned and soughed above them.

"Trinity, I'm sick of this deception, this fear of being exposed as the real Bruce Lockheart. And sooner or later someone is going to find me out for sure. I want to have it out with Maggard." The tone of Bruce's voice betrayed his agony.

"Oh, Bruce, I know it's awful to live like this!" exclaimed Trinity. "But what if you did? It would mean the end for us. He would take you away."

She gripped his hand and they sat in silence. Then she brightened. "Maybe he wouldn't after what you did today. Maybe he would believe in your innocence. Jack told me a lot about the fight—that you had saved Maggard's life twice. I shrieked for joy. I'd prayed for something that'd put him under great obligation to you It worked out. What blessed luck!" Then she stopped. "But we have no proof!" It was almost a sob.

"Trinity, I can always kill him," said Bruce starkly.

"Sure! In the temper I'm in now I wish you would. But for you and me—that's unthinkable."

"Yes, Trinity. Back down the road I had that out with myself—or Maggard and his Ranger guard would be dead and I'd have been fifty miles away in the brakes."

"You thought of me, darling?" she whispered, in passionate significance.

"That was all that saved Maggard."

"I love you more for it," she murmured.

"How long will Maggard stay here?" he asked.

"I heard him tell Dad a day or two, until the crippled rustlers are mended a little. Oh, he's keen to take them to Austin. Keen to spread the news! Keen to get credit for riding down a vicious outlaw band."

"He's getting old," declared Bruce. "Why, he

believed implicitly that Stewart was Bruce Lockheart."

"Bruce, he wants Lockheart bad. Yet he has a kinder, a softer side. He loves me. But I feel helpless now to move him an iota."

They clung to each other there in the cold black night with the wind moaning its indifference.

"Bruce, I don't have to torture myself as you're doing now," said Trinity, at length. "It's come to me all at once."

"What's—come?" he asked huskily.

"Two escapes possible—just two!"

As he did not speak, Trinity went on, "We can take the chance of living together as Lee Jones and wife in a homestead back in the canyon. Maybe no one will ever recognize you. Disguise yourself, and don't meet many strangers." She paused.

"What is the other choice?" Bruce faltered.

"Plan to ride away together. Choose the right time . . . . You go to Maggard—throw your gun on him— fling the truth in his face, along with those bank robbery thousands he sets such store upon. Swear to God that was the only evil act which justified making you an outlaw—that all the rest are lies, crimes laid upon you because you were a fugitive. . . . Tell him but for you he would have been killed by Stewart. Not only once but twice! Tell him any man who was human, even if he was a Texas Ranger, would rise above hate and greed, and set you free. . . . Tell him that I chose to go away with you, and that if he ever rides us down and you fail to kill—him—*I* will!"

All the breadth and strength and wildness of Texas rang in the voice of this daughter of Melrose. Bruce's reception of it was so overwhelming that there seemed to be no power in him to divine its effect, its extent, its

206

consequences.

"Trinity, which must it be?"

"It's for you to choose, Bruce."

They fell upon another long silence, holding each other close, while the wind sang its melancholy refrain through the boughs. The coyotes had ceased their hue and cry, but from far up on the slope the mourn of a wolf floated down, blood-curdling in its remorseless note of hunger, of strife, of self-preservation.

"Bruce, it's late, and I'm dead on my feet," said Trinity finally. "Take me back to the house. You'll have to boost me up to my window. They think I went to bed long ago."

He allowed her to lead him under the trees to where the house loomed up, dark and quiet. How she could find her window in the blackness Bruce could not guess. Still she did. This time it was not she who thought of a good-night kiss, but Bruce, and as he held her long, lips locked on hers, it was as if his heart was riven. His instinct understood that embrace better than his mind.

"Bruce!" she whispered, half strangled as she broke away. "I may love you terribly—but I still have—to breathe. . . . God help you, man! Whatever you decide—I'm with you. Good night!"

Bruce left her, and stumbled along in a tumult. He crossed the flat, passed the bunkhouse, and went out upon the prairie. The cold, the piercing wind, the thick gloom, the loneliness all suited his mood, though he did not think of that.

Behind his tenderness, his beating, pulsing love for Trinity, the spell of her hands and lips, the glory of her woman's surrender to him—behind all these loomed the great decision he had to make.

The second hour saw Bruce's consciousness

absolutely and unalterably refusing to consider a life of deception and fear of discovery. The mere supposition was false. Too long had he been a fugitive, a killer of men, and an outlaw, a man who had to ride and hide, a fugitive so disreputable and notorious that the real desperadoes of the range hid their identity under his name. He could face it no longer. He wanted to live as Bruce Lockheart and be able to hold his head up.

And Bruce passed on to the alternative—a choice that made him writhe with the endless train of thoughts it provoked. What infinite detail he knew of an outlaw's life which Trinity could not guess! To disgrace her there at Brazos Head, to make her name go echoing down the range as a mad girl of true Texas blood, gone to the bad for an outlaw, to force her to share his flight and all the hardships that it entailed for a woman; the constant movement without food, comfort, cleanliness, without sleep and rest; or the hiding in some squalid cabin or cave or covert, to live the life of a savage, and after a short or a long period to be cornered in some hole in some wilderness or on the street of some town where hunger must necessarily drive them; to fight for her, and see her fight for him, perhaps shed blood as good as her own; and surely see him fall at last, riddled with bullets, at her feet; to leave her alone, an outcast, a woman whose infamy and ill-placed loyalty would never be erased from the annals of cowboys' fireside story, and the history of the Texas range—to all this Bruce could not doom his beloved.

Cold dawn broke upon decision. The sun rose in bright glory over range that was to know him no more. Its beauty, its pure and bracing air, sweet and icy off the rolling prairie, the loneliness of its length and breadth, and the thick waving grass so dear to the heart of a cowboy and a cattleman in the making—these lovely things, never so mockingly beautiful and alluring as in the hour of renunciation, were not for Bruce Lockheart.

The black brakes for him—the bitter hiding—the stealth from covert to covert, until they rode him down! What evil, what spirit was left in him to want to fight, to kill before he was killed? That was hate, which had died and was now reborn, flaming up in him against the injustice of life and the brutality of law.

Once more, that day, for Trinity's sake, Bruce Lockheart would stay his hand against the life of his great foe! But never again, never for any Ranger, not even for her.

Curling columns of blue smoke, ring of ax, voices, and whistles proclaimed that the cowboys and Rangers in the bunkhouses had stirred to a new day. As Bruce strode by the open door of the store someone within hailed him, but he gave no sign that he heard. As he entered his room, a smile and greeting on Tex's face froze in its incipiency. Peg, busy as usual, looked up at him, quickly to avert his gaze and look no more. Bruce did not notice the others. He wrapped his few belongings in one of his blankets, and tied it up ready to strap at the back of his saddle. Spurs he buckled on with hard, fierce hands. Then he dragged his saddlebag out from under his bunk.

"Peg, will you pack some dried fruit, strips of meat, biscuits, say about ten pounds? And put in a little salt?" he asked, in a voice that he did not recognize as his own.

"Shore—pard—shore," replied Peg nervously.

"Thanks, old man, for the last of your many favors to me," said Bruce, and taking up his bridle he made for the pasture. As he strode off the porch he heard Peg gasp: "For Gawd Almighty's sake—what—?" and Tex interrupted, cold and hard: "Yore hunch last night was correct. We cain't do nothin'."

As it chanced, Legs, near the pasture gate, saw Bruce and came whinnying to him, reaching for the nosebag of grain. In spite of Bruce's clamp upon his emotions, a pang rent his breast. He cared for this grand horse that had saved his life time and again. But Legs belonged to Trinity. In one of their loving moments Bruce had made a gift of the horse to her.

"Legs, you son-of-a-gun," said Bruce, patting the keen nose. "Take a mouthful of grain for old time's sake, and forget me for your new owner. She'll love you. . . . Legs, I'm riding down the long trail again."

He found a shaggy rawboned mustang he had ridden, and chose him for endurance more than speed.

Bruce let the mustang eat the grain, then readjusted the bridle and put it on. Leading him out and down to the bunkhouse Bruce kept sharp lookout for Rangers.

At the porch rail he saddled the mustang, tied saddlebag and pack, then went into the bunkhouse. All the cowboys were there. All of them knew. If eyes and intent faces meant anything, these riders were for him. Bruce helped himself to some ham, a biscuit, and a cup of coffee.

"Peg, I'm pretty shore to need some of these heah biscuits for lead bullets," he said.

"Yeah, they air tough an' heavy, most as tough an' heavy as life is for some of us."

Not another word was said in that room, where the very atmosphere was charged with suspense.

"So long, pards," said Bruce, strode out, and swung up into the saddle.

Tex came through the door, strapping on his gun belt. Bruce gave him a long look, full of somber disapproval.

"Tex, you stay out of this," he said sternly.

"Wal, pard, how'd you like to go to hell for a change?" drawled Tex, with his slow smile.

"I'll have to go there pronto, whether I like it or not." Bruce rode across the flat without looking back, through the open gate, dismounted and tied the mustang. Jack came whistling down the path, another proof of how fate was favoring Bruce.

"See here, kid, I like you heaps, and I wish we could go on being pards. . . . Will you do me a last favor?"

"Lee? . . . Hell yes!"

"I'm the real Bruce Lockheart and I'm spilling that to Maggard right now. He's there?"

"You . . . ?" Jack paled with astonishment, but finally gasped out, "Aw, pard. . . . Yes, with Dad an' Luke. Nobody else. But heah comes Tex. What's yore favor?"

"Keep Trinity away, even if you have to rope her."

"She's out back. I'll run. . . . My Gawd, this's awful!" Jack went thudding up the yard around the house. Bruce looked back as he mounted the porch steps. Tex was approaching with long strides, a brooding and formidable figure. His gesture seemed as great to Bruce as if gunplay was inevitable. Tex would have embraced that and outlawry for his friend. Leaping across the porch, he threw open the wide door, and left it open as he entered.

Slaughter was lighting a cigar. Melrose stood with Maggard, back to the fire. The Ranger beamed upon Bruce.

"Mawnin', Lee, I shore—" Then he ceased to beam as well as speak. Melrose stared aghast. Luke Slaughter's tanned face suddenly blazed with

211

intelligence.

"Maggard, I've thrown my gun on you," said Bruce in a sinister voice, low and clear as a bell.

"So I see!" replied the Texas Ranger, cool and slow. "Boy, you're shore not drunk, so you must be crazy."

Melrose burst out: "Lee, for heaven's sake—"

"Keep still, you and Luke," ordered Bruce, and he advanced a couple of steps, his gun held low and steady.

Maggard's calm front underwent a stupendous change. His bulk expanded, his tight lips emitted a sibilant hiss, but the stupefying query they framed froze there.

"I am Bruce Lockheart!" Bruce let that statement sink in an instant. *"I'm* the man—the outlaw you've ridden down for years! Hounded for my part in that bank holdup! . . . But that was my only crime. And I kept the money. . . . Every dollar of—my share! Trinity has that money. She'll give it to you. . . . I promised her I'd never kill a Texas Ranger. But I break that promise here and now. . . . Ride your man down again, Captain Maggard—and see!"

Bruce ended his bitter pronouncement and backed out the door onto the porch. Tex stood there and let him pass. Bruce leaped off the steps and ran down the road toward his horse. A scream shook his nerve—Trinity's passionate cry from back there in the living room. Bruce leaped astride, and spurring the mustang he cut across the flat, aiming to come out on the road below the bunkhouse.

Once out upon the level, he pulled the mustang into a lope. He must not run him unless forced to. He did not look back. He could not have seen anyone distinctly. His deadly purpose accomplished, the passionate and terrible betrayal of himself done, never to be undone,

212

loosed a riot in his breast and brain that made him blind and insane and frozen.

Yet he kept his stirrups, clung to his pommel, until his sight cleared and his flaying thoughts grew intelligible. He did not even look back from the bridge where it crossed the Brazos, where he had met Tex and the other cowboys, and where a turn hid the ranch from view.

Ahead of Bruce the prairie dipped gently into a great green-gray basin, divided by the white-streaked road, and marked at the far rise by a patch of trees. Far over the rise the landmark Flat Top Mountain, and to the right ten miles or more, the butte that he well knew gave him exact location. The black brakes were out of sight. Only the stark rim of the Staked Plain marked the barrier in that direction.

His mustang loped on, steady, rhythmic, tireless, down the gentle slope into the basin, and on up the imperceptible incline toward the green rise of horizon. From that rise, still five miles distant, he would look back for the first time. To see—to see if he was pursued!

Was that a hallucination—the pursuing object in his mind? No! It was a horseman! A stream of dust rising behind the flying hoofs!

A hard bitter laugh escaped his lips. Five miles or less back, just this side of the bridge, a rider showed dark and moving on the white road. He was the forerunner of the Rangers, perhaps, Maggard himself. What nerve, what hellish persistence, what slavishness to duty! It wrung unwilling homage from Bruce's heart.

"Captain, too bad it's not in a better cause!" Bruce bit out, with sarcasm. Too bad Maggard should doom himself to death! For Bruce swore he would kill the man if he ever rode near enough.

The pursuing horse did not gain. The distance was far, but even at that range Bruce's experienced eye began to suspect the rider was gaining. Bruce looked back often now. At the rider and beyond, expecting a posse behind!

Suddenly horsemen appeared coming round the bend by the bridge. Four—five!

"Ha! I should have known." Bruce spoke aloud. He spurred the mustang to a run. He cursed himself for not taking to the timber under the rim when he rode away from the ranch. Here he was ten miles, uphill, from any good cover, and more from the brakes. Still for him, mounted on a stanch horse, five miles were as good as five hundred. Those Rangers had heavy horses, weight carriers, chosen for long pursuits rather than short races. They could never catch him. And if his mustang should go lame or if some unforeseen accident should happen, Bruce had a rifle and he would kill this headstrong fool of a captain and his men.

After what seemed long moments Bruce calculated the remaining distance up to the rise of the prairie. Still three miles or more! He had misjudged distance in that rarefied air. The mustang was running easily. Bruce knew how to foster the stamina of a horse in a life-and-death race. That was another of his melancholy gifts.

Again Bruce looked back over his shoulder. "Gaining!" he muttered, in dark amaze. The first horse had gained a mile. It was a big horse and fast. The mustang had speed enough to make the gain of the pursuer something out of the ordinary. The first doubt edged into Bruce's mind, so easy a prey for doubts.

Something else followed, a piercing perception, a suspicion, a certainty—that horse was a bay—a big, long-legged bay.

"My God!" cried Bruce. "It's Legs! That cursed Ranger is riding me down with my own horse!"

Bruce urged the mustang to his limit. Once over the rise of ground he believed he might have time to reach some cover. The mustang could run, but his stride was short compared to that of Legs. Could any fate have been more fantastic and cruel than that of being run down by his own horse, driving him to murder? Bruce rode up the last remaining rods to the rise of land and over it, hating to look ahead.

Level prairie for miles on either side without thicket or clump of trees! Indeed, these would have availed nothing. He needed the timbered bottom lands or the black brakes—both unattainable for him unless he shot this pursuer.

He rode on, succumbing to this decision. That would be the end for him. And at last he accepted it. After all, he could die only once. He would fight these Rangers to his last gasp.

Bruce looked back. The grassy prairie and the white road were clear. He was a mile or more beyond the summit of the basin. But on the instant the bay horse, swift as light, shot into sight and stretched out on the level. His beautiful action wrenched from Bruce all the fine feeling that was left in him.

"Legs, it's settled," whispered Bruce. "I'll ride on with you—soon as I kill that — — — !"

He pulled the mustang to a halt and, dismounting, jerked his rifle from its saddle sheath, and grimly faced back on the road. The mustang heaved and dragged his bridle into the grass and began to graze. Bruce thought he would have time enough to cut his pack and bags loose from the mustang, tie them upon Legs, and get away before the posse came up over the hill. Maggard was as good as dead. His Rangers would find him stretched upon the road, hands and teeth full of dust.

Bruce worked the action of the rifle, throwing in the shell and leaving the hammer back. His hands were like the steel in that weapon. Then he looked up to watch and wait. Legs was carrying that big Ranger as if weight meant little to him. He had been goaded. He was being ridden by a master of horsemanship. This rider hunched low over the pommel, the flaps of his coat flying out at each side. Like the wind in the prairie grass the great horse came on. Like a cloud shadow sailing down the road!

"Yeah. Ride your man down, Ranger!" ground out Bruce harshly, unable to hold back this tribute to his great foe. Maggard had no fear. He did not expect to die. He had forced this outlaw to a stand.

But Bruce expected Maggard to halt somewhere down that road, out of gunshot, though within sound of his stentorian command to surrender. Strange to see the Ranger come on, into the half mile, on to the quarter, with that horse running stretched low, magnificently swift.

On raced Legs. Bruce heard his pattering rhythmic hoofbeats. How swiftly a fool could ride to his death! Was this Ranger as blind in his sight, as in his conceit? Was he not close enough to see Bruce waiting there, rifle in hand? But If Maggard saw he gave no sign.

With a hunter's cool judgment of distance Bruce raised the rifle. It was easy to draw a bead on that big horse, running on the level, coming like a thunderbolt, but hard to align the sights on that hunched rider. Bruce would take risks not to hit that horse.

At two hundred yards or less Bruce froze in his aim

216

and pulled the trigger. A round object—the Ranger's sombrero—sailed off his head away into the grass.

"Not so bad, Cap, at a target on the back of that devil!" muttered Bruce, and throwing up another shell aimed again.

Over the sights he saw a gauntleted hand waved high. Did the authoritative Ranger imagine he could halt destiny with a waved command? Grimmer than ever, Bruce sought to cover that moving figure.

On the instant when Bruce was about to freeze and shoot again he discovered that the rider was trying to pull the horse. He lay back and hauled. But Legs had the bit and he would not stop. Too late! The Ranger saw his blunder. On he rode.

Bruce's sight caught the dark figure. How small—how narrow! So close! Bruce was about to fire when he saw long hair flying in the wind. Then a white face! Trinity!

"So help me God!" The rifle dropped from his paralyzed hands, to explode on the ground. He stood stricken with terror at having come within an ace of killing her. Down upon him flashed the big horse. Trinity was pulling him with all her might. She screamed at Bruce as Legs thundered by. Down the road the horse sped, to break and change, to slow up and plunge at last to a stop, champing his bit.

Bruce came out of his stupefaction. Snatching up the rifle, he ran to mount the mustang. Trinity had caught him to share his flight as she had sworn she would. She had outrun the Rangers. Bruce glanced back toward the line where the prairie fell off into the basin. No riders in sight! His icy veins stung to the release of hot blood. He galloped toward Trinity, who had finally turned Legs.

They met. But Bruce's first utterance was faint,

incoherent. The girl's pallor showed under a flush. Her eyes were great dark holes.

"Well—can I—ride him?" she asked defiantly, panting a little, and with gauntleted hand patted the wet glossy neck of the horse.

"Trinity—you—you—" he gasped hoarsely, then with shaking hand he pointed down the road, in the direction they had come! "Those riders—behind you—who?"

Again Bruce flashed troubled dim eyes toward the horizon. Still the prairie was bare, lonely, with the grass rippling.

"Jack—and the cowboys," she replied.

"Not Maggard . . . Rangers?"

"No, darling," said Trinity, and placed a tender gauntleted hand on his heaving shoulder.

Bruce collapsed over the pommel of his saddle, held on somehow while he got out of his stirrups, and staggered off to sink upon the grass. Trinity was quickly beside him, speaking, holding him. But Bruce could neither see nor hear in that convulsion of emotion.

How soon he recovered he could not tell. Trinity was wiping the tears and sweat from his face. Out there on the horizon he saw five horsemen, halted, waiting at leisure.

"Trinity, what happened?" he whispered huskily.

"I've already—told you," she replied brokenly, and Bruce could see that her courage, her defiance had broken now that the climax had passed.

"But I—couldn't hear you."

"Bruce, I was coming—in with Jack," she began hurriedly, gripping him as if she needed strength. "Through the hall . . . I heard Captain Maggard. . . . You had thrown a gun on him. . . . I couldn't move my feet.

218

You told him! And you left. . . . I came out of it. I ran into my room—got your money belt—and I tore in there—flung it in Maggard's lap. I screamed for Jack to run and saddle Legs. I don't know what I said to Maggard. I raved. I called him terrible things. He grew white—then red. . . . He looked at that money. It transformed him. He beamed upon me. Then he grew stern, alarmed. 'Trinity!' he shouted. 'He's squared himself with me. Ride after him. Take the cowboys. . . . You ride him down!' . . . Crazy with joy and fear I ran to put on these overalls and boots—grab my coat. . . . I ran out, down the yard. Jack came tearing along on Legs. . . . Then! I was up. I told Jack to follow with the cowboys. . . . Oh, it was terrible—terrible—till I saw you—far across the basin. . . . Then I knew I had you, Mr. Bruce Lockheart."

"Yes, you rode him—better—faster than I . . . Oh, Trinity, almost to your death!"

"Almost. . . . When I saw you meant to shoot I knew you'd taken me for Maggard. I waved. I tried to stop Legs. That horse has an iron jaw, and he was mad. I couldn't stop him. . . . Bruce, you shot my sombrero off my head."

"I know. When I recognized you my heart seemed to stop. Of all the horrible—"

"Boy, you missed me. At that I'd rather have had you hit me than desert me. . . . Come, let's walk along, get my sombrero—then ride home."

They led the horses back along the road. Trinity picked up her sombrero, to show a bullet hole high in the crown. She poked a finger through it, and laughed with a ghost of her old audacity. "We'll keep it always. It will be a lesson to you. Never run away from your Trinity again! And always aim low when you *have* to shoot!"

We hope that you enjoyed reading this
Sagebrush Large Print Western.
If you would like to read more Sagebrush titles,
ask your librarian or contact the Publishers:

United States and Canada

Thomas T. Beeler, *Publisher*
Post Office Box 659
Hampton Falls, New Hampshire 03844-0659
(800) 818-7574

United Kingdom, Eire, and
the Republic of South Africa

Isis Publishing Ltd
7 Centremead
Osney Mead
Oxford OX2 0ES England
(01865) 250333

Australia and New Zealand

Bolinda Publishing Pty Ltd
17 Mohr Street
Tullamarine, Victoria, 3043, Australia
1 800 335 364